NOSTRA

EMMA NICHOLS

First published in 2020 by:

J'Adore Les Books

www.emmanicholsauthor.com

Copyright © 2020 by Emma Nichols

The moral right of Emma Nichols to be identified as the author of this work has been asserted by her in accordance with the Copyright, Designs and Patents Act 1988.

All rights reserved.

This book is licensed for your personal enjoyment only. This book may not be re-sold or given away to other people. Except as permitted under current legislation, no part of this work may be photocopied, stored in a retrieval system, published, performed in public, adapted, broadcast, transmitted, recorded or reproduced in any form or by any means, without the prior permission of the copyright owners.

This is a work of fiction. Names, characters, and incidents are either the products of the author's imagination or used in a fictitious manner. Any resemblance to actual persons, living or dead, or actual events is purely coincidental.

ISBN: 979-863-6877899

Also available in digital format.

Other books by Emma Nichols

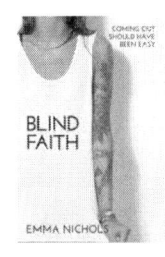

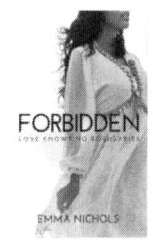

To keep in touch with the latest news from Emma Nichols and her writing please visit:

www.emmanicholsauthor.com
www.facebook.com/EmmaNicholsAuthor
www.twitter.com/ENichols_Author

Thanks

Without the assistance, advice, support and love of the following people, this book would not have been possible.

Bev. Thank you for your contribution chicky, and for your time reading and re-reading the chapters as the book progressed.

Kim and Doreen. Thank you for your instructive feedback and proofreading skills. I am delighted you both enjoyed this story.

Mu. Thank you for your on-going support, creative ideas and nailing yet another brilliant cover. Awesome job. Xx

Thank you to my editors at Global Wordsmiths, Nicci and Victoria. Your coaching and editing input had a significant impact on my crafting of this story. I will be forever grateful.

To my wonderful readers and avid followers. Thank you for continuing to read the stories I write. I have really enjoyed writing this wonderful plot and epic love story.

With love, Emma x

Dedication

To those who need the courage to live the life of their dreams.
Be brave. Be strong.
You will get there.

1.

Maria Lombardo entered her parent's villa and inhaled the aroma. Warmth spread through her as she sighed deeply. Her mother never failed to put a smile on her face with the feast she cooked. She removed her jacket and the Smith and Wesson 637 Magnum holstered at her side. She placed the weapon carefully on the sideboard next to her mother's Beretta .357 Magnum. The difference in their choice of weapon mirrored their life choices. Her mother's sense of cultural loyalty had drawn her to the traditional looking Italian manufactured gun with its long nose, whilst Maria preferred the smaller snub-nose weapon that she could easily conceal and forget she was wearing. She sighed. *Maybe someday I won't have to carry the damn thing at all?* She followed her roused senses. As she entered the kitchen, her smile broadened. Her stomach rumbled as she moved closer to the source of the aroma. "That smells so good."

Her mother turned and smiled as she continued to stir the lightly bubbling liquid. "You're early, *tesoro*."

"I missed you, *Matri*."

Her mother waved her hand in the air. "Pah! You lie too convincingly." She chuckled. "Anyway, what are you looking so happy for?"

"It's been a good day." Maria had spent the afternoon reaffirming her commitment to create a future outside the business, beyond the shores of Sicily where she could be with a woman without retribution, but now wasn't the time and place to have that discussion. And she would rather her father was present to help her mother to understand.

"Don't tell me, you found a nice young man to settle down with? Make a family?"

Maria smiled. It was a question her mother asked frequently, and one she always answered in the same way. "Matri, you know that's never going to happen."

Her mother mumbled in Sicilian as she stirred the pot. "You find a good girl?"

She smiled. Her mother's disappointment with her life choices always paled. Love had that kind of power. If only... "No *good girl* wants to be associated with the business, Matri." The reality of her life and the tricky situation with Patrina that was about to become more complicated brought a wave of sadness that washed over her. Patrina certainly wasn't a good girl. Not even close.

Her mother's head snapped up, a mild look of indignation present before it gave way to a tender smile.

She reached up and stroked Maria's face. "Your matri was one of the good girls, tesoro. You remember that. And your father, he is a good man too."

Maria smiled and kissed her mother on the cheek. She did know that. "You are the best, Matri."

Her mother went back to the stove. "Catena will be late."

Maria shrugged. "She's always late." She had learned to live with her sister's irritating inability to keep to a timescale or a schedule of any kind. Vittorio, her husband, was another matter. She couldn't tolerate her brother-in-law's tardiness. Actually, there was a lot she couldn't tolerate about him, not least the fact that he was stupid. She tilted her head and stretched out the tension that his name created. A lack of attention to detail got those you love killed in this business, and he certainly demonstrated that particular trait a little too regularly for her liking. But Catena loved him, and she loved Catena, so she bit her lip at her sister's choice of husband and pushed her distrust of him to the back of her mind.

She kissed the top of her mother's head, leant over the pot, and dipped her finger. The taste of oregano, sweet onions, and freshly made tomato sauce caused her stomach to growl, and she closed her eyes. "That tastes good."

"You always say this, tesoro. This's why you come to your matri."

She stroked and patted Maria's cheek. The fragility and affection in her mother's touch stabbed her in the chest, triggering the emptiness she knew would one day reside there. *I love you, Matri.* She kissed her mother's flushed cheeks. "You will always make the best pasta, Matri," she whispered.

Her mother inched away from Maria, her discomfort at the affectionate gesture apparent in the stiffening of her posture, and she shifted back to the bubbling sauce.

"Now, I cook. You are in the way."

Maria chuckled at the abruptness in her mother's tone that only partly obscured the depth of her feelings. Her mother was never one for overt displays of emotion, but no matter how hard she tried to suppress her affection, Maria never doubted her love. She knew what it was like to live behind a mask, to deny those you loved to protect them, to protect herself from an inevitable broken heart.

A knock at the door distracted her. Her mother looked at her with a quizzical gaze. They weren't expecting company and unannounced visits often meant trouble. "I'll get that."

"There is plenty food for more guests."

Maria laughed as she went to the door. Her family didn't get their reputation for being the best hosts in Palermo without it having been earned, but tonight was a family only affair.

She opened the door and locked eyes with Capitano Rocca Massina. The intensity in the officer's eyes, her thin lips set in a tight jaw, and the fine lines carved around a concerned expression caused Maria's heart to pound. The Direzione Investigativa Antimafia (DIA) never visited their home without an invitation and not at this time of the evening, and the capitano certainly wasn't on the guestlist for their private family dinner. She swallowed, her chest constricting with increasingly shallow breaths. "Capitano Rocca, what can I do for you?"

Rocca stared across the shallow threshold. She lifted her arm, seemed to hesitate, and then lowered it to her side again. She broke eye contact and inhaled deeply. She didn't smile.

"Maria. I am sorry to disturb your evening. I need to speak with Lady Lombardo...and you."

Maria's heart thundered, and a sudden rush of weakness left her feeling exposed. She glanced at the weapon she had discarded earlier, hoping the news wasn't going to incite her to have to use it, then gave Rocca her attention. "Please, come in."

Rocca followed Maria into the kitchen.

"Matri, it's Capitano Massina to see...us."

"Good evening, Lady Lombardo," Rocca said, bowing her head as she addressed her.

Her mother smiled, though her eyes didn't. "Capitano, good evening."

Maria recognized the lack of inviting resonance in her mother's voice.

"Lady Lombardo. Maria. I have bad news. I am sorry to tell you, but Don Calvino was killed in a traffic accident...earlier this evening."

No! No! No! The screams in Maria's head became one with her mother's gasping sobs and then faded behind her spiralling thoughts. Calmness slowed her, and her focus narrowed. "You must be mistaken, capitano," she said evenly. She kept her posture neutral, giving nothing away, while the torturous assault ripped her heart to shreds with teeth of diamonds, then gnawed at the pulsing flesh until her senses became silent. Numbness quickly consumed her.

Rocca looked at Maria, her head at a slight angle. "I'm sorry, Maria. There is no mistake."

"What happened? How? Where?" her mother asked.

Maria ran her fingers tight to her scalp then clenched her fist around her hair, pulling the roots.

Her mother clasped the kitchen surface, mumbling prayers as she made the sign of a cross against her chest. With an imploring look at Maria, shaking her head back and forth, tears fell onto her cheeks.

Maria pulled her mother into her arms and held her tightly to her chest. "It's okay, Matri. It's okay," she whispered. The words rang hollow. *It wasn't okay.* Her shirt became wet, and her mother's frail body shook in her arms.

"Our understanding is that this was an accident. The car swerved and collided with a lorry about two miles from here, along the beach road."

Maria shook her head. "I need to see my father."

Rocca averted her gaze, hesitated, and then cleared her throat. "I would not recommend that. The car caught fire instantly, and because of a road block it took longer for the emergency services to arrive at the scene. The body...your father...he is not what he was. Of course, if you wish to see him it is your right to do so."

Her mother choked. "Did he...feel anything?"

Rocca shook her head. "No. It was instant." She reached into her pocket and held out a ring. "I believe this is Don Lombardo's?"

Her mother clasped her hand to her mouth, stifling her moans. She lifted the ring with trembling fingers and stared vacantly at the familiar crest, scorched and misshapen by the heat it had been subjected to.

Maria stared at the gold ring, the symbol that now marked her father's death. Slowly, she closed her eyes. Jumbled images and competing thoughts flashed into her awareness, none of which could be made sense of. Everything she had dreamed of became dark and distant; her plans, her future slipping away into a void. She couldn't grasp them. They were gone. And in that moment, it was as if she too had died. She stared at her mother.

"I am so sorry for your loss." Rocca bowed her head to the two women and turned away.

Maria followed Rocca to the door.

Rocca turned and placed her hand on Maria's arm. "If there is anything you need, Maria, please call me."

Ice chased the length of Maria's spine and she shivered. She shook her head, her thoughts with her mother, her sister, their life without her father. The weight in her chest became dull and dense. "Thank you, Rocca."

She walked into the kitchen and held her mother's stiff body in her arms.

"Oh, no, tesoro. Tell me this is not happening. Please?"

She shook her head and stared into her mother's pleading eyes. No words could change the facts or turn back the clock and start the day again. But for a different decision, the door would be opening now, and her father would walk in with a warm smile and a comforting hug. They would be dining together as planned, chatting, and laughing. Nothing could be done to soothe the rawness of the pain that tore her heart into shreds. "He's gone," she whispered.

Her mother took a deep breath and released it slowly. Then, it looked as if she had flicked a switch and the death of her father had been buried somewhere, anywhere, so that it didn't need to be accepted. She resembled Patrina when she had just ordered a hit. Focused. Intense. Dissociated. And then she saw regret in her mother's eyes.

Her mother's eyes narrowed. "You know what this means, tesoro?"

"Yes," Maria said.

"I am so sorry, tesoro. I know you didn't want this." Her mother leaned into Maria's chest. "You will be expected to lead at least until the election, Maria."

"Yes." *That's eight months away.* Anything could happen in eight months. She would make sure someone else could take over from her then. Giovanni was the obvious choice.

Her mother lifted her head and looked at Maria. "The men will want you to go for re-election, you know that. You are the Lombardo future, Maria."

Maria couldn't focus that far ahead. It would destroy her soul to accept that everything she had wished for was now lost. "I know." *I can't accept that. Please, Matri, stop talking to me. I love you, but please stop.*

Her mother stroked Maria's face. "Oh, tesoro, what will we do?"

Maria looked into her mother's red-rimmed eyes, tears spilling freely onto her puffy cheeks, and her own heart ached painfully. She would not cry. She could not cry. Consumed by emptiness, she had no words of reassurance that might console her mother. There was no comforting her own grief either. A sense of profound loss, beyond that which she had expected possible in the event of her father's death, released an unfamiliar emotion inside her. Anger. The title she had no desire to hold, *Donna* Maria, drove a chill through her so terrifyingly potent it rooted her to the spot. Her new role as CEO of the Lombardo construction business she had never wanted to run left her feeling hollow. Her role as boss of the mafia clan she had never wanted to lead made her heart race. She had been trained by her father, yes. But she'd never thought she would ever need to lead. She had always expected Giovanni would be elected, and that would have been with her blessing. He had been the son her father had never had, an older brother to her, but out of loyalty he would never stand against her. She would have to work hard to convince him to put himself forward. *Donna Maria Lombardo.* Who was she? Who would she become?

2.

Maria hesitated, her heart running at a steady beat. She opened the penthouse suite door with a steady hand. Though she expected the overbearing scent of perfume that lingered in the corridor, inhaling the heady aroma inside the expansive bedroom amplified her revulsion. This space, and the fragrance that hung in the warm air, reeked of deception and desperation. That truth didn't prevent the throbbing sensation between her legs from intensifying as she crossed the room. She cursed silently, and not for the first time, her body's acute carnal response to Patrina's sensual presence. She removed her jacket and hung it neatly on the coat stand, then walked with practised confidence to the side of the grand walnut table and removed her holstered weapon. The sense of her every move being watched heightened her arousal. She needed to prevaricate, gather her resolve, to do the right thing. *Damn you, Patrina, for making this so hard.*

She removed the crystal stopper of the decanter, poured herself a large glass of Courvoisier XO cognac, and downed it in one long swig. The fiery sensation clamping her throat was a welcome distraction from the burning gaze calling her. The drink wouldn't defuse her desire, though she wished it could. She willed it to. Tonight, once and for all, she needed to walk away. She moved her hand slowly, tenderly stroking the cloth seat exquisitely decorated with soft tones of turquoise blue and woven with an intricate gold thread.

She took a long, deep breath and released it silently before turning to face Patrina lying naked on the large round bed at the other side of the room. The light always complemented Patrina's olive skin, smoothing the fine lines that would otherwise reveal Patrina's age. Maria had studied the difference in their bodies, the subtle changes over the years as they laid together. Despite over a decade between them, Patrina's body was impressively ageless.

Patrina was waiting for her, wanting her, smiling at her in the way that she always did when getting what she wanted, when taking what she wanted. Determination warred with desire in every cell of Maria's body, and the tension in her jaw reminded her of the ramifications of the decision she'd taken. Patrina wouldn't take rejection well. She parted her lips and inhaled deeply, alleviating the pressure. She stared across the room, her pulse racing. Was she already losing the battle she had come here to fight? Closing her eyes, she committed to her intent. At the very least, she would make Patrina wait.

She averted her eyes and mused her fondness for the private room that had become their haven for the past six years that they had shared a bed. The gold ornate trim of the headboard, a feature of the classical Asnaghi design, handcrafted with elegance, upon which she had rested her head as they had talked about a future *together* all those years ago. The matching armchairs around the table that were identical in every minute detail, on which they had sat and dined *together*. Rare moments of bliss, an illusion shattered by life.

Maria valued precision. It was a demonstration of standards, an assurance in the craftsmanship that had created something distinctive, beautiful, and timeless. Her eyes narrowed as she cherished for the last time the antique Majolica plates characterized by their unique, vibrant shades of green and blue set in an octagonal mural on the wall, and the Sicilian Moorish head sculpture, an exotic centrepiece above the large marble fireplace. She would miss all of that. But she would not miss what this beauty had come to represent. Manipulation. Prostitution. Had she really been bought by Patrina? Had Patrina ever really loved her?

The light evening breeze from the half-open window carried in the faintest pine aroma from the garden below, and she breathed it in, hoping it would lessen her stress. She tilted her head from side to side and ran her fingers through her hair and down the back of her neck, but the tension wouldn't subside. She released a short breath through her nose and turned again to face Patrina as she leaned back on her elbows, her chest rising and falling in a steady, erotic rhythm. Patrina's soft breasts, erect nipples, and dark, hungry eyes held the beauty of a fruit ripe for the picking.

She swallowed and her tongue tingled, piqued by memories of Patrina's soft skin against her lips, salty sweet, sensing the texture of her arousal when it came, as it always did. Maria tried to find that past pleasure in the present moment, but it alluded her. Patrina's eyes weren't bright, although she smiled as if they should be. And they had sparkled in the beginning. They had been the stars existing in a time and space millions of years before now. And Maria had felt the intensity of that look across many a crowded room in a thrill that ignited her core, consumed her in a fierce flood of electric energy, and turned her inside out, stealing her from herself. Maria had given herself completely, willingly...in the beginning.

She had been captivated by Patrina back then, seduced and rendered speechless in the secret moments of affection they had enjoyed together, away from Patrina's husband, Don Stefano Amato. Maria was sure that she and Patrina had shared something special. It would be untrue and unnecessarily cruel to deny that fact. Maria had known intimacy without words, without the overt expressions of love that lovers often use to demonstrate their commitment, promising their souls in return for a lifetime together. So what? She didn't need that. That had never really been the deal, nor would it ever be.

Maria ran her tongue over her lips as she appraised Patrina's shapely hips and soft thighs awaiting her attention. She reflected on the wetness she would find between the silky folds, the treasures that would be revealed at the height of Patrina's orgasm.

She refilled her glass and drank from it in an attempt to still her quivering lips that betrayed her arousal. She swilled the liqueur, her attention on the dark amber liquid as it settled in wave-like translucent form on the inside of the glass. Bringing the glass to her lips, she paused and inhaled before her focus narrowed to her ever-so-slightly trembling fingers around the glass. She moved with urgency and swallowed in haste, clinging to the glass for refuge. Her throat burned as the fiery drink coursed inside her. A shudder passed through her seconds later, making her heart race. There was a time when she would have wanted to be sober making love, but not now, not here, and not with Patrina.

Maria blinked as the burning sensation reduced her to numbness, and she meticulously placed the glass on the edge of the table. Had *she* ever actually loved Patrina? She thought she had, in the beginning. She looked at Patrina and forced herself to smile. Patrina's eyelids fluttered as she smiled alluringly. The attempt at seduction felt feeble and didn't affect Maria. It didn't resonate as it once had. Maybe it was the years that had passed or the impact of their mafia life. Maybe it was simply that they had become complacent with their relationship and grown apart. She had seen the end coming a long time ago, if she were honest. But there was a strong bond and secrets they shared that had stopped her doing back then what she must do now. It would always be complicated. She closed her eyes and made a promise to herself that she intended to keep. This would be their last time.

"Come to bed, Maria. I need you."

The resonance of Patrina's voice slipped through Maria's defences. Maria blinked, trembling, then squeezed her eyes closed again. She reached for the image of a time past, a time when the desire to arouse Patrina came easily. She recalled the soft warmth of Patrina's sex against her fingertips, brought to mind the essence they had once shared. Keeping the image in mind, Maria slowly undid the buttons of her shirt and removed it. She folded it with precision and placed it on the table.

Patrina mumbled in appreciation. Maria closed her eyes, inhibiting the verbal response she didn't want to encourage Patrina with. She shook her head, lifted her chin, and ran her fingers lightly through her hair, briefly massaging her temples. She unhooked her bra, folded one cup into the other, and placed it on top of her shirt. The days of her ripping the clothes off Patrina and herself, flaming desire nullifying her own need for order and precision, had long since passed. Maybe she should have ended the relationship sooner. Maybe she should never have got involved in the first place. God knew, they had been treading a very fine line. And she had prayed every day that Don Stefano never discovered the truth.

With a look that appeared absent of affection, Patrina raised her eyebrows. "You are a tease, tonight. Need encouragement?"

Maria watched as Patrina leaned her head back, parted her knees and unveiled her beauty, and slipped her finger into the glistening, silky juices. With calm consideration juxtaposed against her racing pulse, Maria removed her jeans, folded them carefully, and placed them on the table next to the shirt. She positioned her shoes under the table, turned towards the bed, and inhaled deeply. She closed her eyes momentarily to help the sensual image to linger and Patrina's distinctive scent to come to her. Her skin prickled in anticipation. She opened her eyes and wetted her lips, reminded of Patrina's taste. Maria approached the bed, shifting her attention from Patrina's breasts heaving with her gasping breaths to the glistening wet centre between her legs. Patrina rocked and bucked her hips, bringing herself to just short of orgasm.

Maria knew that deft touch well. She moved to the bed and placed her hand over Patrina's fingers, interlinking with them, revelling in her warmth and wetness. Desire surged through her every synapse, building urgency in her own sex, and sweeping away her doubts, pushing away her promise. She eased inside Patrina's silky softness and bit her own lip to restrain the inevitable groan of unadulterated pleasure. Maria took Patrina's nipple into her mouth, teased and toyed it, and Patrina's sex soaked the palm of her hand. Patrina groaned her pleasure into Maria's ear as she moved with artful precision, slowly and teasingly at first.

Patrina clasped Maria's head to her breast, then tried to pull her up to face her. "Kiss me, *bedda*," she gasped.

No! Maria shook off Patrina's hands and eased lower. Savouring the soft flesh at her lips, Maria moved down the length of Patrina's body. She nuzzled into Patrina's damp curly hair, lowered her mouth over Patrina's swollen clit, and wrapped her arm around Patrina's leg. Maria enveloped Patrina's silky flesh in her mouth, and her tongue enticed and danced across her sensitive clit. Maria moaned at the wet heat at her fingertips as she entered Patrina. Patrina threw her head back and groaned in pleasure. Then her hips slowed, and her body became an exquisite sculpture.

Maria thrust deeper, sucked harder and faster, her body aching with desire that would never be satiated here. She sensed the moment, the rise, Patrina suspended before the fall. Maria held her there, as she always did, her buried fingers softly caressing, the tip of her tongue eliciting tiny shocks with every delicate touch. And then the moment passed, and the trembling eased.

Patrina sighed heavily and laughed, then she reached down to Maria to pull her upward. "Kiss me, bedda."

Maria moved up the bed and looked at Patrina, as she had done hundreds of times before. Only this time she stopped with her head at Patrina's breasts, keeping her distance from the kiss that would be too intimate and wrong. The sheen of moisture highlighted Patrina's flushed cheeks, her pulse pounded visibly in her neck, and the fine lines shaped her face beautifully. Her tapering eyes begged to stay closed, immersed in the pleasure that flowed through her. None of it touched Maria the way it used to. There was no urge to cherish Patrina, to trace a fingertip lightly along her cheeks and jaw, or place soft kisses down the line of her neck and nestle against her chest. That feeling remained a distant memory that would fade with time.

Patrina opened her eyes, gazed hazily at Maria, and smiled. She cupped Maria's cheek, and traced her thumb along the line of Maria's lips. Patrina rose from the bed and came towards her.

Maria froze. Gripped by a sense of darkness, her gut twisted and roiled against what Patrina might want that she wouldn't give her. Maria pulled back. "I have to go."

Patrina stared at her, lips pursed, the hint of a frown narrowing her eyes. "Why the rush, bedda?"

Maria slid from the bed, strode to the table, and started to dress. Bile rose in her throat, and she swallowed it down. She closed her eyes as she buttoned her shirt, irritated by the tremor in her hands that slowed down her progress. Tightness spread across her body, reaching her shoulders and chest, and she inhaled deeply to draw it away. She opened her eyes, turned towards the bed, and stared through the pain of truth. Her heart pounded with the certainty that what she was about to say would only incite Patrina's worst traits.

Maria straightened her back, cleared her throat, and looked at Patrina with unwavering commitment. "I can't do this anymore."

Patrina laughed. She shifted up the bed and leaned casually against the headboard.

Maria had come to despise that wry smile, the way Patrina arrogantly cocked her head in an obvious look of utter contempt. Power. History. Control. That was in the past now. Strange, that the woman she had once cared for, maybe loved more than any other, could derive pleasure from inflicting pain. She clenched her teeth and swallowed the fire that would propel her to fight back. Patrina had a knack of conveying emotional blackmail effortlessly through her natural demeanour. How long had it been this way? "I'm serious, Patrina. This." She pointed between them. "Us. It's over."

Patrina tilted her head and considered Maria, as if looking down her nose at something of disgust that she needed to wipe from her shoe.

"You think it is this easy, ma bedda?"

Maria looked away, rolled her tongue over her teeth, and swallowed past the constriction in her throat. She turned towards the door and started to walk. As she turned the handle and opened the door, she took one last inhalation of Patrina's unique combination of scents. She looked over her shoulder and saw the tightness behind Patrina's smile and her eyes that looked at Maria without truly seeing. She met Patrina's gaze and matched her in combative intensity. "That was the last time, Patrina."

Patrina stiffened her jaw, and her lips all but disappeared. She released a dismissive huff, threw her head back on the pillow, and placed her hand between her legs.

Maria was unable to stop herself from watching as Patrina drew her fingers in circles around her clit.

"What is the saying, Maria? About keeping your enemies close? You don't want to make too many enemies so early in your leadership. Men are so..." She moaned and bit down on her lip.

Maria rolled her neck and looked away. It was so like Patrina, using seduction to leverage control. But she was done with that tactic.

"They all think they can be the boss. They get impatient, you know." Patrina moaned in pleasure, started to shudder under her own touch, and then her fingers stilled.

Maria clamped her jaw tightly and shook her head almost imperceptibly. She stepped into the hallway and closed the door softly. She leaned against the chamfered wood and sighed. The bright yellow walls and aroma of freshly laid carpet intensified the nausea clawing at her throat, and she swallowed back the urge to scream.

She pushed away from the door and strode towards the lift. She thumped the call button repeatedly, cursing beneath her breath. She looked back to the penthouse door that she would never open again. The ping announced the arrival of the lift, and before the doors had fully opened, she stepped inside and pressed her thumb firmly on the ground floor button. The lift doors closed all too slowly, eventually hiding the vibrant colours of the penthouse foyer behind the sheet of silver-grey. She stared at her reflection in the highly polished metal. Nausea gave way to relief, and the stiffness in her shoulders eased slightly. *I am free.* The thought settled in a moment of lightness that quickly transformed into a low-level hum of something akin to anxiety. Patrina would not accept the relationship was over. But Maria would deal with the fallout of that later. She'd at least shattered the toxic chains that had linked them and severed the rope that had become a noose around her neck. She swayed on the balls of her feet as the lift started to descend then watched the numbers light up, floor by floor. She looked down at her shaking hands then back to the numbers, and as the lift dropped level by level, emptiness claimed her. *What have I done?* With Don Stefano serving multiple life-sentences, Patrina held the Amato's power, and there was no doubting she could be dangerous. *Will she put a hit on me?* No, she would back Patrina to fight. She closed her eyes, slowed her breathing, and rolled her shoulders. The descent slowed, and she opened her eyes, lifted her chin, and inspected her smile in the mirrored walls. Did she look older or was that an illusion? Tired and wasted. Her smile lacked something. Joy? Her passion for life had died the night her father passed, the same day she had decided to end the relationship with Patrina. She wetted her lips, took a deep breath, and smiled again. *Better.* The outside world must never discover what had existed within the walls of the penthouse suite. The lift arrived at the ground floor. She exited the partially opened doors and strode towards the glass-fronted hotel entrance. She needed time alone to think, to process. Patrina Amato knew how to win, and losing wasn't an option for either of them. Like it or not, Maria would need to fight.

3.

Simone ambled across the cobbled square, the sun warm on her face, and her smile growing wider as she drew closer to her brother standing outside the cathedral. The dimples on his cheeks became more pronounced as his grin widened. He had always been a good-looking boy. Now, he was a handsome young man. She took the tie from around her neck as she stepped up to him, lifted his shirt collar, and placed it around his neck.

"Mama will turn in her grave if you go to church without a tie on."

He gave her a cheeky grin. "It looks funkier on you."

She straightened his jacket and frowned at him. "The satchel, really, Roberto?"

"You sound like Mama." He held out his hands in a placating gesture. "I bought pizza for after."

"I hope you paid for it."

"Stop sounding like Mama." He grinned. "They give us pizza for free."

She stared at him and smiled. She never doubted his honesty these days though he had learned the hard way. Lying about the brawls he had got into at school, lying about his attendance, and then being expelled as a result of his disruptive behaviour. He had challenged her tolerance in the months following the death of their parents, but she had been hurting too and hadn't been of much help to him. Had she failed him? Now, working delivering pizza, he seemed more settled. He had grown up fast. She kissed his cheek. "Right, shall we go in?"

He turned towards the doors of the cathedral and held out his arm. "This sure is a strange birthday present."

She linked arms with him and tugged him to her. "I just want to say hi to them on my birthday, that's all."

He shrugged. "I hate churches."

This particular visit to the cathedral to pay her respects was momentous. Today, she crossed a threshold from twenty-nine to thirty. It felt like a final goodbye, a cord cut. She couldn't explain it, and Roberto would just shrug if she tried. He had never needed rituals to get over his grief, though Simone had questioned whether he might have rebelled less if he'd had a different outlet for his anger. Today was a stepping stone to a new future, though she had no idea what that looked future looked like. She worked for people she didn't like and had no one to go home to at night, except Roberto, of course. But that was different and with his working hours, they could be like ships passing in the night. Anyway, he had his own life and more success with women than she had. Was she deluding herself? Patrina's behaviour at work didn't feel like she was on a new and exciting venture. In fact, Patrina had been more challenging than normal and for no explicable reason. She took a deep breath. She didn't want to think about Patrina Amato or Café Tassimo. She wanted a nice birthday lunch with her brother. She patted him on the chest and straightened his jacket at the front.

"Stop whining. We won't be long." She reached into her pocket and handed him a five euro note. "Put this in the box when you take a candle."

He took the money. "Sure."

The cathedral bells rang out across the square. They were chiming again when they walked out of the cathedral fifteen minutes later. "See, wasn't so bad was it?"

He shuddered. "Why is it always so cold in church?"

She smiled at him. "So, how about pizza then?"

They wandered to the fountain and perched on the concrete ledge. Coins glistened in the shallow water. She threw a euro into the font and closed her eyes.

Roberto removed the satchel and pulled out a box. "What did you wish for?"

"Can't tell you." She looked into the box. "Yum, you got my favourite."

"We use the best salami this side of the mainland. I got them to put all the anchovies on your side." He picked out a slice of pizza and handed it to her with a grimace.

Simone took a large bite and moaned in pleasure. "This is the best birthday present ever," she said, wiping a trickle of oil at the corner of her mouth.

Roberto handed her an envelope. "I bet that tops the pizza."

She saw kindness and anticipation dancing in his eyes. It was a loving mischievous look that made her heart sing. He was looking expectantly at the envelope in her hand as she ripped it open. "A ticket for the opera." He beamed a satisfied grin, and a tear slipped onto her cheek.

"I knew you would cry," he said. "You always cry."

She wiped at her face and frowned at him. "How can you afford this? A hundred euros."

He shrugged. "I've been getting good tips." He shoved a piece of pizza into his mouth and continued to speak. "Really..."

"Don't speak with your mouth full."

He swallowed. "You're sounding like Mama again."

Simone sighed as she chewed. "Do you miss them?" she asked quietly.

"Sometimes."

"When?"

"I miss Mama's meatballs."

"Seriously." Simone chuckled. Their mother hadn't been known for her cooking skills. Their father had been the keen chef of the family, and it had been through him that Simone had discovered her passion for food. "We used to throw them to the birds at the pond."

"Even they refused to eat them." Roberto laughed. "You know, fish died as a result of chewing on those meatballs."

Simone laughed, enjoying the light airy feeling that came when she was around Roberto. He seemed to have a way of making her feel relaxed and frivolous.

"How was work?" he asked.

She didn't want to talk about Patrina's foul mood, or Alessandro's growing addiction, or the fact that she felt trapped, despite her dreams of a new future. She saw a hint of frustration flash across his eyes.

"You don't have to stay there."

She smiled through sealed lips. She couldn't leave the job at the café without there being some kind of price to pay. There was always a price to pay with the Amatos. If she had realised what she was getting into from the start with Patrina, she might have made a different decision. Maybe? *Dream on. I never had a choice.* At least she got paid well for the work she did and nothing *else* was expected of her. Their arrangement worked on that level, and she had been able to protect Roberto from being dragged into the mafia. That fact alone made the work situation bearable. Better the devil you know, her father had always said. And the Amatos were certainly the epitome of that trait.

"I do." She looked into Roberto's eyes and smiled, hoping he didn't notice the weariness she felt. He didn't reciprocate. "Tell me about your day."

4.

Faint scratching noises streamed into Maria's awareness, and she smiled. With a light thump, Pesto landed on her, punching a groan from her before she opened her eyes. She chuckled, and her arms flailed to guard her face from him as he sought to lick her to death. "Hey, boy." She yawned and ruffled his short coat. "All right, all right, I know." She bundled him off her, sat up in the super-king bed, and yawned again.

He inched his nose towards her, tail wagging energetically, then barked twice.

She smiled at the familiar routine. He was her rock, her sanity inside the insane world she'd been born into. She had rescued him as a puppy, a scrawny greyhound-looking mongrel with a chocolate and coffee-coloured short coat. It was the white patch over his eye that captured her heart and the way he had tilted his head and yawned at her. They had instantly bonded, and he had learned quickly. "I need a pee. Be patient." She patted his head as she climbed out of bed and stretched her arms as she walked to the en-suite bathroom, her nakedness revealed to no one in the privacy of her bedroom. She enjoyed the sense of ease that came with solitude, something she had never experienced with Patrina. Promises had been made but in reality, their relationship had been founded in the worst kind of secrecy; the hiding kind. And hiding meant someone had something over you. There was always a risk of the wrong person finding out. In this case, Stefano, and that would cost her life, and Patrina hers.

Seclusion had been a reason she had chosen the beach house, along with its isolation and the beauty that surrounded it. The single story open-plan villa was modest in both size and design by her family's standards, and she liked it that way. She was protected and free to live a normal life. With a gated entrance and the fencing monitored by CCTV on the inland boundary, and the seafront and vertical cliffs surrounding the deep set cove, she could run for miles along the webbed pathways and not see, or be seen by, anyone. It was safe.

Pesto dropped one of her training shoes at her feet as she sat on the toilet.

She chuckled. "So much for patience."

He ran out of the room, and she waited for him to return with her other shoe. It was the same routine every day. She stood, flushed the toilet, splashed water on her face, and picked up her running gear. "Come on, then. Let's go."

He barked at her while leaping from his front to his rear paws, span around in circles, and jumped up at her with his tongue lolling from his mouth. Maria laughed. It took more effort to avoid his increasingly enthusiastic affections than it did to get dressed. Shoelaces tied in a double knot, she cupped his ears, and stared into his big dark eyes. "You ready to run, Pesto?" He tugged away from her and ran to the door. "Wait, I need water." She jogged to the fridge, grabbed a bottle, and twisted the cap off. She took a long slug as she made her way to the door.

Squinting into the early morning sun, she stepped onto the beach terrace overlooking the cove. She tipped water into his bowl and threw the bottle into the bin, but Pesto was already at the sea's edge, nosediving the shallow water exploring as if it had never existed before this morning.

She visually traced a line from the tall cliffs bounding one side of the bowl-shaped cove to her cruiser, the Bedda, moored at the edge of the cove on the opposite side. The fine sand beneath her feet to the stark blue line defined the meeting of sea and sky, and the light gold of the shallower waters became teal and then a deeper shade of blue. The sea was picturesque, giving the illusion of stillness, sufficiently silent for Maria to notice the pounding of her heart. She had always enjoyed these moments of silence. Being in nature energized her. She sighed. Her father had joked that she had a greater love of wildlife than she did for her fellow man. It was true. She felt a particular affinity with sea. Nature wouldn't break her heart as people did, as her father had done when he died. He had smiled tenderly the day she lectured him on the merits of nature over man, the glint in his eye shining brighter with every statement she put to him. Nature just is as it is. It doesn't judge, doesn't criticize, doesn't alienate. It doesn't fear.

She pinched the bridge of her nose and stemmed the tears that welled in her eyes. *I miss you.*

She looked down the beach to her right from the Bedda along the arc of the cove to see Giovanni standing barefoot in the shallower water at the beach, fishing rod in hand. He delved into a sack attached to his belt, attached bait to the line, and cast the rod in the direction of the rocks that fed the base of the cliff. He hadn't spoken to her about Don Calvino's death, and although he concealed his emotions well—as was necessary in this job—she had noticed the strain on his face. The taut flesh pulled across his cheeks, his strong jaw more defined in shape, the hollowness behind his eyes more pronounced. He had become distant and his thoughts impossible to read in the way they hadn't been before. She had always been able to read him instinctively, and he her, but not so much now. Muted conversation and unwarranted hesitancy divided them. He too had withdrawn.

Maria sighed, the calmness of the sea unable to ease the niggling sensation in her gut that wouldn't go away whenever Patrina came to mind. *Patrina, Patrina.* All those years with Patrina as her lover in an affair that never existed beyond the walls of the penthouse suite. False promises had turned to convenience. The relationship had suited them both. Patrina didn't have the courage to leave Stefano. Had she been naïve to think things might change and that Patrina would pick her over her loyalty to the business? Patrina had stopped talking about a potential future together after Stefano was sentenced, when her power at the helm of the Amato enterprise increased. Maria's heart still ached with the illusion of what might have been. Even though the reality hadn't been perfect, Patrina had been her first and only lover, and that was something special. *These feelings will pass with time.*

She shifted her attention to the sun rising in the sky. "It's going to be a hot one," she said for no one to hear. Pesto entertained himself in the water, already a hundred metres up the beach to the right. Watching him exploring made her smile. She held onto the balustrade with both hands and stretched out her shoulders. She continued to hold onto the support with one hand while lunging gently to stretch the tired muscles of her legs, hips, and lower back. Even following an extreme fitness regime, there was always residual tension that needed easing out. Stress came with the job. She stepped onto the beach and started to jog towards the sea. Finding damp, solid sand, she maintained a steady pace heading away from the villa in the opposite direction to Giovanni and towards the cliff.

Pesto bounded back towards her, nose in the air. He ran straight past her, dipped his face into the shallow water, and then sprinted back past her again. He picked up a stick the sea had cast off, dropped to his haunches, and chewed on it then ran with it for a while, juggling it between his teeth. Unceremoniously, he dropped it in front of Maria as she jogged. She skipped over the obstacle before she stopped and threw it back into the sea. He swam after it and returned it to her feet again. She ignored the stick, upped her pace to a sprint, and when he caught up with her, stick in mouth, she slowed down again. They continued with the game until the edge of the cove at which point Maria took the path leading inland. Pesto abandoned the stick and sprinted ahead of her to take their usual route, up and around the front of the estate in a loop that would bring them back to the villa after eight kilometres.

Maria looked at her watch as she jogged the last few paces to the veranda. *Forty-two minutes.* "Good job, Pesto." She stood recovering her breath, hands on her hips, while Pesto lapped from his bowl and flicked water across the veranda. She wiped the sweat from her face, the gentle ebb and flow of the sea encouraging her pulse to slow. Giovanni was still fishing. The cruiser's white bows glistened against the rising sun, and there was a little movement on the water. Maybe she would dive later.

She went to the side of the house shaded by the terraced roof, put her boxing gloves on, and started to spar. She pounded the hanging bag with short, fast punches in a steady, even rhythm. She shifted to faster movements in a pattern of two-to-one, jab-jab-cross, bouncing on her toes to adjust her position and enable maximum impact.

She began to grunt with each punch, becoming louder as she pushed the boundaries of her comfort until she let out a final shout as she landed the last punch. She bent over, fighting for breath. "Fuck, that hurts, but it feels fucking great." Pesto's ears flicked, but his eyes remained closed. She straightened up, puffing hard, and pulled off the gloves and placed them on the bench. She made her way to the kitchen, pulled a bottle of water from the fridge, released the cap with shaking hands, and emptied the bottle in one hit. She reached for the box of dog biscuits on the countertop, and as she tipped some into Pesto's metal bowl, he came running into the house. He sat to attention, waiting. She ruffled his neck as she lowered the bowl to the floor. "Not much escapes you, does it, boy?"

She loaded the filter with coffee, flicked the switch, and waited for the aroma. She poured a small glass of orange juice from the fridge and drank it, then filled the creamer with milk and set it to heat. She poured the coffee and went to the veranda. The routine was comforting and the vista calming.

Giovanni cast his line into the water. Pesto looked up at her. She smiled. "Come on, boy, let's take Giovanni a coffee."

Pesto jumped to his feet and ran onto the beach.

5.

Light grey, matt painted walls towered the corridors that led to a web of cells sprawling across the footprint of the prison. From the west wing to the east wing, metal railings defined boundaries, and steel doors segregated individual spaces; every man's cell a prison within the prison. Stefano had described it to her, complained about the ringing and clanging and the constant echo that reverberated around the inner walls of the prison. But what he had to endure was nothing by comparison with the incarceration in which Patrina existed. She was a mafia boss's wife. That was her destiny. This prison, this corridor, was no colder and no more austere than her life had become. At least Stefano lived within a community here, respected by those who surrounded him. At least most of them did. She had no one.

She imagined the softness of Maria's lips, her tongue driving her to a state of senseless ecstasy, and she felt instantly enveloped in a fuzzy sense of hope and expectation. *Maria hadn't meant what she had said at the penthouse suite.* She shook her head. They would find their place, together again. They always did. Maria needed her as much as *she* needed Maria.

The guard's heavy footsteps and the clip of Patrina's heels resounded in the corridor. They passed through a door and an offensive, overpowering, musty male odour hung in the air, and disinfectant gave off a nauseating aroma. *Always smells like piss.*

"Lady Amato."

The guard addressed her with her formal title though he didn't bow his head as others would feel compelled to do in her presence.

He held open the door to the small room. "You have ten minutes."

A dense Perspex screen split the room in two with her chair on one side and his on the other. She welcomed the physical barrier that separated them. As she made herself comfortable, the seat effused a new perfume. *A wife? A lover?* She played both parts, though favoured the latter, and only with a woman. She sighed and closed her eyes. *Maria.* She couldn't imagine taking another lover. *No.* She blinked her eyes open and took a deep breath, then straightened her posture. She needed to portray strength to Stefano, though he always made her feel weak. She was in control. She was the voice of the Amato business. Though she sensed it slowly slipping through her fingers with Alessandro's increasing involvement. No one must know she was losing control. It would be the death of her.

The door closed with Stefano Amato facing her on the other side of the screen. He moved in the silence the barrier created between them and sat. He picked up the phone on the wall that linked to the phone on her side then indicated with his cold stare for her to pick up the handset.

"You had a haircut," she said. The short white hair, tight to his scalp, matched the length of the stubble around his chin. He looked younger for the close trim. She smiled. He didn't.

"How is business?"

His deep, commanding tone hadn't changed since his incarceration. The tingling in her neck crept down her spine as it always did. She tried to breathe softly to abate the trembling in her stomach. She adjusted her position in the seat. Nothing worked. "Business is good."

He nodded. "How is Alessandro? You are teaching him well, I hope?" He leaned towards the screen and glared through narrow eyes.

Had he always been as menacing? As handsome as he was, the sight of him now made her heart thump, and her instincts urged her to escape his presence. The Perspex didn't stop her fear. That he was a brute, she had always known. He had been charming...once. Even so, the best part of a lifetime together, and she had never known the tenderness with him that she had experienced with Maria. She craved the gentle touch of a woman...one woman.

She softened her smile and pouted. It was a game. Men were so easily distracted.

He licked his lips.

"Alessandro is like his uncle. He has a strong will," she said.

He leaned back, nodding his head and smiling smugly, before he crossed his arms. "He has a good brain for business."

He doesn't. She smiled. "He is ambitious."

Stefano looked vacantly. "That's good. Very good. He will learn quickly."

He's as thick as shit. She wanted to tell him about her concerns and that Alessandro was impulsive and likely to bring down the Amato empire. But that could make her look weak, and if Stefano lost faith in her, God only knew what he would do. He would think the worst of her long before he could see his nephew and heir's reckless behaviour clearly. Blood was thicker than water. If Stefano wanted to, he would ensure Alessandro was elected Don in his absence. And if that happened, she would be history. *Over my dead body.* "How are you, darling?"

"I'm okay." He looked away. "It's getting tougher in here." He closed his lips tightly together and leaned closer to the screen. His eyes widened, and he pressed his mouth to the mouthpiece. "The new regimes are entrenched."

He was referring to the fact that the prison governor and guards couldn't be bought easily. The same was true of the police now. Times had changed. She smiled inwardly, the thought of his suffering lifting her spirits. *Keep to the script.* She frowned, hoping her eyes conveyed tender concern. "They are treating you well, though?"

He rubbed his ribs. They wouldn't leave visible scars, though part of her wished they would. Retribution came in many forms and from many directions, and since she couldn't exercise revenge on him, it would be sweet justice if someone else did. The unified image they had presented to the world, and the pretence she had endured in the name of loyalty to him as his wife, she would no longer tolerate. She would support the Amato business, always. That was the code she had signed up to. But they were working in a new era now, with new rules, and this was a game Stefano wasn't aware he was playing. If she had her way, Stefano would spend the rest of his life in prison, thinking he had control when he hadn't, but she was under no illusion that if he had good reason to get to her, he had the means, and he would make the call. For the foreseeable future, she needed him.

His muscular frame dominated the screen between them as he leant forward. "You look distracted."

She shook her head and put on a smile she hoped would absorb him.

His eyes narrowed.

"Do you need anything, *amore mio*?" She didn't care, but she had to ask.

"Send Alessandro to me, bedda."

Her mouth went dry. She pressed her lips together and nodded. Alessandro having direct contact with Stefano could confuse the chain of command further. Stefano would big up the boy's ego, and she didn't need Alessandro thinking any more of himself than he already did. *Fuck!* She smiled, forcing her grin to stay in place. He looked away from her. She cleared her throat. "Tell me what else you need?" She softened her smile, and he stared intently into her eyes. She maintained the warmth in her expression despite the tingling creeping down her spine. She swallowed and wetted her lips seductively.

"I only want Alessandro to visit," he said. "There are things he needs to learn that only I can teach him."

Shit! She blinked. He was smiling at her, and the tingling intensified and moved into her legs. She rubbed her forehead.

"I'm glad he has you too, bedda." He pressed his palm against the window.

His hands looked too big, too harsh. They reminded her of Alessandro's. Stefano's hands had stolen the lifeblood from many men, but that was expected in his job. Her hands weren't clean either. Whose were? The thought of his hands touching her made her stomach cramp. She placed her hand opposite his, and the Perspex seemed to become less dense. He was closer than she wanted him. His heat, his touch couldn't reach her, though she imagined it did, and her stomach flipped. "I wish you weren't stuck in here," she said softly.

He returned the handset and stood.

With shaky legs and using the table to assist her, she slowly rose from the seat, and the other woman's perfume left the room with her. She inhaled short, shallow breaths as she followed the guard to the prison entrance. Her heart thundered. *Get me out of here.* The guard opened the steel doors to the outside world, and even though the air was humid, she inhaled it deeply and lengthened her stride.

6.

A haze of warm air hovered lazily over the lower parts of the city of Palermo and car headlights ghosted past the shadows of the buildings. The night sky seemed to expand at the outer reaches of the city and darken to near-blackness as it reached out into the stars. Maria smiled at the view that seemed more alluring at night.

She heard the door close and the sharp clip of multiple leather and metal soles on the highly polished wooden floor. She didn't turn to face the three approaching men. She knew exactly who they were and why they were there. Instead, she kept her focus on the white, round cotton cloth in her hand. *Tending plants is so much easier than this.* Dealing with her idiot brother-in-law's behaviour was an annoyance she could do without. She took a deep breath and tamed the rage she wanted to launch at him. He wasn't worth the effort, but he was a loose cannon, and she couldn't afford for him to start a bloody war with Alessandro Amato. And now she had to assert her authority in a way that Vittorio would respond to.

The footsteps stopped, and Maria half-turned to see them stood just before her large, solid mahogany desk. Vittorio looked skittish and out of control. Beads of sweat seeped through his skin and slid down his temples and neck towards the blood-stained collar of his otherwise well-pressed, white shirt. His slight sway and reddened nose told Maria he'd been drinking too much again. If he wasn't her sister's husband, she would consider taking a hit on him herself.

Giovanni Grasso stood stiffly to Vittorio's right-hand side. Maria acknowledged him with a small nod. He would be as pissed with Vittorio's behaviour as she was, though his flat features obscured any thoughts he might have about Vittorio's current state. He looked the epitome of calmness, loyalty, and focus. Angelo, Giovanni's younger brother, stood closer to Vittorio on his left, allowing Vittorio to lean on him lest he should fall over.

"Did you know the orchid has been around for a hundred million years?" Maria asked, her voice soft. She caressed the dark green, rubber-like leaf with a cloth before she threw it in the bin and pulled out another clean one. "And yet, it's a highly specialised pollinator: extinction of the insect means extinction of the orchid." She leaned closer to the vase on the window ledge and traced the symmetrical face of the blood red flower with her fingertip. It resembled the silky flesh of a woman's sex, open and inviting. With tenderness, it becomes pliant and responsive to the touch. She rested the delicate soft petals lightly in her hand as if caressing them. Show a plant love and it grows. Treat it badly, you destroy it. So intricate, so striking in every way. *Discipline is about taking control of your urges. You cannot take that which is not willingly given to you.* Did Vittorio not realise that a lack of discipline was the quickest route to the grave? "The orchid is designed to attract a mate who will pollinate for them, you see."

Vittorio's right eye twitched violently, and he stretched his neck upwards. He tilted his head side to side before returning to a static stance. His arms hung down either side of his body, and he picked at the skin around the thumb of his right hand, something she noted he did when intensely uncomfortable. He looked down at his hands. Blood crusted darker in places across his knuckles and dirt and grime contaminated the open wounds. He was nothing more than a streetfighter and a poor reflection of the Lombardo clan. What in the hell did Catena see in him?

"They live in symbiosis with fungi, did you know? Very clever." Maria picked up the water bottle that sat next to the plant and softly squeezed the trigger. A light spray rained onto the leaves. She watched a trail of water slide the length of a leaf, lingering at its tip before it dripped onto the window ledge. She wiped the water away with the cloth. "Many are so beautiful. Some consider the orchid is parasitic, but they are not. They never take what is not theirs to take. They don't harm another for their own gain." *Unlike you, Vittorio.* She placed the bottle back on the ledge, positioned the handle at an angle of precisely forty-five degrees from the window to the right side, and threw the soiled cloth into the bin.

This wasn't the first time she had had cause to address Vittorio for his indiscretion with respect to the Amato family, and most likely it wouldn't be the last. Maria walked slowly from the window to the front of her desk. She ran her finger along the carved and polished lines in the wood that defined the desk's outer boundary, then continued another three paces until she encroached on Vittorio's personal space and forced him to look up at her. Pesto rose from the basket at the far side of the desk and growled at the men. She clicked her fingers to silence him.

Vittorio glanced towards Pesto. He blinked several times, his vision appearing unfocused. Maria stepped closer, and he shuffled a pace backwards. Angelo stiffened his arm around his back to steady him. Vittorio shrugged the assistance off and clenched his jaw in a mild act of defiance as he regained his balance.

Maria saw the raw graze blotting his clean-shaven cheek and the swelling and purple shading around the socket of his right eye. She winced at the smell of alcohol and the bitter, rancid hum of cigar on his breath. "You lie without opening your mouth, Vittorio. It's a weakness we can't afford in our business." She pointed to the trickle of blood on his face.

He wiped the back of his hand across his misshapen nose. "I..."

She flashed him a look. He should know better than to speak unless invited. Maria shook her head. "You reek." She stepped back, plucked a handkerchief from her pocket, and held it to her nose. "You're a disgrace." She looked at Giovanni, who shrugged almost apologetically, but he was not Vittorio's keeper. "Now, tell me. How the fuck did Don Stefano's nephew end up in the hospital two hours ago?" She clenched her jaw and waited for him to answer.

Vittorio looked to the floor at her feet. "I didn't mean to hospitalise him. He must've hit his head when he fell."

She considered Vittorio's excuse. His manner was far too casual. He lacked respect. Alessandro Amato had come off a darn sight worse in this exchange. She didn't care about Stephano's nephew. The ramifications that would be sure to follow were what concerned Maria. Patrina would want revenge, and she always got what she wanted. "Severe concussion and under close observation, Vittorio. That's one hell of a fucking fall."

"He was hitting on our territory, Maria. Bragging. He's making us look like dicks. What was I supposed to do? Just let him walk over us?" He wiped at the stream of blood that trickled from his nose.

Maria looked to the painting on the wall of the Madonna with baby Jesus cradled in her arms. Family was everything, but her brother-in-law wasn't *her* family. "What do you suggest I do, Vittorio?"

Catena could have done so much better than this pathetic excuse of a man, a man that couldn't be trusted in a business where trust was golden was a liability. Respect was their bond. And he knew nothing of either. She would have to face Patrina to repair the damage caused by his stupidity, which would have been difficult enough before their split. The family didn't need this kind of inconvenience, and she didn't need any more of a fight with the Amatos than she already had with Patrina.

Vittorio remained silent, seemingly unable to find an answer.

"This is not the way we do business with anyone, and it is especially not the way we do business with the Amatos."

Maria noticed Giovanni tense. Was he expecting her to order him to terminate Vittorio? She looked back at Vittorio and took a deep breath. This was Catena's husband, the man her sister was in love with. He had developed an uncontrollable shake in his hand that mirrored the twitching at the corner of his right eye. He looked an unholy mess. "You're still drunk, Vittorio. Look at you." She waved her hand at him, and he flinched. "You do not lay a finger on an Amato again unless I say so. Do you understand me?" She turned, too disgusted to continue to face him. Her hands shook with the restraint she had executed. "Go and tidy yourself up."

Pesto growled as Angelo escorted Vittorio from the room. As was expected, Giovanni waited.

"Want me to keep an eye on him, Donna Maria?"

Maria nodded. "Can you make sure a box of Dom Perignon gets to Patrina today?"

"I already sent it."

"Good."

"It was returned."

"Shit."

"All the tops of the bottles were smashed, Donna Maria."

"Fuck. That idiot. Yes, guard him, Giovanni. Anything he does, let me know. He so much as shits in the wrong toilet, I need to know. And for fuck's sake, teach him how to behave. We can't have a loose cannon in our ranks."

"Yes, Donna Maria."

"I need to invite Patrina to lunch at The Riverside on Monday." She glanced at the wall clock. The fact that it was 10:58 p.m. was of little concern to the matter of honour that was at stake. "Will you see if she can make it?"

Giovanni nodded. "Give me an hour. Donna Maria?"

She looked up to see his eyes full of concern and a smile of genuine affection. "Yes, Giovanni?"

"Are you okay?"

No. "Any progress with that kid you spotted?"

Giovanni cleared his throat. "I've been watching him. The boy has skills."

"What do we know about him?"

"He's Adrianu Di Salvo's youngest. You remember his parents and older brother were killed, must be eight or nine years ago, leaving him and an older sister? His name is Roberto."

She blinked as she recalled the time. What she remembered most was her father's disgust at Stefano's sloppiness. The man is losing his way, her father had said. There was often collateral damage, with the end justifying the means. Everyone knew the rules. But Amato had been wild and careless, and their close relationship with the Amato family had become strained. It had come as a surprise within the community that Stefano had gone down for the hit and was another sign of the changing times. There was a tangible shift in the power they had once enjoyed. Legitimate business was the best way forward, her father had said. She agreed with him but clans like Amato made legitimate business difficult to achieve.

"What does he do?"

"He coordinates a gang of pick-pockets from what I've seen. And delivers pizza."

She smiled. "Pizza?"

"He handles a scooter well."

"He must know the city."

He nodded. "He seems popular... There's something else."

She frowned. It wasn't like Giovanni to be evasive.

"His sister, Simone. She works at Café Tassimo. She's worked for Patrina since the death of their family. She brought up Roberto. Patrina has helped. Blood money."

Maria bit her lip and made a soft sucking noise through her teeth. "Is Roberto not working for Amato?"

Giovanni shook his head. "No. He looks to be operating independently."

"He's just a kid, right?" *Independently operating could get him killed.*

"There is something about him, Donna Maria. He's street-smart for sure. He's never seen doing a job, but he collects the proceeds. It's only small stuff, but he seems to be well respected."

"Why hasn't Patrina picked him up?"

He shook his head. "Maybe it's just a matter of time."

"If you think he's worth it, test him. See if he wants to wash cars for us. When you're happy, I'll see him."

Giovanni smiled. "I'll bet this kid can fix cars too."

She smiled. Giovanni was a good judge of character and abilities, and he was already convinced of the boy. Taking Roberto on could cause an issue with Patrina though. *Not my problem.* The thought still settled in an uneasy feeling. Would she ever get used to not giving a shit? Patrina would make it a problem if she found out, and Maria would need to deal with the consequences. She swallowed down the bitterness. The business was her life now, and not for the first time in the past three months of her tenure as the donna, emptiness filled her. "Let's find out what his interests are."

Giovanni's lips moved slowly into a half-smile. "Yes."

"Goodnight, Giovanni."

"Goodnight, Donna Maria." He bowed his head and turned away.

The door clicked closed, and Maria turned to face the window. Patrina's image came to her again, and an electric pulse fired through her. She cursed the involuntary response. How long it would take for that old stimulus to die out? Self-betrayal was irritating. It showed a lack of control. Three months without sex was a long time, though. She rubbed her hands vigorously up and down her thighs to dissipate the energy. She needed a distraction. She picked up her phone and dialled. She was just about to end the call when it was answered.

"Donna Maria," Rocca said.

"Capitano, good evening."

"How can I help you, Donna Maria?"

Maria hesitated. It was too late for second thoughts. "I am…struggling to sleep at night."

"You need to see the specialist?"

Maria bit down on her lip. "Yes."

"I will make arrangements. When?"

"Saturday?"

"Saturday."

Maria ended the call. She squeezed the phone in her hand while the surge of discomfort blossomed in a sheen of moisture on her skin and then dissipated, leaving her with a feeling of disgust. Is this what her life had come to? Paying for sexual gratification. Not much had changed since Patrina then, though at least she was the buyer now and not the bought. Keeping a distance from the world, a life spent in isolation with no lover to come home to or share a life with, wasn't what she'd hoped for. Her heart ached. A woman—a wife—wasn't an option. It was bad enough being a Catholic in a society that frowned deeply on such an arrangement. But a mafia boss? Not a chance in hell. A scream burned inside her chest, and she buried it.

The unexpected click drew her attention to the opening door. She smiled at her mother who had not long returned from her evening at the opera. "Bona sira, Matri."

"Bona sira, Maria."

The delicate sound of her mother's stiletto heels seemed in conflict with the serious tone in her voice and the deep frown that made her eyes look too heavy for the rest of her delicate features. The sound should be heavier and her pace quicker, if it were a true reflection of her mother's obvious disquiet. Her mother's efforts to conceal the innermost workings of her mind might foil the men that surrounded them but not Maria. She always noticed incongruence. It was a skill that served her well. It had become second nature to her to pick up on the suppressed emotions and the unarticulated concerns of others. Her mother was no different from the rest, hiding her true feelings inside a calm exterior. You need to see beyond that which your enemy wants you to know, her father had often said. "Look into their eyes, Maria. Deep into their soul. You will sense the truth there. You will know who to trust." Deep affection moved through her, molten, bathing her in warmth. She leaned forwards and placed a kiss on her mother's cheek then smiled.

"I saw the office light on. It's late to be working."

"How was the opera, Matri?"

She stroked Maria's cheek. "Is everything in order, Maria? Vittorio looks as though he got badly stung."

Maria tilted her head at her mother's lack of interest in small talk. "Did you know there is a bee orchid, Matri?" she asked.

"Yes. It's sneaky. Its flower mimics a female bee, so the male tries to mate with it and in doing so they pollenate it. I don't understand."

"Vittorio is the foolish insect, always attracted to the wrong plant. The orchid is smarter than he."

She sighed and placed her hand on Maria's arm. "Darling, he's your sister's husband."

"He drinks more than he can handle, and he spends too much time on the wrong side of the casino tables. He is causing us a problem, Matri. And we can't afford his kind of problem."

Her mother let Maria go and turned to face the window. "Do you think he needs to feel respected, that you consider him family?"

"He wouldn't know respect if it were the bee that stung him on the arse."

Her mother chuckled. "Can you not give him responsibilities? So he can prove himself to you? The men look up to you, but they are still men and need to feel...useful. They're not comfortable with a female boss. It is alien to them, a threat to their masculinity. They are more familiar with fighting for their honour than sending gifts of apology," she said.

Maria clenched her jaw. Though her mother was not running the family business, it was clear she still knew exactly what was going on at any given moment. Had Giovanni told her about the champagne?

"Who knows? It might help us all. If Patrina is making a move, maybe we do need to reinforce our presence."

"Patrina will not take this incident well, Matri."

Her mother turned back to face the window. She stood in silence for a moment. "Are relations still good with her?"

"There are new challenges."

"Can we resolve the tension, Maria?"

"Not easily." Maria recalled their last tryst and shuddered. "Patrina wants what she can no longer have."

Though her mother's features remained still and passive, Maria knew that the meaning of her words were clear. Her mother knew about her relationship with Patrina though they had never spoken of it. Had her father known about the affair? No. He would have challenged her directly.

"I know this is the right thing for you, tesoro, and I confess I am relieved. But it does change matters. Can you handle the situation?"

"I will deal with it."

Her mother sighed. "And is Vittorio safe?"

"I am watching him." Maria turned to face her mother. "I want to trust him, Matri, but he is wild. He has no sense. I'm worried he will give Patrina a reason to escalate."

Her mother reached out, and took Maria's hand. "You will do what you need to do, Maria. Your father would have done the same."

Maria nodded. The rules were simple. She would do what was needed to protect those she loved, and Vittorio currently sat outside that circle. Minded of the conversation she had had with her father at her sister's wedding, she winced. "It's going to be difficult for you, not that I'm planning to go anywhere," he had said and laughed. Then he had become serious. "Vittorio is the type of man who will think that the reins should automatically be handed to him, but I would never condone that, and it must not be allowed to happen. It's the old way. He doesn't think clearly and is quick to anger. He is not a Lombardo, and he has too much to learn. This is the Lombardo family business, and we do things our way. It's the new way, Maria. The bloodshed must stop. I believe in you. Vittorio, he is your sister's choice. He is not mine. He is not ours." But that was the point, wasn't it? Vittorio was Catena's choice, and she needed to respect that fact and help Vittorio to become family. If she failed to do that, she was no better than Vittorio.

Maria rubbed at her tense jaw.

Her mother turned from the window and smiled. "Anyway, I have some good news. Catena is pregnant. You are going to be an auntie."

Shit. Maria took a deep breath. Vittorio, who had stood before her looking pitiful and broken an hour ago, was going to be a father? God help them all. "I didn't expect that."

"Be nice. Your sister is very excited."

She needed to speak to Patrina. Whether Vittorio deserved it or not, she couldn't let Patrina take revenge for Alessandro. If she did, Vittorio might not live to see his first child.

"What are you going to do about Vittorio?"

"I need to visit Patrina and make sure this doesn't escalate."

Her mother stroked Maria's cheek with tenderness. "Remember what I said about giving him responsibility. He sees how you treat Giovanni. Can you not give him something to be proud of?"

"I need to think about it." Maria couldn't think of anything more dangerous than giving Vittorio responsibility in the family business right now. "He has aspirations, I can see that."

"Yes, he's ambitious. Our men are. We live in a changing world, Maria, a world that I don't necessarily agree with, but it is what it is. Women bosses still aren't commonplace, and most men would feel castrated by working for a woman. Years of tradition has been turned on its head in such a short space of time. You—even Patrina now that Stefano is in prison. The rules are changing, and women like Patrina are finding positions of power before they are ready. But remember, family is family. *Omertà* is still our law. If we lose that, we have nothing. We will be annihilated."

Maria frowned. She curled her fingers into a fist at her mother's words, *"Before they are ready."* Did her mother think Maria wasn't ready? Maybe she wasn't. The acts of violence she needed to instruct and the bloodshed that would result caused her gut to tighten. And the law of silence wasn't *her* law. She had never seen the sense in loyalty for loyalty's sake and neither had her father. Loyalty that had been bought was fickle. Loyalty earned lasted. Her mother's insistence that the code to remain silent be preserved at all costs caused the tiny hairs on her neck to rise.

"You were trained by your father, Maria, and trained well. The same is not the case for others, and violence and retribution are increasing across the city. Stability requires order and respect. Lose respect, and you lose everything. You must not lose the respect of the men, Maria."

I never asked for this. I never wanted this. Maria shook her head. She was well versed with the ways of the Cosa Nostra; the expectations, the image, and how quickly it could all turn. People would disappear. Accidents would happen. She had been fortunate to follow in the footsteps of her father, and Giovanni and Angelo were trustworthy and loyal to her. But it could quickly turn. One wrong foot, one decision that called her leadership into question, and she too could disappear. It was clear that Vittorio would be the first to jump at the chance of taking control of the business, and he was amassing followers. "I'll let you know if I need any help."

Her mother smiled, turned away from Maria, and headed to the door.

"Bona notti, Matri."

She glanced back over her shoulder. "Bona notti, tesoro. Sleep well."

Maria doubted sleep would come easily. The clock on the wall reading 1:28 a.m. told her it would be a short night. She plucked her phone from her pocket and read the text message from Giovanni: *Patrina prefers the taste of the coffee at Café Tassimo at lunchtime.*

Maria smiled. She hadn't expected Patrina to agree to meet at a restaurant on Lombardo turf under the circumstances, and Café Tassimo was the latest Amato acquisition. It would be interesting to see what she had done with the rundown ex-nightclub on the outskirts of town. Her smile faded with the thought of meeting with Patrina on Amato turf after months of no contact with her. Maria was the prey and Patrina the serpent that had struck a casual blow and was now preparing a full-on attack. Her heart pounded. She swallowed, and her thundering pulse quickened. She challenged her fears with images of the tenderness they had once shared. Patrina may want to lash out but deep down, Maria refused to believe Patrina would seriously hurt her even though her body seemed to think differently. She would prime herself for whatever Patrina might throw at her. Having the problem go away was of paramount importance. *Damn you, Vittorio.*

7.

Simone stopped drying the glass and looked up from behind the bar. The throaty roar of the Maserati as it pulled slowly into a space at the front of the café before the engine fell silent attracted the attention of the Amato men outside.

The two Romano thugs in their car outside the restaurant looked out through the plumes of smoke they generated and stared in the direction of the vehicle. Alessandro's runner leaned over the petrol tank of his motorbike and smiled as if admiring a woman he would like to bed. It didn't take much to work out their thoughts. Simone laughed to herself. There wasn't one of them who wouldn't want the Maserati, let alone the woman who was now walking towards the café's entrance. *In your dreams.*

Donna Maria Lombardo bore no resemblance to their standard guest. For one thing, the café's clientele was almost exclusively male. And for another, *they* didn't dress like *that*. There was no doubting the quality of the dark blue suit. Ten thousand, she reckoned. The perfect cut exemplified the image of Maria Lombardo she had seen portrayed in the newspapers, elegant and sophisticated. She was more handsome in person than any picture had managed to convey. Awe radiated through Simone, and she looked away, acutely aware of the heat flushing her face. Only after Donna Maria had walked past the bar did she swallow hard and look up.

She watched through the corner of her eye as she slowly dried the glasses. Donna Maria looked out of place in this cheap, pretentious setting, with its plastic seating in shades of coffee and brown reminiscent of 1970s décor. Alessandro was equally fake, with the grossly oversized gold chains that had to fight their way past the layers of fat that concealed his chin and neck, the large gold signet ring bearing a coin that adorned the chunky little finger of his right hand, and a gold band encrusted with diamonds circled the thumb of his left hand. He thought he was the king. The gold bar that pierced his right eyebrow and the cosmetic white-toothed smile that concealed the ruby piercing in his tongue she had seen when he laughed, just made him look like a punk. No better than the majority of men in their late twenties in Palermo. The bruising that marked the smooth skin of his right cheek and temple bore a remarkable resemblance to the indentations on the sole of a boot. It was less than Alessandro deserved but Simone applauded the person who had given it to him.

Maria stopped just short of the table at which Patrina, Alessandro, and Beto were sitting drinking wine. Alessandro stood as swiftly as his clinically obese body would allow and lumbered towards Maria with a conceited smile on his face.

The glass fractured with the tension in Simone's grip. She looked up. No one had noticed. She restrained the urge to run out and defend Maria's honour. The odious man galled her. Her heart raced and her breathing felt tight, even though Maria appeared to be calm and unphased by Alessandro's attempt to intimidate her.

Alessandro looked up to meet Maria's eyes. "Donna Maria."

"It's been a while, Alessandro. You've grown into quite the young man."

Simone smiled at the subtle insult. He would be too stupid to notice.

He stood taller and flashed a grin. "Yeah, I have."

He pointed towards Patrina, indicating for Maria to take a seat at the table. As he turned, the injury that had been inflicted to the back of his head made Simone smile.

Maria stood at the edge of the table.

"Are you carrying?" Patrina asked.

Maria shook her head. Patrina got up, moved around the table, and stepped in front of her.

"You won't mind if I check, will you?"

Patrina half-smiled. It looked as though she was goading Maria to challenge her authority, testing to see how far she could push her. Surely Maria wouldn't react? She was smarter than that.

Maria held out her arms. "Be my guest."

An intensity built quickly within Simone and she clenched her jaw, then the metallic taste of blood alerted her. She had bitten her lip watching Patrina run her fingers around Maria's shirt collar, down between her breasts, around her waist, and down to her hips. As Patrina moved lower, she leaned into Maria's body. Simone couldn't take her eyes off Maria. There was *something* about the casual way in which Maria and Patrina communicated. Simone frowned and looked fleetingly to the two men at the table. They seemed oblivious to the obvious intimacy between the two women. Were the men blind, or was it her imagination?

Patrina backed away quickly, looking flustered and flushed. Maria must have whispered something personal to her. Simone had never seen Patrina looking embarrassed before. Simone could barely breathe. She turned away, her hands trembling, and poured wine into a carafe and prepared a basket of bread.

Patrina cleared her throat and returned to her seat. She gestured to an empty spot at the table. "Sit."

Maria acceded. She looked across the table at Beto picking at a scab on his knuckle.

"Beto." Patrina tilted her head indicating for him to leave the table.

He promptly stood and made his way to the back of the restaurant and through a door that led into the kitchen.

Simone took the bread and wine to the table on an imitation silver tray. The closer she got, the faster her heart raced. She stood in front of them, her heart pounding, and smiled weakly. Maria's soft smile eased Simone's anxiety. Then Simone became aware of Alessandro staring at her, and a bolt of fire shot through her.

His eyes were on her breasts. He licked his lips and grinned, his possessive intent clear and vile. She wanted to smack that grin from his face. She forced a smile, hoping her detest of the man didn't show. *Smug, revolting arsehole.* Something flashed in Maria's eyes that told her she had a similar opinion of Alessandro.

As Simone lifted the basket of bread from the tray and placed it in the centre of the table, Alessandro reached around her with his fat hands, grabbed at her arse, and pushed her short skirt upwards. She jumped, and the carafe slid across the silver tray, rocked, and spilled its contents. She tried to steady it whilst shifting away from the unwanted physical contact. Alessandro wrapped his hand between her legs and tugged her closer, trying to force her to sit on his lap as she placed the wine on the table.

Maria glared at Patrina, but she casually finished her drink and poured herself another one. Simone looked pleadingly from one woman to the other. *Please, one of you intervene.* Maria looked incensed by Alessandro's behaviour, but she wasn't in a position to tell either Amato how to treat their staff. Maria must have picked up on her silent plea, because she looked intently at Alessandro and drew his attention away from her.

"Alessandro. I owe you a sincere apology."

Alessandro laughed, and he gripped Simone tightly. "You like pussy, Donna Maria? Simone here is a lovely example."

Simone froze. Had he noticed the connection between Patrina and Maria? Maria gave her a quick empathic look that eased her concerns, though her chest remained constricted.

Alessandro tilted his head to the side and stared at Maria as if he held some power over her. Maria sighed. She seemed unmoved by his provocation. In fact, if anything she looked subtly bored. *She's in control.* Simone felt a flicker of something warm settle inside her.

Maria cleared her throat. "Alessandro, perhaps we could arrange to dine together one evening, and you can tell me what it takes to be a real man. I would be interested to know what makes you so popular with the women. You clearly have something special."

Simone concealed the smile that Alessandro would punish her for if he saw it. Alessandro's ego had been sufficiently massaged, and he was a sucker for a compliment even if laced in sarcasm. It was how Patrina operated with him, and the only thing that caused him to back down. He was weak and stupid when praised.

He puffed out his chest and grinned, then with a flick of his hand he cast Simone free as carelessly as he would kick the dirt from the soles of his shoes. She took a couple of small steps to regain her balance, straightened her skirt, and glanced briefly at Maria before walking to the bar, aware that Alessandro was still leering at her.

Maria watched and waited for Alessandro to shift his attention from Simone, breathing deeply to stem the unexpected warmth the barwoman's presence had elicited in her.

So, you are Roberto's sister.

Maria had sensed Simone scrutinising her from the moment she walked into Tassimo. There was an openness in Simone's eyes that summoned something deeply inside Maria. The overwhelming desire to protect Simone didn't make sense. The despicable way Alessandro treated Simone tempted Maria to exact retribution on Simone's behalf without a second thought for the consequences. But that wasn't the reason. He was just a pig, and she would defend any woman abused by him, even if she couldn't do it in the moment. She could and would deal with him. This feeling though, and her intense reaction to Simone, defied logic.

Alessandro's eye piercing caught Maria's attention, and she cleared her throat. "Could I get some water, please?"

"Simone. A jug of water, please," Patrina said.

"Alessandro, I have come to see how we can we repay you for the debt we have incurred."

Alessandro leaned forward, squeezing his stomach to the table as he reached for the wine and poured. "Vittorio did a bad thing, Donna Maria."

Maria remained motionless. Acquiescence was always the best policy with men like Alessandro. They had to feel as if they were in control.

Simone delivered a carafe of water to the table and returned to the bar. Maria poured herself a glass and sipped, then resumed the visual duel with Alessandro.

He was relishing the power. One way or another Maria would strip it from him. It was just a matter of time. She wished she wasn't on the back foot from the start though. Vittorio had made a mess of Alessandro's head and while she could see what had driven him to violence, this was now one hell of a developing problem. *You fucking idiot, Vittorio.*

"A very bad thing, Donna Maria." Alessandro broke eye contact with her and grabbed at the bread.

He broke off a large piece, dipped it in his wine, and rammed it into his mouth. He shook his head and dark red crumbs skittered across the table. For a brief moment, Maria imagined drawing a knife across his stomach and watching his guts spew from him, as they surely would at some point in the future. She watched him dip, eat, speak, and spray. *Fucking pig.* "Vittorio was misguided, Alessandro."

Alessandro swung an arm in Maria's direction, pointed at her, and then at the food. "Eat. The bread is freshly cooked, and the grapes are the finest in Sicily."

Maria glanced at Patrina, who plucked a small piece of bread from the loaf and dipped it into her wine. Maria watched as she put the bread into her mouth, then she too broke a piece of bread, dipped it, and ate. "These are good grapes, Alessandro. A good crop this year, yes?" The lie slipped effortlessly, and his smile demonstrated he was a man of little taste.

"It could be achieving more."

Now they were talking. "How? What do you need?"

He smacked his lips as he ate, spoke around the food turning in his mouth. "The Riverside."

Maria slowly dipped her bread. He wanted to take over the management of the Riverside, one of their key accounts, as retribution for the injuries he sustained at the hands of Vittorio. It was an outrageous act of dominance, one that, if she acquiesced, would send a message across the patch and call her credibility into question. She leaned back in the seat and placed the bread in her mouth. Though she was finding it hard to swallow, refusing their hospitality would be disrespectful.

"The Riverside would allow us greater access to the market." Alessandro chuckled and wiped his chubby fingers across his too-wide mouth. "With grapes as good as these, more people should benefit, don't you agree, Donna Maria?"

She was well aware that this transaction wasn't about the Amatos running their wine distribution through a wider network. The Riverside would enable them to expand their drug distribution and cut through the centre of Lombardo territory. It would be like handing them a license to print money. And to do so would be signing her own death warrant. "The Riverside isn't that profitable, Alessandro. I can find you a better business to supply wine to." It was a lame card to throw, but she was playing for time with a shit hand.

He rubbed his palm over his chin. "A bad thing happened, Donna Maria. A very bad thing." He shook his head, and his eyes darkened.

Patrina stared, her eyes as dark as her nephew's, and her features revealing nothing that would indicate that leniency might be negotiable.

Maria glanced away from the table to Simone. Simone didn't look away when Maria caught her staring at her intently. Maria broke eye contact and turned back to face Alessandro. "Alessandro, can I have a moment with Patrina? Alone."

Patrina reached out and cupped his face. He looked at her like a puppy waiting for an opportunity to please. She leaned across and kissed his puffy cheek. He stood, clicked his fingers, and the men who had been sat at the window left the room. He clicked his fingers at Simone.

Maria watched Simone closely, concerned as to what might happen behind closed doors as she was ordered into the kitchen. She swallowed back the acid burning her throat and fought the overwhelming urge to rescue Simone from Alessandro.

Silence surrounded them oppressively. Maria needed a shred of their intimacy to equal some leniency here, but even she couldn't feel it. "What will it take, Patrina?"

"You make your bed uncomfortable, bedda Maria, and now you want me to sleep in it for you?" She dipped a chunk of bread in the wine and ate it.

Maria turned her head slowly. "You know I can't give you the Riverside."

Patrina lifted her chin, her focus distant. "Alessandro is his uncle's nephew, Maria. What can I do?"

Maria wasn't going to be drawn into Patrina's mind games. Patrina was Stefano's voice on the outside. No matter who the delivery agent was, the instructions always led back to her. She desperately needed their history to mean something, to cause Patrina to reconsider. "What can I do to help with this, Patrina? How can I make the pain go away?" For a split second, Maria was certain she could see a shred of compassion. She felt it in the familiar ache in her heart that always came with her hope that Patrina truly cared. In an instant it was gone as if it had never existed, and the ache turned to steel.

Patrina looked away. "Let me think about it."

Maria released a slow breath. "Thank you, Patrina." She was under no illusion that Patrina would make her pay a hefty price for the reprieve she had begged of her.

"I will be in touch."

Maria stood, and Patrina remained seated. She walked from the restaurant and got into her car. She removed her weapon from the glove compartment and holstered it. As she turned the engine, she saw Simone staring at her from a room at the far side of the restaurant. A bolt of electric energy shot through her. *Who are you?* Maria smiled, hoping to convey her sympathy and hide her blush. Simone turned away. Maria shifted the Maserati into gear and slowly drove onto the main road. Then she hit the accelerator hard, cursing her brother-in-law as the car roared down the road.

8.

Maria stood with her back to the window and brushed at a fleck of dust on her tailored, black tuxedo jacket. Patrina hadn't taken long in getting back to her to suggest a meeting at the opera. She had a proposition to discuss. Other than the penthouse suite, it was a place they had enjoyed together and where they often concluded business.

Competing emotions warred within her. Irritation at Patrina's passivity, contempt for Alessandro's revolting behaviour, and fear that if Patrina lost control of him, this would be a dangerous situation for them all. She expected Patrina to handle him, and she had done nothing of the sort. She had placated him, and Maria had left the café wondering. *Did he have power over Patrina now?*

Seeing Roberto's sister had thrown her though. Simone had quickly become a distraction to the matter of the business at hand. She had emitted vulnerability and strength, and Maria had the impression that Simone felt oppressed. The desire to protect Simone had struck Maria with the force of an unexpected uppercut. The pain of Simone's apparent suffering and the shock of the strong emotional impact of her own response were equally debilitating. The residual effect of the punch had remained with her long after leaving the café, and thoughts of Simone hadn't strayed too far from the front of her mind since. Simone wasn't safe.

The office door opened, and Giovanni came in. Maria adjusted her red silk bow tie.

"Good evening, Donna Maria."

He looked as he always did, calm and focused. She relaxed a little, though Giovanni wouldn't know the difference. No one would ever know what was going on beneath her skin unless she wanted them to know. Despite her preference for non-violent methods and to work in harmony with Amato, Maria was not a woman to be underestimated. Neither would she underestimate Patrina.

"We need to take on extra staff at the Riverside, Giovanni. It's going to be a busy summer."

He cleared his throat. "Roberto?"

She shook her head. Roberto wasn't quite ready for this kind of responsibility, and more importantly she had a job she needed him to do. She turned back to Giovanni. "You said he can fix cars. Does he do a good job?"

"He's a talented kid, Donna Maria. He learns quickly and has a keen eye for important details. He fixes cars well."

"Good. I have a job for him."

"He is ready for whatever you throw at him."

She knew she could trust Roberto. He had proven himself when he came to her house and washed her Maserati. She had placed three thousand euros in an unsealed envelope down the back of the front passenger seat. He had brought it to her immediately. She had locked eyes with him and asked, "Do you know how much money is in here?" He had nodded hesitantly, clearly unsure as if having checked the money would count against him. She'd offered him one thousand euros from the envelope, but he had refused to take it. Yes, she could definitely trust Roberto. "I like him."

Giovanni looked out the window. "How was diving today?"

"The reef is stunning this time of year. I spotted red starfish and damselfish."

"Incredible."

"Who would have thought such biodiverse beauty could exist inside the depths of an underwater volcano? And Octavia was there." She smiled, recalling the octopus she had named since discovering it as a baby.

"It is a magnificent place," Giovanni said. "Discrete. A great escape, yes?"

"Perfect. Which reminds me, can you make sure our donation to the Marine Centre is increased by thirty percent please? They do an excellent job of keeping the reef safe from unwanted visitors."

He tilted his head in a slight bow. "Of course, Donna Maria."

"We must remain vigilant at the port, Giovanni. I have concerns that the staff there are overstretched with the recent increase in Amato shipments." They owned the port and imported their construction supplies; cement, sand, and steel, but unfortunately, it didn't mean they had full control of everything that went through there. They had shipping agreements with the authorities, as did the Amatos, that had always been respected. "I'm concerned that Alessandro might make a move on the harbour to take more than belongs to him."

"I will see to it."

"Thank you, Giovanni."

He gestured towards her outfit. "You look good."

Before she could respond, there was a knock at the door and it opened to reveal Roberto, dressed in a pressed white shirt, dark grey trousers, and highly polished black shoes.

"Bona sira, Donna Maria." He lowered his head. "Giovanni."

Maria turned to Giovanni. "Can you collect me from the theatre at eleven thirty and take me home?"

Giovanni smiled. "I will be there. Carmen is spectacular, I understand."

She smiled. "So Matri says." Maria straightened the front of her jacket even though it sat perfectly against her breasts and tucked in at her waist and headed to her car.

Roberto moved ahead of her and opened the door.

"Thank you." She slipped into the driver's seat, and Roberto closed the door before coming around to sit beside her. She drove in silence through town.

Roberto started fidgeting and seemed uncharacteristically tense. She looked across at him, and he avoided making eye contact with her. She smiled internally. This was the moment that always came with ambitious kids like him. They wanted to do more, often before they were ready. It was her job to keep Roberto safe until that time.

She smiled. "How are you enjoying your job here, Roberto?"

He kept his eyes on the road ahead. "It's good. I am learning quickly, Donna Maria."

"And the pizza delivery?"

"It's..."

He looked across at her as if judging whether the moment was right to say more. She smiled as she guided the car slowly to the front of the opera house. "Yes, Roberto?"

"It's just...I just want you to know I am ready for more responsibility, Donna Maria."

"In good time, Roberto. Your time will come." She eased the car up to the curb, put on the handbrake, and turned to face him. His hazel brown eyes, rimmed dark, somehow managed to convey his honesty. Trust. Honour. "Roberto, I have an important job for you. Would you like to do it?"

He nodded quickly.

"Good. I need you to be my eyes at the Amato hotel, Hotel Fresco, close to the port. You know the one?"

"Yes, Donna Maria."

"Roberto, can you do that for me and do it well? I need to know who Patrina is meeting. Any new faces, I need their names. Patrina will need to join forces to protect her interests. I need to know who she talks to. You talk to no one else about this. You come to me."

"Yes, Donna Maria. Talk to you only."

"Good. Take the car to my home and go to your work. *Capisci*? You can tell them you quit. You work full-time for me now."

Roberto beamed a grin and his face shone. "I understand, Donna Maria."

"And, Roberto."

"Yes, Donna Maria."

"Simone must not know you are working for me. You understand? She works for Patrina, and you working for me makes the relationship...tricky. You know what I'm saying, Roberto?"

He looked towards the opera house with a frown before ducking his head a fraction. "Capisci, Donna Maria. I understand. You should know that Simone is at the opera this evening."

A rush of blood assaulted Maria's ears, and she cleared her throat. Her intense response to hearing Simone's name lingered. She blinked, dimming the vivid images of Simone and the exhilaration that simmered inside her, and looked at Roberto. "Right. You had better go." She stepped onto the street, straightened her jacket, and walked towards the grand entrance of the opera house without looking back, her heart running a faster beat. She heard the roar of the Maserati as Roberto drove away. She glimpsed Angelo in the corner of her eye, chatting with a small group of people mingling outside the opera house. Ignoring him, she entered the building. She had always refused to have a minder at her heels, on account of her belief that Patrina wouldn't actually take a hit out on her. But Alessandro couldn't be trusted, and now either Angelo or Giovanni had eyes on her whenever she was out and about. She hated it.

"Bona sira, Donna Maria," the man attending the door said, and smiled.

She slipped a fifty euro note into his hand as she shook it and patted him on the arm. He escorted her into the building. "Thank you, Enzio. I will make my own way." She dismissed him and entered the bathroom.

She stood at the mirror assessing herself, then straightened her bow tie once again even though it didn't need any adjustment. As the door opened she turned on the tap and ran her hands under the cold water and watched in the mirror's reflection as a woman entered a toilet cubicle behind her. Her heart beat heavier. She'd never been like this before. She hadn't felt the need to look over her shoulder every five minutes. She hadn't given people a second glance. Now, she looked at everyone more than once, and this kind of interest wasn't driven by lust and desire. *Fat chance*. This feeling was driven by the most primal of needs: survival. Although Simone added further complexity to the Amato situation. *Was Simone here? Was she about to walk into the bathroom?* The fluttering in Maria's chest intensified. She patted cool hands to her face, tucked her hair around her ear, and exited the bathroom. Acutely aware of the increasing number of people in the foyer, she made her way to her private box to the right of the stage and closed the door behind her.

A bottle of Dom Perignon rested on a bed of ice in a silver bucket to the side of the two satin-clothed chairs that looked out over the auditorium. The hum and low rumble of competing voices ricocheted around the tiered structure as people located their seats. Low lighting veiled the curtained stage. Spots of light illuminated the pit, and the flicker of movement and the tuning of violins attracted her attention. At least her heart had slowed to its normal rhythm. The theatre was filling quickly, and the heat began to rise, making the air in the box heavily perfumed. She stood back from the front edge observing and appraising. It was a learned habit. Familiar figures adopted their regular seats in the stalls at the front of the stage: Mayor Marino, his wife, and his two high ranking councillors; the chief commissioner and his wife; and the chief prosecutor. Capitano Rocca sat at the end of the front row with her new sidekick, Detective Tomasso Vitale, by her side. Rocca glanced up at her, locked eyes, and bowed her head.

The box door opened, and Maria turned towards it as Patrina entered. Struck by the long, straight black dress that accentuated Patrina's shapely figure and removed years from her age, Maria smiled. "You look good, Patrina."

Patrina's lips twitched into a smile. "You always look good, bedda."

Her tone seemed to carry on a sigh. The look in her eyes pierced through the professional barrier Maria needed to maintain between them. "Let me get you a drink." Maria lifted the champagne from the ice, ripped the foil from the cork, and unhooked the wire cap. She twisted the cork, and it emerged with a crisp pop. Maria picked up a glass and tilted the bottle to its lip. Slowly, she half-filled the tall glass and handed it over.

Patrina took the glass and lifted it in a toast. "*Â saluti*, Maria."

"*Â saluti*." Maria lifted her glass and watched Patrina.

She used to see a sparkle of life in her eyes, open and inviting. Now, shadows fell across Patrina's eyes and obscured her feelings. Maria sighed. Why did she feel sorry for her? This was the woman who had promised her so much and failed her, the woman who would sit back and allow a pig of a man to belittle an innocent woman. That was exactly how Don Stefano had treated Patrina. Could Patrina not see she was condoning the same behaviour she had been subjected to by her own husband? Patrina had lain in her arms many times before Stefano was imprisoned and wept. She had nursed Patrina, held her close, and showed her the love she deserved. What about now?

Patrina's enticing lips were perfectly accentuated by the evening shade of pink lipstick rested delicately against the tip of the glass as she sipped. Soft lines fanned from the edges of her eyes as she smiled. She looked attractive enough to be a model, though distant and emotionally unreachable. Maria's guard lowered. Perhaps she had misjudged Patrina. They lived in a harsh world. She took a sip of her drink and admired Patrina's dress. She had worn a similar one the first time they attended the opera together, elegant and carrying to the floor, and Maria had been suited in her black tuxedo, crisp white shirt, and a red bowtie that had perfectly matched the rose in Patrina's hair. *Were they just playing a game?* Maria felt the sexual tension increasing and tried to push it away. *No.* She couldn't let Patrina have that power over her. She was here purely for business and to clear her fucking brother-in-law's debt. *Their* relationship was over.

The violins started to sing, the house lights went down, and the stage came to life in a spot of light, prompting the audience to silence. Maria held out her hand and Patrina sat. Maria took the adjacent seat. The curtains swung back, and light danced across the tobacco factory and the square depicted in the construction on the stage. Maria, determined that Patrina's attention had shifted to the opening scene, scanned row by row; the lower stalls in front of the box, the rows of the circle that spanned to the left of them and formed an arc around the stalls to the opposite side of the auditorium, then the front two rows of the upper circle above them to the left forming a shorter arc above the lower stalls. Was she looking for Simone? Carmen started to sing, but Maria continued to scan the rows.

Patrina leaned towards her and whispered, "You seem unsettled."

Maria shook her head and turned towards Patrina. "It pays to be vigilant."

Patrina smiled. "Maybe that's why I always feel safe around you, Maria."

Maria kept her expression blank, unmoved by the compliment. "What's the price?"

"Shh!" Patrina brought her index finger to her lips and smiled. "I want to enjoy the opera." She turned to the stage, closed her eyes, and swayed her head, drifting with the resonance of the song.

Maria watched Patrina, the gnawing in her gut reminding her that Patrina would decide when she would reveal the price and nothing Maria did or said was going to speed up that process. Powerlessness fused with rage, and she gritted her teeth. She turned to face the stage and tried to distract her growing irritation with Patrina. Any other time, with anyone else at her side, this would have been a poignant and pleasurable evening. Instead, she was a caged tiger, trapped in the illusion of safety and comfort, and fighting an overpowering drive to leave its enclosure. As the music gave way to dialogue, unable to settle, she looked around the auditorium again.

Maria squinted to look more closely at the woman in an exquisite red dress seated in the back row of the stalls, bounded on both sides by men in black evening suits. The light from the stage danced off her, drawing Maria's attention only to her. The dress reminded Maria of the vibrant red of the Love Couture orchid, bright and alluring. She narrowed her eyes further and refocused. *Simone?* She shuddered. Simone moved to sit upright and craned to see the stage, clearly engrossed in every detail of the performance. She made small movements, as if breathing through the emotion of the song. Her lips parted, her fingers moved to cover her mouth, and she brushed at her cheek just below her eye. She toyed with the wavy bangs that hung full and freely to her neck. Maria watched her, absorbed by the beauty that radiated from her. Simone rubbed at her eyes again, though they never left the stage.

Maria's heart raced, light and airy, as she watched Simone enjoying the opera. There was something pure and innocent about her. She wondered if she had ever been to an opera before, and a prickling sensation jabbed Maria in the chest. She felt the ache in her heart rise to form tears. She swallowed hard, snapped her head towards the stage, and took a deep breath. *What the fuck was that about?*

Patrina wiped a cotton handkerchief at her tears, but her practised show of emotion failed to touch Maria in the same way watching Simone had. The realisation clamped hard against her chest.

As the curtains closed for the interval, the lights came up, and Maria's attention was drawn to the movement at the back of the stalls. Simone was making her way out of the auditorium. There was no mistaking her. Simone glanced up to the box. A shiver passed across Maria's skin, and she became aware that Patrina was watching her.

Patrina stood but not before scanning the stalls and frowning. Maria rose and made her way from the box down the stairs and towards the bar, searching for sight of Simone's distinctive dress. She saw a flash of red disappear into the bathroom and felt her breath swiftly leave her.

"Bona sira, Mayor. Contessa," Patrina said. "How are you enjoying the opera this evening? Do let me get you both a drink."

Maria smiled cordially at the mayor and his wife. "Good evening, Mayor. Contessa."

"Good evening, ladies. How very kind of you, Lady Patrina. I have some good news regarding your new development plans," Marino said as they made their way through the crowded space.

"That is excellent news, Mayor, excellent indeed. Don Stefano will be pleased to hear that things are progressing."

They approached the bar. Maria placed a hand on Patrina's arm to get her attention and smiled at Marino and his wife. "If you'll excuse me, I need the bathroom."

Patrina nodded and continued attending to the drinks.

Maria made her way back through the crowded bar with a sense of urgency. She went through the bathroom door so quickly that the woman stood at the sink jolted and snapped her head up sharply. Maria smiled as she took in the stunning red dress and then her smile faded. Simone's cheeks were tear-stained, and the tenderness in her dark eyes clearly affected by the performance. Something moved inside Maria, and the disconcerting feeling was accompanied by an uncharacteristic surge of heat to her cheeks. "Sorry, I startled you."

Another woman entered and shuffled quickly into a toilet cubicle.

Simone gripped the sink with her right hand. "Donna Maria."

Simone's response was clipped and mildly accusatory. She could understand Simone being pissed at her for not standing up for her at the café, but if she had threatened Alessandro on his turf it would have made matters far worse for them both.

"I...I'm sorry, we haven't been properly introduced." Maria never stuttered. Simone inhaled through her nose and drew herself up in stature. She looked as though she was trying to be strong.

"I'm Simone."

Maria took a step closer, and Simone flinched. "I won't hurt you," Maria whispered. She pulled the silk handkerchief from her breast pocket, stepped closer, and held it out. Simone didn't move. "Please, take it."

She took it and pressed it against her face. She seemed to inhale before opening her eyes and becoming suddenly self-aware. She held the handkerchief out in front of her for Maria to take.

The toilet flushed and the woman made her way to the sink. She smiled at Maria. "Good evening, Donna Maria," she said.

Maria didn't know her but smiled politely. "Good evening."

Simone withdrew her hand clasping the handkerchief, and Maria smiled at her. The woman stared at Simone as she washed her hands. Simone seemed to resume breathing after the woman left the bathroom and held out the handkerchief again. Maria smiled. *So innocent.* "Please, keep it."

"Thank you," she said softly.

Maria gestured to Simone's face. "Are you okay?"

Simone lowered her head. "The story of Carmen is very sad."

"It's very romantic too."

"It is about betrayal and a crime of passion." Simone laughed gently.

Maria tilted her head to the side. The lightness of Simone's response had an uplifting effect. "You are right, of course."

Simone appeared to assess Maria, perhaps reconsidering her perspective from the café. Maybe one formed even before they had first met. Maria stared at her, wanting desperately to know her thoughts. She trembled inside. And, if she wasn't mistaken, there was an emotional connection between them in the way Simone looked at her. And the way Simone's eyes evaded hers and yet her skin flushed, and her lips quivered as she spoke.

"You enjoy the opera?" Simone asked, and her blush deepened.

Maria smiled. *Usually.* "Yes. You?"

"I have never been before. This is a birthday present."

"Are you here with anyone?"

She shook her head. Maria observed the softness of Simone's skin, the tenderness of lips that seemed fragile, and her bright eyes now the dampness from the tears had dried. She wondered what had caused the faint scaring over her eye and felt a twist in her gut. She glanced away to control the protective instinct before returning to face Simone. "You were given a wonderful gift."

"I should get back. It will be starting again soon."

She picked up her clutch bag and seemed to hesitate before taking a step towards the door that Maria stood in front of. Maria realised she was blocking the exit, cleared her throat, and stepped aside. "I'm sorry." She reached into her pocket and pulled out a business card. "Please, take this. If you ever need help, call me."

Simone took it. She looked up at Maria and slipped the card in her bag.

Maria leaned towards her. "Promise me you will call."

Simone avoided Maria's eyes. "I will," she whispered.

Maria opened the door, and Simone disappeared from view. She closed the bathroom door and leaned against it, recovering her racing heart. The silky feeling flowing through her was alien and alarming. She rolled her tongue around her dry mouth. She went to the sink, and ran the cool water over her hands, then patted them dry with a towel.

She returned to the bar, thoughts of Simone distracting her from conversation which passed over and around her. Why did it feel like she was swimming in shark infested waters without a harpoon? Simone was no physical threat. No woman was. But that wasn't the problem. Simone was far more dangerous. Simone had awoken something within her that she hadn't felt before, not even with the woman smiling at her now with a quizzical look. She smiled at Patrina, hoping not to reveal the weakness she felt.

They returned to the box to watching the remainder of the performance. When it ended, everyone rose for a standing ovation before the curtains closed, and the lights came up. The auditorium was alive with an excited air of appreciation as people rose slowly from their seats and started to make their way out. Maria watched Simone staring, looking almost bereft, at the stage, and then she glanced towards the box. Maria felt Simone's intensity in a silent gasp and quickly looked away. Patrina was looking at her again, and she turned to face her with an affected smile.

Patrina eyed her suspiciously. "You see something of interest?"

Maria's lips thinned as she shook her head. "No. You?"

Patrina's eyes hovered on Maria's breasts before descending to her crotch. She raised her eyebrows. "Always."

Maria released her tension through a long breath grateful that Patrina hadn't noticed Simone. She reluctantly pulled her thoughts back to business and ignoring Patrina's attempt to seduce her, she plucked the champagne from the ice bucket and poured them a final drink. She wanted to give Simone time to leave without being seen by Patrina, who was clearly enjoying making Maria wait for her decision on retribution for Vittorio's transgression. "So?"

Patrina sipped at her glass. "This is a good year."

Maria glimpsed Simone exiting the auditorium through the corner of her eye and smiled at Patrina. Now she could concentrate. "You are right. It's the best."

Darkness appeared in the emptiness that sat behind Patrina's eyes. *This is it.*

"I needa favour, bedda."

"What do you need, Patrina?"

"Alessandro is very upset. Inconsolable, in fact."

Maria would have rolled her eyes if it hadn't given away her contempt for the fat pig. "What would make Alessandro happy, Patrina?"

Patrina looked away. The last few people milled around in the stalls below them, and the air was cooling considerably.

"He wants to make the business a success, Maria. You know how it is. Increasing profitability is important to him. He needs to show his uncle that he is a good businessman, and that he can handle the responsibility his birth has afforded him."

"You know I can't let him supply the Riverside."

Patrina sighed heavily. "I know, I know. That leaves us in a tricky position, Maria. What can I say?"

Maria remained silent, knowing Patrina's question was rhetorical.

"Alessandro has a strong mind. He gets ideas in his head, and it can be hard to deflect him."

"If anyone can refocus him, you can, Patrina. He will listen to your reasoning."

Patrina winced. "Well... maybe, before..."

Before the night I walked out on you. Patrina was never going to take the spurned woman role easily. Patrina closed the space between them, forcing Maria to the back of the box and into the closed door, obscuring them from the view of potential onlookers.

Her warm breath brushed Maria's cheek, starting a war between the sick feeling in her stomach and the throbbing sensation between her legs. Maria held back a groan as Patrina's soft lips skimmed her neck. Hairs rose up her neck, and her spine tingled. Patrina eased Maria's shirt from her trousers and slipped her hand beneath the sheer material. Maria tensed. Patrina grazed the skin around Maria's waist with her fingertips, and Maria couldn't stop a soft moan escaping.

Patrina unzipped Maria's trousers with her other hand. Maria's body betrayed her head, and she gave Patrina the warmth she'd clearly hoped had called her there. Patrina eased her fingers into Maria's silky wetness, drawing a restrained gasp.

She leaned closer to Maria, nibbled her ear, and whispered, "We have unfinished business, bedda."

Maria winced. Hate rose inside her for what she knew she would have to do to settle this fucking debt, hate for Vittorio. But even more excruciating was the hate she had for herself. The only real power Patrina held over her she would willingly execute, and if Maria didn't comply, there would be bloodshed. This was about Maria's family. Stability. Stopping a war between their clans. Simone's image came to her and self-hate turned to revulsion. *Fucking Vittorio.* "Not here, Patrina. Not now."

Patrina removed her hand from Maria's crotch, slowly did up the zip, and brought her fingers, slick with Maria's wetness, to her mouth. "Sweet."

Maria feigned interest, trying not to vomit the bile that had crept into her throat. *This is the price. This will always be the price.*

Patrina pressed her finger to Maria's lips. "The penthouse suite. Tomorrow at two."

The aroma of her sex wafted temptingly in the air, and Maria nodded.

Did she have a choice?

9.

Ten kilometres in a record time of forty-seven minutes and twenty-six seconds. Maria stopped the clock and breathed deeply. She could never work hard enough for long enough to rid herself of the anguish that meeting Patrina brought, but she could sure as hell burn off sufficient rage to keep her cool. She started to spar. Something didn't feel right about the meeting. Patrina didn't feel right. The vivid memory of their intimate exchange brought disgust and tightened her stomach. She trusted her gut. She punched the bag harder.

Competing thoughts challenged her. If she could stop this now, they could go back to the harmonious relationship they enjoyed before her father died. Was that delusional? Was it possible to recreate the past? Not if Alessandro was taking a lead in the Amato business. He was on a different page. Simone was in danger. She drove a hard punch into the belly of the bag. *That one's for you, fat boy.* She landed another hard punch that created a deep dent in the surface. She watched the bag slowly regain its shape. Minded of Alessandro's stomach pressing against the table in the café, she punched the bag with as much force as she could muster. Her arms fell limply to her side, and she bent over. Her lungs burned as she inhaled deeply. She regained her breath, stood, and wiped the sweat from her face. The urge to punch Alessandro's smug face flooded her again. She raised her fist to hit the bag again and stopped. Boxing in anger was never good practice. You could injure yourself. *That's the last thing I need.*

Arms drained of strength, she ambled into the villa and set the coffee to percolate, Simone's eyes and the depth of emotion she had seen in them haunted her with an unsettled feeling. She picked up her phone to see a missed call from Giovanni. She would deal with that later. She typed out a text message to cancel the specialist appointment she had asked Rocca to arrange for later that evening and pressed send. Her phone beeped a response.

Would you like me to rearrange?

No.

She slid her phone onto the breakfast bar and finished making coffee and looked up to see Giovanni's car on the CCTV. No need to make that call. She ground more coffee beans and waited.

He knocked as he opened the door and entered the villa. "I tried your phone. Is everything okay, Donna Maria?"

"I was just about to call you back. I needed to train."

"There's been an incident."

She took a deep breath and looked into his eyes. "Alessandro?"

"The Riverside just received a delivery."

Maria clenched her jaw. Was Alessandro working on his own or did this have Patrina's blessing? "Go on."

"A hundred cases of wine. Antonio refused it, and they shot him."

"Shit. Is he okay?"

"Shoulder wound. He's being treated at the hospital."

Maria paced the kitchen. "Send him a get well gift. Make sure his family know we are looking after them."

"I will take care of it... We are to expect twelve-hundred bottles of wine every week, Donna Maria. They are invoicing at six euros a bottle."

"Fucking hell. There's no way we are selling that crap." She ran her fingers through her hair and rubbed at her forehead. "The bastard is trying to bring us down."

"That's just the beginning. The driver said to expect tobacco in next week's delivery. At five euros a pack, that's double the cost price."

Maria slammed her fist down on the breakfast bar. She took a deep breath and looked at Giovanni. "I have to meet Patrina at the penthouse suite this afternoon."

"Is that wise?"

She winced.

"Sorry, I didn't mean to question."

She lifted her chin and sighed. "No. You are right. This meeting was arranged yesterday, but the reason for it has just changed. I need to go. Patrina is losing control of the Amato business, Giovanni. Alessandro doesn't know the rules. We need to get rid of this merchandise. Send it back to him and invoice him double."

Giovanni nodded. "Alessandro will be very unhappy."

Maria's thoughts shifted to Simone, and a dull ache weighed heavily in her chest. "I'm concerned about Roberto's sister. Roberto is our family now, and we need to make sure she is taken care of too." In truth, there was more to her reasoning, but she hadn't the time to label her thoughts and feelings about Simone. Her urge to protect Simone was too compelling to ignore, and she trusted her instincts.

Giovanni looked at her quizzically.

"Should we send a stronger message to Alessandro?"

If they did that, and Don Stefano traced his death back to them, it would start an outright war that would never end. She shook her head. "That is not our way, Giovanni. If we retaliate like that, things will escalate quickly. Alessandro is a street fighter, not a warrior. And we need our house in order."

"We need to protect our business, Maria. The men will want to."

"Yes. And *I* need time to think and to plan the consequences."

Giovanni held her gaze. "You know permission for the Amato casino was given?"

Maria looked away. "Yes. The mayor mentioned it to Patrina at the opera."

The Amato's acquisition of the development site didn't sit right either. Her father had put in a bid to construct the tech park on the same ground and had been all but assured his application would be accepted. But that was before he died. Had she dropped a ball, not appreciating the gravitas the Amato's plans had managed to leverage? Money must have changed hands at the top of the chain on this one. Digging deeper would need to wait.

"Amato are taking care of construction themselves and will be increasing consignments through the port."

"Yes, I know."

"This is a threat to business, Donna Maria, a grave threat."

"I know, Giovanni." Maria's head was spinning. None of what he was saying came as a surprise. And she was sure her mother would also have something to say on the matter. But she needed to prioritise. Decision making would be a lot easier if Simone hadn't entered the picture. How had Simone become a priority?

"What do you want me to do, Donna Maria?"

"Make sure Simone is safe. I will go and talk to Patrina. Then I will decide what action we take next."

Giovanni waited.

Maria poured two coffees and passed a cup to him across the breakfast bar. The casino would be an economic threat to the Riverside, which was currently the largest restaurant and casino in Palermo. However, it would take months to build, and the timescales could be significantly delayed if they could slow down the transit of materials through the port. And then, she would get the planning quashed and her father's plans reinstated.

"Donna Maria?"

"Yes."

"Should we arrange a family dinner to celebrate your sister's good news?"

Maria groaned. *Shit.* Catena's pregnancy had completely slipped her mind. It would be entirely appropriate for the family to celebrate and incumbent on her to arrange the party. "Yes. Let's arrange an evening at the Riverside. Invite our cousins and their families and our closest friends this coming Friday."

"Leave it with me, Donna Maria."

"And don't serve that fucking shit Alessandro is trying to pass off as wine. Just send it back to him. No. Actually, send it to his clients as a gift. They will be very happy, and they won't need any stock from him for a while. Alessandro will find his business grinding to a halt very quickly. We're not paying any invoice." She smiled.

Giovanni grinned. "Consider it done."

Maria sipped her coffee. "Roberto wants more responsibility. Use him. But keep it low key. He still has a lot to learn."

"Very good, Donna Maria. As you wish." Giovanni placed his empty cup on the breakfast bar, turned, and walked towards the door.

"Giovanni?" She waited until he turned back to her. "Thank you."

"I will be close by."

Maria smiled through thin lips. Giovanni closed the door behind him. She watched the CCTV camera and his car approaching the gate. As it closed behind him, she became acutely aware of the deep, rhythmical pounding in her chest. She looked down. Her hands were trembling. Patrina was out of control, that much was clear, but she was feeling equally threatened by the swift escalation of events. She might want to avoid violence, but this feud was only heading in one direction. Men like Alessandro didn't know when to stop battling and start talking. It always ended in annihilation. *What I wouldn't give to run the hell away from here and never come back.* The image of Simone came to her. A scream boiled inside her, tried to be heard, and she swallowed hard to stifle its voice.

She gritted her teeth, picked up her phone, and sent a message to Rocca to meet at the Riverside. *Monday at noon.*

The confirmation came quickly.

*

It looked as though Patrina had gone to a lot of effort providing a luscious spread of fresh caviar, king prawns, ricotta-filled arancini, and aubergine caponata accompanied by the vintage wine from her personal collection. She needn't have bothered. The delicate aromas from the freshly prepared food would have excited Maria's senses under normal circumstances, but the veiled act of manipulation had already filled Maria's stomach with a vile quality that stripped her of her appetite. Either Patrina was clearly oblivious to Alessandro's attack on the Riverside or she was playing games. With Patrina it was never clear. Either the pretence had to stop, or Patrina needed to admit she was no longer in control.

"Bedda, come eat."

The smile on Patrina's face turned Maria's stomach sour. If Patrina wanted games, she would give her fucking games. The edginess that had stalled Maria outside the room had lifted. The power Maria experienced looking at Patrina, she didn't recognize. An intense thrill laced with absolute determination. She walked to the table as she removed her jacket, making no effort to conceal the weapon holstered at her side nor to remove it. She had seen Patrina note the fact too, and Maria smiled internally. She plucked a prawn from the plate and ate it, then picked up the crystal glass and swirled the wine before taking a sip. "Tastes good." She smiled.

Patrina let her robe slide open at the front and reveal her naked body. Maria dismissed the visual intrusion that curdled the contents of her stomach. She rested her hands on her hips and looked around the room. "We had some good times here, didn't we?"

Patrina sipped her drink and smiled. "We can have those times back again, bedda. I've been thinking."

Maria lifted the Moorish head sculpture she always admired and ran her finger across its glazed surface. She couldn't connect with the piece and put it back. She turned to face Patrina. "I am here to repay a debt, Patrina. I want to settle this problem with Alessandro once and for all."

"Let's eat first. I ran a bath."

Patrina closed the space between them and the perfumed scent from Patrina's body intensified. Maria smiled, pleased to feel unmoved by the sensual offering being laid on a plate for her to dine from. She had feasted from Patrina's menu for the last time. There was nothing of interest to her. "I need an assurance, Patrina."

"I have control of Alessandro, bedda. You can rest assured." Patrina pressed her body into Maria and breathed into her neck. "You can trust me, bedda. I have always had your best interests at heart," she whispered. She kissed Maria's neck and then her cheek.

Maria pulled back. *Liar.* "I know you have, Patrina and I thank you for everything you have done for me. Those bad things happened a long time ago. We needed each other then." She wasn't going to let Patrina bring up the past and use that against her. She wouldn't be blackmailed.

Patrina's eyes narrowed, and she stared at Maria through a veil of darkness. Her demeanour had shifted, becoming instantly unrecognisable, and then there was another swing, and she smiled affectionately. "We could go to Paris, or Sydney, or Los Angeles and live together, bedda. We could be happy together. Just imagine, away from this world that you detest."

Maria had imagined that world, but for a long time now, Patrina hadn't been at her side in that picture. Maria had been alone and happy.

Patrina allowed the robe to slip from her shoulders and stood naked. Maria averted her eyes and turned away.

Patrina lunged for Maria and pawed at her. "Please, bedda. I need you."

Maria lifted her arm sharply, her clenched fist catching Patrina squarely on the nose. Patrina fell to the floor, and Maria stared at her. *Pathetic.* "You think you have control, Patrina. You don't."

Patrina lay on the floor, dazed and bleeding. Maria moved to stand over her and watched Patrina wipe the blood that seeped from her nose. Maria had crossed a line that couldn't be uncrossed. The look on Patrina's face confirmed the fact that she had effectively signed her own death warrant. Maria had never seen such darkness, such pure evil, emanate so effortlessly from any living being. Even Don Stefano had been seen to demonstrate something akin to compassion. It was obvious Patrina didn't know the meaning of the word. Patrina cared about no one other than herself.

"You are history, Patrina." Alessandro was calling the shots now, and other than having Patrina baying for her head, what could be worse?

Patrina cupped her trembling hand to her face and shook her head. "You know nothing, bedda," she whispered. "Nothing."

"I know that Don Stefano would be very interested in your extramarital activities these past years, Patrina."

Patrina spat blood up at her. "He will have you killed."

Maria put her foot on Patrina's chest and pressed her firmly to the ground. "Maybe it would be a price worth paying.

I'll see you in hell." It was an idle threat but sufficient for Patrina to know that she would do whatever was necessary to protect her family and the business and end their toxic relationship. Maria would wager Patrina feared Stefano more than she did.

"Fuck you, Maria. You're nothing but a fucking whore."

Maria stamped her heel hard into the soft flesh just below Patrina's ribs, winding her badly. Patrina curled up on the floor. She looked a pitiful mess, choking blood and cursing Maria, and then Patrina started sobbing.

"You think I won't resurrect your past for those who would be interested to know?"

Maria crouched down and whispered, "I pity you." She stood silently and picked up her jacket. The threat of blackmail fell from Maria like water off a duck's back. She had nothing to lose that she wasn't willing to give. She smiled at Patrina and walked out of the penthouse suite for the last time.

10.

Maria wound down the window of the Maserati, keyed in the code on the security pad, and waited for the garage gates below the Riverside to open. She drove into the underground garage, parked up, and headed for the ground floor restaurant. Antonio, his arm in a sling, came to greet her. "Antonio, what are you doing at work?" She put her hand on his good arm.

"It is just a graze, Donna Maria. Nothing to be concerned about," he said, brushing off the severity of the situation with a casual air. "Please, I have your table ready."

She smiled warmly, then followed him to her private table in the back corner of the expansive restaurant. A life size statue of Archimedes at one side and a large rubber plant at the other made it all but impossible to see into, or out of, the space.

"Thank you, Antonio." She took her usual seat with the most advantageous view over the dining area. Antonio bowed his head and excused himself to return to the bar. She watched him continue with his duties.

A young waiter appeared with a carafe of red wine, two cut-crystal glasses, and a sterling silver basket loaded with freshly baked chunks of bread. He placed the items on the table, bowed his head, and retreated back to the kitchen. A man and woman entered the restaurant and were shown to their seat. A second group of four men entered and took a table at the front of the restaurant. The place would be full within another thirty minutes.

Maria looked around the room that honoured her father's commitment to the city of Palermo. It had been one of his first construction projects, built before she was born, and was the flagship of what later became his construction enterprise. He had insisted on maintaining the traditional Sicilian Baroque style architecture, and the inside walls were lavishly decorated with coloured marble and mosaic inlays. Vivid colours complimented the soft textured stone walls and pillars. A modern ventilation system kept the air at the perfect temperature, fresh and clean. It was also one of only a few smoke-free restaurants in the city and had been since the day her father had opened it. Both the architecture and the restaurant's three Michelin star status resulted in an air of exclusivity. To eat at Maria's prestigious restaurant meant a wait of three months. Above the restaurant, refreshments and entertainment in the form of the casino with bar and dance acts by invitation only, kept the hosted business meetings companionable. The Riverside was a relaxed and informal venue, and that was the way Maria wanted to keep it. She looked at her watch. *Noon*.

She watched Rocca enter the restaurant, nod to Antonio, and walk towards her. She made no effort to hide the bulk protruding from her side. Firearms were not permitted inside the building, unless of course you were the police, in which case the rules didn't apply. Or to Maria herself, who had a holster and loaded Smith and Wesson permanently fixed to the underside of her private table which never seated anyone else.

Maria stood to greet her. They air-kissed on both cheeks.

"Donna Maria, it is good to see you looking so well."

"Please, take a seat." Maria looked the capitano over with a view to returning the compliment, but she sported dark shadows under heavy lids that pulled her eyes almost closed. "You look jaded, my friend. You are working too hard."

Rocca smiled. "Never a dull moment in the city of Palermo."

Maria indicated to the bread. She poured them both a small glass of wine. Rocca broke off a crust and took a bite. Maria did the same.

"The best bread in the city," Rocca said.

"The best wine too."

"I heard you have a new supplier."

Maria shook her head. "You heard incorrectly. We were approached with an offer, but the wine wasn't of the standard we expect."

"That's reassuring to know. Has Antonio had an accident in the kitchen?"

How the hell he would injure his shoulder in the kitchen wasn't in question. "Yes. He fell and landed awkwardly. He is strong. He will heal."

"That's good."

Maria watched her dip the bread in her wine.

Rocca looked up at her and smiled. "You know there are new friendships being formed with the mainland."

Maria had heard. She picked up the glass, sipped the wine, and waited to find out what Rocca knew.

"The 'Ndrangheta business is growing, and they are looking to form strategic partnerships."

Maria inhaled slowly and deeply. Everyone was aware that the 'Ndrangheta were becoming the most powerful crime syndicate in mainland Italy. She knew Alessandro was forging relationships with them to help secure his transit of merchandise into Sicily. There was no way she would involve Lombardo business in anything the 'Ndrangheta had to offer. That would be akin to siding with the Devil himself. Clearly Rocca didn't know everything that was going on. "That isn't good for our economy."

Rocca shook her head. Maria leaned across the table. "I need a favour," she whispered.

"Whatever you need, Donna Maria."

"We need customs controls to scale up. I want them to double the number of searches and slow the transit of materials through the port. Can you see to this?" She waited until Rocca nodded. "The increase in cost for the additional staff will be adequately compensated. I will ensure funds are transferred this afternoon."

Rocca looked at the bread she was dipping into the wine, turning it to absorb as much fluid as she could before lifting it into her mouth and chewing slowly. "Everything will be put in place by the morning."

"Excellent."

"Very good wine, Donna Maria. Very good indeed."

"I'll have a small selection sent to your house this evening."

Rocca shook her head and raised the palm of her hand to Maria. She lacked conviction.

"I couldn't possibly accept such a gift, Donna Maria."

Maria smiled and rested her hands palm down on the table. "Think nothing of it."

Rocca picked up her glass and finished the wine in one swallow. She looked at Maria and smiled. "How are you sleeping?" she asked quietly.

Maria looked away. "I'm managing."

Rocca lowered her head. "You know where I am, should your needs change."

Maria sighed. The last thing on her mind was sex. "Thank you." She reached across the table and put her hand on Rocca's arm. "I need to focus on the business."

Rocca swallowed hard, seemingly thrown by the unexpected contact. "I...I am *always* here to help, Donna Maria."

Maria let go of her arm and leaned back in the seat. Rocca's apparent discomfort was new. There was vulnerability there and such a weakness could be exploited if necessary. She smiled. "How did you enjoy the opera yesterday?"

*

As Patrina entered Café Tassimo, Simone stopped cleaning the bar and started to make Patrina her usual coffee.

Simone noted her purposeful stride as she crossed the room to join Alessandro and Beto at the oval table. Patrina's heels seemed to clip the stone floor with more weight than normal. She seemed different, and Simone couldn't put her finger on the change. Focused, maybe? Determined?

"Auntie, join us." Alessandro said and waved Patrina to the table.

Simone held back a scowl. He had been sitting on his arse for the past two hours making demands, drinking wine, and bragging to Beto about the deliveries they had been making. His business was doing well, by his account. She was sick of the sound of his voice and the sight of his face, and as she watched Patrina pull him into an embrace, kiss his cheeks, and look at him with apparent tenderness, her stomach churned.

Patrina smiled at him. "We got the planning, Alessandro. We got it." She kissed him again, and he clung to her like a child in need of approval and comfort.

Simone shuddered at the thought of close physical contact with Alessandro. She placed the coffee and a dish of olives on the tray and took it to the table.

"Thank you, Simone," Patrina said and smiled at her.

This is new. Patrina was never overly polite. She nodded and went back to the bar.

Alessandro beamed his cosmetic smile at Patrina. "Sit. Let's celebrate."

Patrina sat, and Beto poured Alessandro another glass of wine, who clicked his fingers at Simone.

She looked at him and smiled. "What can I get you, Alessandro?" She hoped her flat tone held sufficient respect even though she had none for him. He didn't seem to notice, though Patrina stared at her oddly for a moment.

"Three steaks and a bottle of champagne, now."

"Of course, Alessandro." Simone flashed a look at Patrina as if appealing to her as one woman to another to teach her nephew some manners. She went into the kitchen and placed the food order and returned to the bar to collect the champagne.

Alessandro was looking at Patrina, his chin up and his head leaning back on a tilt. Patrina was frowning and had a tight-lipped appearance.

"What is it, Auntie?"

Patrina leaned towards him and stroked his face. "It's nothing, Alessandro, nothing. There's just some personal business I need to sort out. I have a lot on my mind, that's all. You have to take care of things here. How are the wine sales going?"

Simone returned to the table with a bottle in an ice bucket and three champagne glasses. She went to uncork the wine, and Alessandro snatched the bottle from her and proceeded to rip the top from the neck. She made a fast retreat back to the bar.

Alessandro laughed and nudged Beto. Another private joke, undoubtedly offensive towards her. Simone rolled her eyes.

The image of Maria's business card came to her, and she was thankful she'd left it in her clutch bag at home. If the Amatos found the card in her possession, they would ask questions she couldn't answer. And the last thing she needed was to make a real enemy of Patrina or worse still, Alessandro. Her special night at the opera had turned out to be more than she could have imagined.

She had become aware of the two powerful women sitting in the box enjoying the opera together just before the interval. She had noticed Maria watching her, and her dress had become overbearingly hot. Then, Maria had entered the bathroom. Her eyes had been dark and conveyed such tenderness, and the closeness of her hadn't felt close enough. Simone's heart had raced, and her mouth had become dry, and she had struggled to hold herself up. She wanted Maria, and the feeling had been so overpowering it had rendered her senseless.

She closed her eyes and inhaled. The desire was still with her. The unique scent of Maria's handkerchief lingered in her memory.

She hadn't meant to appear rude and had carried her embarrassment at her clipped and incoherent responses home with her. Maria had made her feel giddy and weak. Maria had thought she was scared. And she was. But not for the reasons Maria might assume. The Amatos were pretty much who they had always been, as were the Lombardos. She was familiar with their ways.

What was disconcerting, and what had kept her from a deep sleep since the opera, was the dull ache in her chest that wouldn't abate. Maria's kindness had slipped under her skin and formed a tingling warmth that had comforted and settled her. For the first time in her life, she felt the absence of something she desired. And it wasn't a pleasant sensation.

Alessandro's raucous laughter filled the room. She glanced across to the table to see the three of them laughing and drinking. Had Patrina changed in the time since she had started working for the Amatos, or had she just not noticed how cruel and heartless the woman actually was?

She sighed, wondering whether there would ever be a time when she could leave their employment and feel safe. *Their* idea of protecting and looking after her family resembled blackmail more than it did support. She had been weak back then and with a younger brother to look after, she had taken the easy option. She hoped she wouldn't regret that decision for the whole of her life.

Alessandro uncoiled the metal sleeve around the bottle and ripped it off. He shook the bottle and thumbed the cork from its neck making sure that it fired with the crack of a bullet, skywards, and so the foam would spill profusely over the rim.

Laughing raucously and moving clumsily, he tumbled the champagne into each glass. Froth plummeted from the rim of the glasses, creating a gush of liquid that pooled on the table. He lifted his glass in a toast.

"To the demise of Lombardo."

Simone flinched, and her spine turned to ice. She continued to listen to Alessandro bragging about his deliveries to the Riverside and his plans for expansion. His eyes looked wild and frenzied, on account of the cocaine, no doubt. A wave of sickness rose within her, and her chest constricted.

Patrina clinked her glass against Alessandro's and smiled. "Don Stefano will be very proud of your business acumen."

Alessandro leaned forward. He waved his hand for Patrina to move towards him. "Auntie?"

Patrina leaned closer. "What is it, Alessandro?"

"I have more good news. The car has been scrapped."

Patrina's eyes widened, and then she looked away from Alessandro. Simone noticed Patrina's skin pale, and a flash of recognition passed across her eyes. That information had meant something significant to Patrina and landed very uncomfortably. Why?

"That's very good, Alessandro." Patrina cupped his cheek and stroked his face. "Well done."

Simone frowned. Patrina was behaving very oddly. A car being scrapped meant nothing to Simone, but it sure as hell was of interest to the Amatos. Alessandro looked smug.

Alessandro threw himself back in the seat and broke into a beaming grin. He slapped Beto on the arm. "Business is fucking good, eh?" he said.

Beto laughed loudly, then sipped his drink as his eyes briefly settled on Patrina. He too had a look of mild concern. Patrina smiled at Alessandro, who cupped his hand over the firmness at his crotch and growled.

Pig!

Patrina sipped her drink, watching her nephew. "You're a good man, Alessandro. Here's to your success."

The words sounded hollow.

Alessandro's upper body shook as he fervently nodded. He took a gulp from his glass. "I have big plans, Auntie."

Patrina's smile seemed contrived.

"The wine, the development of the casino, they are just the tip of the iceberg. I have links with the mainland now. Business is growing quickly. They will supply everything we need."

The tone of the conversation didn't sit well with Simone. She went quietly into the kitchen and returned with their food. Silently, she placed it in front of them, avoided eye contact, and returned to the bar.

She had been drying the same glass for some time, rooted to the spot as the droning from Alessandro's mouth faded in and out of her awareness. The realisation that the Amatos had a keen interest in the disposal of a vehicle that had been held by the police rattled her thoughts. Surely, this wasn't the car in which Donna Maria Lombardo's father had died? *Holy Christ.* She closed her eyes and swallowed hard, opened her eyes, and looked down at her trembling hands. Knowing information of that nature could get her killed. Feigning ignorance was her only defence, and she'd better hope she was believed.

11.

Maria walked the length of the banquet room examining the sumptuous spread and nodded her approval. She plucked a black olive from a dish and ate it. "Excellent, Antonio." She squeezed his arm. "The guests will be arriving anytime now. Thank you."

He bowed his head and left her alone with Giovanni.

"Giovanni."

Giovanni glanced at the food and smiled warmly. "You have done Catena proud."

"You think she will like it? I don't know whether she has any cravings or dislikes at the moment, so I went with something of everything, then she can choose."

"I'm sure she will be delighted."

Her mother entered carrying a large wrapped gift, closely followed by Catena, Vittorio, and Angelo loaded up with similar sized boxes. Her mother claimed a table for the presents, and they offloaded them before approaching Maria and Giovanni.

"I forgot to get a gift," Maria whispered to Giovanni.

"Antonio will bring your special gift up shortly."

She smiled at him then took a pace to greet her mother, who waved her arm in the direction of the expansive spread, the one-hundred soft pink and light blue balloons, and the light display that flooded the dance floor area. The pianist was setting up at the grand piano at the entrance to the room, preparing to kick off the event with a more sophisticated musical recital. Every possible taste was taken care of.

"Bedda, this is so beautiful. You have done your sister a great honour."

Catena rolled her eyes at Maria and shook her head. Maria went to her and pulled her into a long, rocking hug and whispered into her ear, "There is a circus act for later."

Catena eased back. She teased the hair from Maria's face then kissed her on the cheek. "I love you, Maria."

Maria turned to Vittorio and held out her hand. He took it. She placed the other hand on his shoulder and kissed his cheeks. "Congratulations, Vittorio." She squeezed his hand and shoulder firmly. "A new baby will keep you on your toes, eh?" She laughed as his eyes widened and his cheeks lost their colour.

More guests entered the room: Mayor Marino and his wife, the Commissioner and his wife, the Chief Prosecutor and his wife, and Capitano Rocca Massina. Maria glanced towards the dignitaries and excused herself to go and welcome them.

Piano music resonated gently in the background. Quiet conversation, laughter, and a warm embrace greeted every guest as they arrived. The table was soon overflowing with gifts. Antonio entered the room with the special gift Giovanni had bought on her behalf placed under the table. She laughed. *A motorised car.* The kid wouldn't be able to use it for three years. As gifts go, it wasn't the most thoughtful. She shook her head. She should've remembered to get something.

Catena looked at the car, shook her head, and laughed. "A black Maserati. Really, sister?"

Maria shrugged. "Could be worse. It could be a Fiat Panda."

"I agree," Vittorio said. "Who doesn't want a Maserati for their birthday?"

"In your dreams," Catena said, rubbing her belly. "You've got schooling to pay for."

"I'll have him driving before he gets to school," Vittorio said.

He was probably right. Maria smiled at her family's gentle banter. That Catena wore the trousers in their relationship was no surprise.

Maria moved around the room to welcome everyone personally and encouraged them to eat and drink. Her sister looked happy, talking animatedly with some of the other wives. Her mother was occupied, chatting with the mayor and his wife. Vittorio and Giovanni stood apart from the group in deep discussion. She approached them and raised her glass in a toast.

Vittorio took a pace as if to leave her with Giovanni. She stopped him.

"Vittorio, I need you to do something for me."

He nodded. "Whatever you need, Donna Maria."

She smiled. It seemed the orchid was learning the art of pollination. She scanned the room, making sure no one was close enough to hear their conversation. "The 'Ndrangheta."

"They are expanding their reach," Vittorio said.

He was aware of what was going on. That was good. "Our *friends* are helping them to grow."

Vittorio slowly sipped at his drink.

"I need to know who is talking to who and about what. We need our ears to the ground." She looked at him for a long moment, hoping she was making the right decision to trust him with a job that required some delicacy and subtlety.

Vittorio leaned closer, put his hand on her arm, and kissed her cheeks. "Leave it with me, Donna Maria."

The darkness and depth she saw in his eyes sent a chill through her veins. Vittorio seemed to derive great pleasure from the kill, as if taking another's life didn't touch him. She would never understand that. It wasn't the Lombardo way. Though if their hand was forced, she would do what was needed.

She watched him go to the group his wife was entertaining and put his arm around her waist. For all his faults, he did seem to dote on Catena, and she was clearly in love with him. He had also managed to keep clean and follow instructions since the incident with Alessandro. Perhaps he could grow up after all.

"He could get killed," Giovanni said.

"We all could."

"Alessandro is very busy moving merchandise."

Maria looked around the room and smiled at guests who acknowledged her as she spoke to Giovanni. "Yes."

"His clients were happy with the gift we donated."

Maria smiled. She lifted her glass towards Rocca who was watching them from across the room, and Rocca approached them.

"Want me to do anything?" Giovanni whispered.

"Not yet." She smiled broadly and held out her hand to receive Rocca. "Bona sira, capitano. I do hope you are enjoying the hospitality this evening."

Rocca smiled as she squeezed Maria's hand. "Thank you for inviting me, Donna Maria." She glanced over her shoulder around the room before continuing. "There have been very long queues at the port this week, Donna Maria."

Maria raised her eyebrows and sighed. "Ah well, the imports business does not always flow easily."

"The union is not happy," Rocca said. "There are rumours of potential strike action."

"That will impact construction across the city. It could be devastating for smaller businesses."

"Yes, it will have a significant impact."

"I'm sure it will get sorted in good time." Maria pointed to the overflowing gift table. "Capitano, did you see the car I got for my sister's child? They will be driving before they get to school." She laughed. Maria's phone buzzed in her pocket. "If you will excuse me, capitano."

Rocca tilted her head in a slight bow. "Of course, Donna Maria. You have a party to attend to. I will keep you updated with activities at the port."

Maria walked away, stepped out of the room, and headed to the bathroom. She pulled the phone from her pocket.

I am scared

She didn't recognise the number, but there was only one person who would send such a message. Maria unlocked the phone and typed: *Where are you?*

The Cathedral

Stay there. I'm coming. Don't speak to anyone.

Maria pocketed her phone. She splashed her face with cool water and patted it dry. She studied herself in the mirror to be sure the sensations that gripped her stomach weren't revealed in her expression. She exited the bathroom and headed through the restaurant, stopping briefly to explain to Antonio that she felt unwell and had to go home. Her family would understand the message for what it was: something urgent had come up that she needed to attend to personally.

She headed straight to the cathedral. After circling the area looking for a parking spot in heavy traffic, she chose to abandon her car at the closest point and hurried across the cobbled plaza. She pulled open the heavy wooden doors and stepped over the threshold, forming a cross at her chest while she hastily scanned the pews. There was a small scattering of people kneeling in silent prayer, and crops of candles flickered along the sidewalls of the church reinforcing the sombre mood in the dimly lit space. She shuddered.

Simone stepped out from behind a pillar, and Maria went to her. She registered Simone's dishevelled state of dress. Her lip was swollen, bruising was beginning to show on the cheek under her left eye, and her shirt was torn. Maria removed her jacket and wrapped it around her shoulders. She took her by the arm and guided her out of the cathedral. Without speaking, she led Simone to her car and helped her into the passenger seat. She got in the driver's seat, turned the engine, and switched on the heat when she noticed Simone shivering.

Simone remained focused on the windscreen in front of her.

"Alessandro?"

One name and a flood of tears streamed down Simone's cheeks, falling to the torn white shirt at her chest. Maria's nose flared, and she locked her jaw. She blinked several times and took a deep breath to calm herself then shifted the car into gear and slowly applied pressure to the accelerator.

12.

The trembling hadn't subsided on the journey from the cathedral to the gated villa. Haunted by Alessandro's wild eyes and the anger in his sharp tone, Simone sat in silence staring out the windscreen. His hands were clumsy because of the alcohol, so thankfully he hadn't been able to get a proper grip on her. She just hadn't moved quickly enough when he lashed out and caught her face. If it hadn't been for Beto coaxing him away, he might have come for her again. He was strong and when angry, dangerous.

The metal gates slowly opened, and the villa came into view. On the inside of the secure complex, Simone breathed more easily. Maria stopped the car on the driveway, and she continued to stare out the windscreen, a new kind of stress seeping into her muscles. This response had everything to do with Maria's scent and proximity. Another tremor passed through her, and she clenched her fists to stop it showing in her hands. Maria was watching her intently. "I'm sorry," she whispered.

Maria squeezed Simone's hand. "Come inside."

The kindness in Maria's voice brought tears to Simone's eyes, and the warmth of her hand and the pressure of her grip was comforting. "I feel such a fool."

Maria shook her head. "This is not your fault. Come." She got out of the car, opened the passenger door, and held out her hand.

With weakness affecting her legs, Simone staggered to her feet. The sadness she saw in Maria's eyes made her own burn, and she looked at the villa behind Maria to avoid locking eyes with her. The intensity with which Maria looked at her would lead her to sob, and she didn't want Maria thinking of her as fragile and needy. Yes, she was concerned and shaken from the events of earlier in the evening. Alessandro was unpredictable and more aggressive, and Patrina was doing nothing to control him. No, she had never feared for her safety as she did now. And, she wasn't alone in that fear either. She had seen it in the eyes of others who served Alessandro, including Beto. But feeble and needy she was not.

She looked around the villa as she followed Maria. *Impressive.* The air was pleasantly warm and sombre lighting cast shadows over various artefacts positioned around the room. In front of her were two large windows either side of a glass door that overlooked the beach. The glass frontage framed the giant cliffs beyond the beach and the deep cove shrouded in darkness. *Beautiful.* Two low backed, leather couches defined the lounge space to the right of which a breakfast bar indicated the start of the kitchen area. Behind her was a corridor with three doors leading from it.

Maria was watching her closely. She could still see sadness in her eyes, but there was something else there too. Caring?

Maria smiled. "Please, come through."

Simone continued to the breakfast bar. Maria went into the kitchen, opened a cupboard, and retrieved a green box with a white cross on it. She put the box on the table and opened the lid.

"Please, sit." Maria pointed to the box as if to ask permission to tend to Simone's wounds.

Simone sat. She looked around, taking in the objects in the U-shaped kitchen; a professional coffee machine that would have dominated her whole kitchen was entirely in keeping with the expansive surface that ran from the breakfast bar around to the sink. The pristine black hob formed a feature on the furthest wall, an extractor fan above it tucked against the wall like a piece of art. Her eyes settled on Maria, who was staring at her. Her racing heart made it hard to breathe. "You have a beautiful home."

Maria removed the antiseptic wipe from its wrapper and handed it to Simone. She gently administered it to her lip. It stung, and she winced as she wiped the clotted blood from her mouth. Her hand started to shake, and tears welled suddenly, and then she started crying.

"Hey."

Maria closed the space between them. Slowly, she eased the wipe from Simone's hand and dabbed the cloth gently to her lip. She tilted her chin upwards and stared into Simone's wet blinking eyes. Maria took a slow deep breath, lifted the loose strands of hair from Simone's face, and repositioned them at the side of her head.

"You have a bruise developing here." Maria pointed to Simone's cheek.

No wonder my face hurts. She watched Maria's frown deepen as she checked the side of her face. She melted at the warmth of Maria's fingertips against her skin, moving lightly along her neck, and then the way Maria glanced at her breasts, revealed beneath the gaping shirt, caught her by surprise, and she struggled to breathe.

Maria tilted Simone's head to the side and continued her inspection. Her eyes narrowed. Her skin looked darker, and her jaw was clamped tightly. Her lips formed a thin line and then she swallowed.

"Did he *touch* you?"

Maria's tone sent a shudder down Simone's spine. There was detachment in Maria's gaze and a chilling void that revealed her disturbed thoughts. What if Alessandro got to Maria first? A gasp resonated deeply in her throat.

"Did he?"

Simone shook her head. It was the truth. He hadn't *touched* her, not in the way Maria implied.

Maria's jaw slowly relaxed though she didn't smile. "Are you okay?"

Simone shook her head. *No.* She closed her eyes as Maria reached out and touched her cheek. She sighed at the warmth of Maria's palm against her skin, and then moaned when Maria's thumb tenderly caressed her damp cheek. Then her skin became cool, and she opened her eyes, disappointed at the distance lying between them.

Maria smiled softly. "Would you like a drink?"

Maria moved away before Simone responded. Simone noted her tone was deeper, her voice quieter.

"Coffee okay?"

"Thank you." She watched as Maria selected a blend of beans and diligently measured them, placed them into the grinder, and flicked the switch. She admired the strong shape of her as she glided around the kitchen, sourcing the cups, spoons, milk, and sugar. And then the aroma of fresh coffee filled the room and comforted her. Then the vibrations began in her stomach again, subtle at first, building and flowing through to her hands, and her teeth chattered as she trembled.

Maria turned to face the muffled sounds coming from Simone, then rushed towards her. She held out her arms and slowly closed them around Simone's convulsing body. Simone leaned into Maria and tumbled from the seat. Maria held her tightly. Simone's eyes closed as Maria's hot breath reached her scalp. Simone inhaled deeply in the comfort. The tenderness eased the trembling, and then Maria moved away from her and a chill passed through her.

She stared into Maria's eyes; her mind awash with confused feelings. The event with Alessandro paled by comparison with the turmoil that Maria's presence elicited in her. She knew now that she had never been caressed before. She had never been *held*, not like Maria just held her. And that was more frightening than the threat of Alessandro. Need, desire, and want were in the throes of a battle against her fear of a broken heart. Her chest thumped, and her thoughts conflicted.

Maria's eyes conveyed deep concern. "Would you like to rest on the couch?"

Simone nodded.

"I'll fetch the coffee over. Would you like sugar and milk?"

"Yes, thank you." She went to the couch and sat. Leaning back, the shivering returned.

Maria took the coffee to the couch. She handed Simone a cup and sat next to her.

"You're staring at me."

"You look like you're in shock."

Yes.

Maria reached out as if to touch Simone, then stopped. She cupped both hands around her drink and sipped. Simone sighed. She wished Maria had swept her into her arms and kissed her. She sipped her drink, the caffeine and sugar instantly providing a surge of energy. She toyed with the idea of heading home but didn't want to leave. She sat in silence, trying unsuccessfully not to think about Maria, and drank her coffee. She stared out the window into the darkness, the cove and the giant cliffs that defended it, aware that Maria was watching her. The heat that rose to her cheeks was a pleasant respite from the shivering. She finished her drink and rested the cup in her lap. *I should go home.* Her heart sank. She continued to look out the window. "It is very beautiful here. Peaceful."

Maria smiled. "It is," she whispered.

Simone's throat constricted. Maria's considered tone caressed her like silk against her skin. "It feels safe here." She turned her head and looked into Maria's eyes.

"It is. It's what drew me here. The sea is an excellent defence, and the cliffs are impossible to climb from the other side. CCTV is helpful, of course." Maria smiled.

Warmth tingled across Simone's skin.

"I have always felt safe here," Maria said. "It's a sanctuary."

Maria's eyes lit up as she talked with fondness about her home. She looked different and unguarded.

Simone sighed. Had she ever felt truly safe? Staring at Maria, she reflected on the time since her parents had died and before then. She had felt safe as a child but no longer felt the same security since she had returned from university to look after Roberto, and not recently since Alessandro started playing a bigger role in the Amato business. It was he who insisted she move to Café Tassimo and take care of the front-of-house. She had been content working in the kitchen in their smaller restaurant on the other side of town. Patrina hadn't fought for her then either.

Maria bit her lip and lowered her head. "What happened this evening?"

Simone looked away and back to the window. "He had the crew with him at the café and was high on coke, and he'd been drinking a lot. He always drinks too much. I had just finished my shift and was about to leave when he made a pass at me. I fought, he grabbed me and ripped my shirt, then he hit me. I hit the ground hard. Beto distracted him, called him for another drink, another snort, and the promise of more interesting women he had lined up for later. Alessandro fell for it, and I ran."

Maria stared at her hands as she wrung them together in her lap, cracked her knuckles, and flexed and curled her fingers. "Okay."

Simone saw Maria's back stiffen and bit her lip. There was never a good time to say what she needed to say, but Maria needed to know. "They were talking earlier."

Maria lifted her head and looked at Simone with a slight frown. "Talking?"

Simone took a deep breath before continuing. "About a car that had been released by the police."

Maria sighed. "My father's car."

You know. Simone swallowed. "Alessandro was talking about it as though he had gotten away with something. He intends to bring you and your family down."

Maria reached out, took Simone's hand, and smiled. "Alessandro's eyes are bigger than his belly." She chuckled at her joke.

There was a distance in Maria's eyes that Simone couldn't fathom, thoughts that Maria concealed even though she jested about the fat boy. It was the unspoken that lodged inside Simone. "What will you do?"

Maria wrapped her hands around Simone's. "He will bite off more than he can chew one day, and he will pay the price. It's what fools like him do."

The comforting touch didn't release Simone's discomfort. "I'm sorry."

"Simone?"

She looked into Maria's eyes, gripped by the kindness she saw there, and when Maria smiled at her, her heart gushed love and bathed her in a warm glow.

Maria's eyes narrowed. "Can you go back to work at the café?"

Simone's stomach dropped as hard as a stone, and her heart flooded her in a different feeling; terror. As she gasped, Maria stared at her with a look of concern.

"I know, it's difficult. But if you don't go back, they will come after you."

Simone felt reassurance in Maria's firm grip. Maria was right. They wouldn't think twice about coming after her. *I do trust you.*

"I'll have one of my men keep an eye on you. If Alessandro makes a move again, my man will stop him."

Simone nodded.

"I'll get you out of there, Simone." Maria took Simone into her arms and held her. "I promise. I need a little time, but I promise."

Simone moved away from Maria and held her head in her hands. "I am sorry to burden you. I should go home."

Maria wetted her lips and cleared her throat. "You can stay here tonight. I'll have a car collect you first thing, so you can be ready in time for work tomorrow."

Simone shook her head. As much as she didn't want to leave, if she got too comfortable in the safety of Maria's house, she would never leave.

"I would prefer that you stay here tonight," Maria said softly.

"My brother will worry if I'm not at home when he gets in."

Maria tensed. She turned to look out the window.

"He will be expecting me."

Maria frowned.

"Can you not send him a message to tell him that you are staying with a friend?"

She stared at Maria with a blank expression.

"You can't tell him you are with me. He could be compromised."

Simone still looked confused.

"You work for Amato. Any association with me is a threat to them. It would be better if he didn't know that you were talking to me. For his safety, and yours. Silence is golden."

Simone knew that. She rubbed her forehead.

"Let's get you to bed." Maria stood and held out her hand.

Simone stumbled and swayed as she stood. "I don't feel well."

Maria put her arm around her waist and led her down the corridor to one of the guestrooms. "Can you undress yourself?"

Simone slumped onto the bed, willing her legs to regain their strength. Maria came to her, lowered to her knees, and stroked her cheek with tenderness. Simone saw sadness in Maria's eyes again, and then it had passed.

"Please, Simone, I need you to be strong," she whispered. "I'll run a bath. You will feel better."

Maria entered the en-suite. The sound of running water and the gentle aroma of jasmine wafted over Simone. She inhaled the soothing scent, stood, and walked slowly into the bathroom. She would be strong for Maria.

Simone started to undo what was left of her shirt, and her fingers fumbled with the small buttons.

Maria turned away from Simone and closed the taps. "There's a nightshirt in the top drawer if you would like one. I'll leave clothes on the bed for the morning, and I'm in the room next door if you feel scared."

Simone looked up as Maria's eyes lifted from her partly exposed breasts. Simone's breath caught and heat prickled her skin. Maria looked away.

"You are safe here, Simone."

Simone could barely breathe, and her heart pounded. "Thank you, Donna Maria," she whispered.

Maria left, and the door clicked softly closed.

13.

Maria stifled a yawn as she gazed through her office window. The city of Palermo hadn't changed overnight. But she had. Sleep had evaded her. She'd listened for the slightest movement from the guest room, and hoped that Simone would come to her, then hoped that she wouldn't. She wouldn't be able to resist the warmth of Simone's body lying next to hers. The scent of her had lingered. She had imagined it on her pillow, and her body had come alive with energy. When her thoughts shifted, the pain of loss slipped tension into her muscles. Her father's shell of a burnt car. The accident that wasn't an accident. Surely, Patrina hadn't ordered a hit on her father? That didn't make sense. In anger, she had paced the room for the best part of the night.

Now exhaustion threatened her as her adrenaline waned. She turned back to her desk, opened the desk drawer, pulled out her Smith and Wesson, and slid it into the holster on her left side. She put her jacket on and buttoned it closed before returning to the window and looking out over the city, the new movie of her father's assassination running in repeating cycles.

She turned as the door opened. Giovanni, Vittorio, and Roberto approached her desk. She moved towards them and focused her attention on Roberto. She was impressed with the stillness in his posture, the straightness of his spine, and the angle at which he held his head with his chin slightly raised but not so much that he would look like an arrogant teenager. He looked like a young man who knew how to remain inconspicuous in a crowd. His eyes were clear, bright, and alert, making it clear he didn't use drugs. *Excellent.* His jaw remained steady and strong, neither tense nor slack. He looked her in the eye without flinching and without threat as she looked at him. He was perfect for the work she needed him to do. "Roberto, I have an important job for you. Do you think you are ready for an important job?" She asked the question though she knew he was. She knew her men's strengths and weaknesses. When she asked them a question it was to test how they responded, and to read their body language or spot any incongruence that would become a problem.

"Yes, Donna Maria."

His response was quiet but carried conviction. She liked that. Respect and confidence. He was like Giovanni. She could see aspects of herself in him too. "Good. You are sure, Roberto?"

"I am very sure, Donna Maria."

She smiled and glanced at Giovanni who looked pleased with his protégé's speedy progress. Giovanni nodded at her, affirming the plans she had asked him to arrange. "Roberto, do you know the scrap yard, north of the city? Rekogest?"

"I know it, Donna Maria."

"There's a car there; a black Alfa Romeo." She handed him a piece of paper with the number plate on. "The car belonged to my father." She swallowed.

"I know the car, Donna Maria."

His features remained unmoved, his focus steady and on her eyes. "Good."

"You want me to look for evidence?"

"I have reason to believe my father's death wasn't an accident, Roberto. I must find out if evidence has been...overlooked. And, if it has, I will seek justice for my family. You understand this?"

"Yes, Donna Maria. Capisci."

"The yard manager will be expecting you." Maria paused. She wanted the truth, and she would then work out how to handle the consequences. "He will turn his head while you look over the vehicle. You will have one hour."

"I know where to look, Donna Maria. I will find what you need."

"Go."

He bowed his head, turned, and strode from the room. She turned to the two remaining men.

Giovanni smiled softly. "If there is evidence, he will find it, Donna Maria."

She turned and went to look out of the window. "Alessandro's business activities are becoming a problem for the city of Palermo. This new alliance with the 'Ndrangheta will destabilise economic security. The port is in chaos because of the increase in imports from the mainland, and the workforce are taking strike action."

"Chico Calabrian has agreed to a meeting," Giovanni said.

Maria turned to face him. "Good."

"I have eyes on Alessandro, Donna Maria," Vittorio said.

She stared at him. "We are guarding Simone?"

Maria had entered the contact details of the man who would keep an eye on Simone into Simone's phone and instructed her to call him immediately if Alessandro became a problem to her. She wasn't to leave a message. She didn't have his name. It was better for everyone that way. If she called, he would be there in seconds. The Amatos would not know him or that he was watching them.

"Yes, we are watching her."

"Good. If Alessandro makes one wrong move towards Simone, we will take appropriate action. Vittorio, you understand what I am saying."

Vittorio smiled. "Yes, Donna Maria."

She looked to Giovanni. "When is the appointment on the mainland?"

"Tuesday."

She brushed the front of her jacket with a calm hand, the weapon under her arm reminding her of the dangers of a meeting with Chico Calabrian. He could blow her away as soon as look at her. "Do we know what they are willing to trade?"

"They are on a fifty-fifty split with Amato," Giovanni said.

"And they will take sixty-forty?"

Giovanni nodded. "I believe so."

"I want a better deal." He was staring at her quizzically. "Is there something else?"

"I should be the one to go, Donna Maria."

Warmth flowed through her. Her focus softened, and her heart beat a quiet rhythm against her ribs. Giovanni was probably right that he should go and speak on her behalf, and if Chico got what he wanted, he wouldn't care who the messenger was. But there was more at stake now, and she needed to be the one to look the Italian boss in the eyes. Chico would expect a demonstration of loyalty and strength. Boss to boss. He would get both from her and neither from the lily-livered Alessandro. "No. We will both go."

Giovanni's lips thinned and his shoulders dropped as he sighed.

She took a deep breath and released it slowly. Don Chico Calabrian, boss of the 'Ndrangheta, had no loyalty to anyone outside his closest crew members. What mattered to him was his bottom line and gaining easy access into Sicily. She had both of the things he needed.

"Firstly, we need to secure the business with 'Ndrangheta and take it from Alessandro, then we will work out how to prevent Chico using the new channels for the transportation of drugs into Sicily. All good?"

Trading building supplies was one thing, but illegal trading was not the Lombardo way. She didn't have a plan for the second problem. First thing's first.

Giovanni nodded. Maria looked at Vittorio.

"Thank you for the party last night, Donna Maria. And your wonderful gift," Vittorio said.

"Have you driven the car yet?" Maria laughed.

Vittorio tilted his head and laughed. "I had to check that it worked."

Giovanni patted him on the back. "You know, it does eight-kilometres an hour but not with your hefty weight in it."

They laughed.

"Everyone was very generous," Vittorio said.

Maria smiled. He seemed genuinely gracious. She patted him on the shoulder. "You will be a good father, Vittorio." A warm feeling moved across her chest, and she cleared her throat.

As Vittorio left the office, he had a skip in his step that made him lighter on his feet like a boxer hyped for a title fight. God help Alessandro if he got in Vittorio's way today.

Maria turned to Giovanni, revealing her concern through an intense gaze. "Alessandro will be finding business difficult with the strike action. I need to know if he is planning to sort the problem out himself." It wasn't that she didn't trust Vittorio, she just trusted Alessandro less.

"Angelo has ears to the ground too," Giovanni said.

"Good."

Maria jerked her head in the direction of the door as it burst open. Angelo strode across the room, his face like thunder.

"The Riverside has been hit."

Maria gritted her teeth. Blood rushed to her head. *Fuck.* "Is anyone hurt?"

Angelo glanced from his brother to Maria. "Antonio is in hospital. He will be okay. Two women are being treated for shock. They made him pay the invoice, Donna Maria. And a second one. Payment on delivery. They dumped more stock on us."

Maria inhaled deeply and turned away. Her spine stiffened. This attack was down to her decision to not pay the invoice and redistribute the stock. Her employees were suffering because of her. A sharp pain jolted her from her thoughts, and the taste of iron slid down her throat. She couldn't even hear the two men behind her breathing. Their silence was a clear message that they needed instruction. She continued with her back to them.

"Give the stock back to his clients."

"Yes, Donna Maria."

Giovanni's tone was quiet. He wanted more. She turned and looked at him. "I will sort out the imports. They won't have any stock to distribute. Tell Vittorio to deal with the delivery guys once and for all."

Giovanni smiled.

Maria turned her back to both men. Their footsteps quieted, and the door clicked shut. She looked at her trembling hands. The aching in her chest spread. Her knees buckled, and she grabbed the desk, cursing the gun as it jabbed her side. Whether she took the hit personally or not didn't seem to make a difference. She clenched her fists. *Control, Maria. Discipline.* Her father's words echoed. *Simone?* Her chest expanded sharply, and her thoughts tumbled with reasoning. How could she get Simone out of Café Tassimo? What if Patrina found out about them? What? *Them.* She rubbed her closed eyes and pinched the bridge of her nose.

The war had begun.

14.

Maria paced the floor as Roberto crossed the room and stood at her desk. She took her place behind the desk and stared at him. He bowed his head. She opened the drawer and took out a buff envelope, and placed it on the desk in front of Roberto, making sure to position it precisely between the picture of her parents and the leather-bound diary. "What did you find?"

"The brakes had failed, and the steering had been tampered with. The driver will most likely have lost control as a result."

"You are sure, Roberto?" she asked calmly.

"Yes, Donna Maria. There is no doubt."

This evidence should have been found. She frowned. *Is Rocca behind this?* She lifted her chin and inhaled through her nose. "Thank you, Roberto."

Roberto waited.

I'll deal with the car later. I need to sort out the imports. She looked at Roberto. He was frowning at her, and she saw concern flash across his eyes. The urge to keep him safe was as strong as it was with Simone, but *he* wanted to be involved. And he was good. He moved around the city without a trace. And, like a well-trained puppy, he was up for any challenge she could throw at him. And, most importantly, she trusted him.

"Is there something else, Donna Maria?"

She moved to the other side of the desk and looked into his eyes. "I need you to do another job, Roberto. It is dangerous work."

He nodded, unmoved by the potential threat that came with the job.

Good.

"Yes, Donna Maria. I am ready."

"The manager and two innocent women were hurt today in an attack on the Riverside."

Roberto shook his head. "This is very bad news."

"We need to send a message to the people who did this terrible crime."

"Yes, Donna Maria."

She stared at him. "The Amato fleet will be forced to park up at the docks tonight. The vehicles need fixing." She nodded her head once as if to confirm his understanding of her request.

"I can do that, Donna Maria. I can fix vans as well as cars."

"Good." She continued to stare into his unflinching eyes.

"Is there anything else, Donna Maria?"

She looked into his eyes. "Your sister is going to be at greater risk after tonight. Alessandro will lash out. He does not discriminate. I want you to know that I will handle the situation with Simone, so you can concentrate on what you need to do. She will be safe, but she may need to stay away from the café for a while...maybe permanently."

"I understand, Donna Maria."

She handed him the package containing fifteen hundred euros. He had earned it.

Roberto pocketed it without question.

"You are a good man, Roberto."

He turned away from her and left the room.

Maria walked to the window and looked out over the city. Darkness couldn't come quickly enough. Her chest still hindered her breathing. The tightness wouldn't lift. The explosion, when it came from the east coast, would wake those sleeping, and the flames would be visible across the city. That Alessandro would wake to the decimation of his business with 'Ndrangheta brought a small wave of satisfaction. He wanted a war, and she would give him a bloody war if she had to, and even though she resented having to give the orders and detested the bloodshed, putting Alessandro out of action would certainly simplify their negotiations with Chico Calabrian. And, when the Amatos eventually came for her, she would be ready for them.

As her thoughts drifted to Simone, a sudden urge to see her caused her hand to come to rest on the gun tucked into her side. The protective instinct subsided, leaving her vulnerable to her emptiness, and heat flushed her skin. Simone hadn't needed to call the number, and that was a good thing. Her man on the ground had also confirmed Alessandro's attention seemed distracted by business matters. That business would have been the Riverside. *The bastard.* She stretched her fingers and clenched them, the scenarios they might face as Alessandro sought retribution coming as a sequence of images. They needed to increase security at all their restaurants, but their crew were already stretched. They had been overpowered at the Riverside two-to-one. She had underestimated the fire in Alessandro's belly. She wouldn't get caught out again. She needed to ensure her own family's safety and Simone's. Alessandro would think nothing of coming after her mother and sister. There was only one way this problem was going to go away and that was to get rid of the source. If Alessandro was taking control of the Amato business, he was an increasing threat to Patrina too. It was a long shot, but maybe she could leverage Patrina to help with the problem. Her stomach twisted. It was unlikely after their last encounter. She looked at her watch, and her thoughts switched to Roberto. Would Simone worry about Roberto? With an explosion of this magnitude, every parent in Palermo would be concerned for their child on the street this evening. She plucked a set of keys from the desk drawer and headed for the silver Alfa Romeo parked in the garage below the building. She would cruise around the city, go to the cathedral, and drive to see Simone. Why? She didn't have an answer, just a strong desire to pray...and an even stronger need to be close to Simone tonight.

Maria had found Simone's address and watched her from a distance since not long after their encounter at the opera house. She had driven past the house half a dozen times since and justified her uncharacteristic behaviour as being in the interests of Simone's safety.

Simone had taken over the rental of the terraced property after her parents died. It was one of a small cluster of houses on the southern edge of the city, constructed in the 1920s. The properties in the row were well looked after, the street located on the better side of town. Simone's house was two-hundred yards up from the main road on the left-hand-side opposite an artisan bakery. Access to Palermo was easy via the underground or bus services. For her journey to work, Simone took the bus from outside the restaurant and then walked up from the bus stop on the main road. The details were important in understanding a potential threat, Maria had told herself.

This was her third swing past the house this evening, and Maria's justifications were utter fabrication. This was about fascination and…affection. Yes, she was attracted to Simone. Her heart raced whenever she thought about her and in those moments of exhilaration, she even dreamed they could be together, though not in Sicily. That Simone might not want to leave the country hurt too much to entertain. She had seen something in Simone's eyes. But she hadn't had the chance to talk to her yet. If it hadn't been for this damn war, she would have already taken her to dinner, courted her, and made love to her. *No good girl wants to be associated with the business.* She took in a deep breath and switched her focus to the night ahead.

Maria parked up in the city centre, crossed the cobbled square, and entered the cathedral, drawing a cross on her chest with her fingers. She sat at a pew, lowered her head, and clasped her hands together in prayer. The foreign feeling inside the cool building prickled her skin. She had never found comfort here, though she admired the architecture. Her father had only gone to church at her mother's insistence. She recognized herself in him and tears formed at her father's image. The outburst from her heart flowed silently down her cheeks. She watched her tears darken the stone tiles at her knees, and an aching sensation clamped her throat and burned like a furnace. In the absence of thought, she became aware that her shoulders were rising and falling as she sobbed. *I miss you, Father.*

She pinched the bridge of her nose and wiped the tears from her face. She remained bowed until the tears stopped. As she lifted her head, the image of Patrina came to her with Alessandro at her side wearing a smug smile that barely made an impression on his bloated reddened face. She moved her lower jaw from side to side to release the tension. If ever there had been a chance of negotiating with Alessandro, which she doubted, one thing was certain, there would be no talking to him after tonight.

Her phone vibrated in her pocket. She looked at the screen. Simone was outside Café Tassimo waiting for a bus. It was time to go.

She stepped outside the cathedral and inhaled the mild evening air. The fumes from passing vehicles and wafting tobacco smoke spewed from rolled-down car windows and caught in her throat. They really needed to address the pollution issue inside the city. She vowed to speak to the mayor about it and get a petition raised.

15.

The bus tilted slightly as Simone climbed the three steps and smiled at the driver's familiar face. She turned to the hissing of the door as it closed behind her, her palm against her chest. There was no one behind her. Did Maria's man still have her in his sights? Was Patrina watching her, as she had in the restaurant for most of the day? The palpitations in her chest slowly settled. She turned to the driver and flashed her ticket. He smiled and bid her a good evening, but the words were hot air and absent of resonance, and she didn't respond to him. She took her usual seat just behind his cab, looked out the window into the passing headlights, and took a long deep breath.

Maria, Maria, Maria. Donna Maria. She played with her name silently on her tongue, and her heart danced in her chest. She touched her bruised lip, and a tingling tremor moved through her in waves of increasing intensity. Reflecting on the tenderness with which Maria had tended to her injury the previous evening, a soft chuckle bubbled inside her. Maria had looked at her with a pained expression and kindness, and she'd appeared more hurt by Simone's injuries than she had. Maria was hard to read; the epitome of respect. But with every touch, every look, and every unarticulated thought, Maria had revealed deep concern and behind that, she had noticed flashes of desire. The same desire that now fizzed through Simone as she sat staring out the window, the image of Maria firmly fixed in her mind. She felt the moan rumbling softly in her throat, and then heat coming swiftly to her cheeks. She looked around the bus. No one was taking any notice of her. She sighed and settled back in the seat. It was hard to breathe and impossible to focus on anything other than Maria's sensual touch. Her stomach flipped, and she sat on her trembling hands. Her legs felt shaky even though she was seated. And then an image of Maria lying dead jarred in her chest and strangled her breath. *I don't want to lose you.* As she chased away the horror, a tear slipped onto her cheek.

She was being child-like and delusional. There was no way she could be with a mafia boss, though she never looked at Maria as a mafia boss. *You are though, aren't you?* She shook her head. *Why do I have these feelings for you? Why you?* Reality was truth. Heaviness swamped the sweet, light feelings and cast a shadow of darkness and doom over her.

Now, her feet bloody throbbed even more than they had during her working day and reminded her of her place in this society. She was a waitress in a café, a nobody. She looked out the window without seeing beyond her reflection in the glass. A hot bath would help her disquiet, and then a drink would relax her for what was left of the evening. She looked forwards to two days off work. At least she wouldn't need to deal with the crazy, fat pig or second guess Patrina's increasingly edgy responses. The woman was fast becoming as unpredictable as her nephew.

Maybe she would go to the park tomorrow and then wander around Palermo on Monday. Perhaps that might get Maria out of her head. She leaned against the cloth seat. Stale smoke filled the air, and she closed her eyes. *Was Patrina watching her?* She flashed her eyes open and looked around the bus, her heart pounding. She didn't recognise any new faces. She released a tight breath and leaned back into the seat, willing her heart to slow and her shoulders to relax. Eventually, both eased and she closed her eyes, and the white noise inside the bus took her into a light sleep.

Simone blinked at the faint squealing of the brakes and opened her eyes as the gaseous hiss indicated the doors were opening. She stepped off the bus and set off up the main road. She crossed just short of the turning that would take her home as she always did. A thunderous crack split the night sky, and she spun her head around in the direction of the noise and screamed. Another booming roar went up and then another. She stood, frozen, with her hands covering her mouth and her eyes glued to the flaming light in the near distance. When someone grabbed her arm, her screams became lost in another explosive crack.

16.

"Hey, it's okay. It's me."

Simone looked at Maria with wide eyes and screamed again.

Simone's body stiffened in Maria's arms, and her breathing was shallow and fast. "It's okay, you're safe." Maria held her tightly and pressed her lips to Simone's head. She whispered, "Breathe slowly, nice and easy." She held Simone until her body softened and her breathing slowed.

The sirens became louder, and then a series of blue flashing lights whizzed past them. Maria noted the familiar unmarked car following at the rear of the convoy. Capitano Rocca was heading to the port. *Good.* She watched the taillights disappear into the distance. The explosion would be put down to a fuel leak, a problem with one of the vans that had caused a fire that had then spread and set off a domino effect across the fleet of parked vehicles. If anyone suspected differently, no one would challenge the word of the DIA, or any subsequent press release confirming the facts as instructed by Capitano Massina.

Simone eased out of Maria's embrace and looked at her with a growing frown. Then a fire flashed across her eyes and she gasped. "What if Roberto has been killed?"

Maria shook her head. "I'm sure he's fine."

"He could be delivering pizza over there. What if he's been delivering pizza and got caught up in it?"

Simone lifted her hands sharply and jolted away from Maria. She held her head, in her hands and her garbled noises increased in volume. It sounded as though she was choking.

Maria bit her lip, frustrated by her need to remain silent. "He will be fine, Simone. Come, let's get you home."

Simone flinched away from Maria. "How do you know? He could be dead."

Maria's heart ached as she watched Simone shaking with worry and growing in rage. She couldn't tell Simone she knew for sure without telling her that Roberto was working for her, and she couldn't do that. "Can you text him? I'm sure he is fine."

Simone grabbed her phone and tapped out the message with shaking hands. She stared at the screen. "Come on, come on."

She started shaking the phone and stopped when Maria's hand closed around hers.

"Let's get you home," Maria said softly, though she didn't smile.

Simone's phone pinged. She sighed. "He's okay."

Maria smiled. The tightness in her chest slipped away in a long deep breath. *Thank God.* She took Simone by the hand and led her up the road. Simone held out the keys, and Maria let them into the house and turned on the hallway lights. Closing the door behind them, she locked eyes with Simone who was staring at her, open mouthed. "Are you okay?"

"What are you doing here?"

Maria felt the energy quiver from her stomach to her chest. Her heart was racing, and she hoped she didn't look as awkward as she felt. She looked away, wetted her lips, and then turned back to Simone. "I wanted to see you...to make sure you didn't worry." The last bit wasn't technically a lie. She cleared her throat, watching Simone's frown deepen as she registered the truth.

"You knew about the explosion?"

Maria's lips thinned, and her jaw tightened as she looked at Simone. "Yes, I did. It's just business."

Simone turned away from Maria. She walked into the kitchen. "Can I get you a drink, Donna Maria?"

The formality in Simone's tone landed like a boulder in Maria's stomach, and she squeezed her eyes closed. *Fuck.* She took a deep breath and went into the kitchen. Simone turned to face her with glassy eyes, and she felt it in the sharp pain that pierced her heart. "I'm sorry, I should have asked before just showing up."

Simone shook her head. "It was a shock, the explosion. I wasn't expecting it."

Simone's quiet calm tone softened the tension a little. Maria nodded. But for a few minutes, she would have already escorted Simone home, and they would have been inside the house together as the bombs went off. "I thought you would be worried about your brother."

Simone looked away.

Had she hoped for a different reason? Maria hesitated. "And I didn't want you to be alone."

Maria hoped that was longing in the softness in Simone's expression, and the quiver returned to her stomach.

"Thank you for your concern."

Maria's stomach dropped. The formality was back in Simone's tone, and Simone looked at her as if from a distance. She turned from Maria and went to fill the kettle.

If Maria didn't ask now, she never would. "Would you like to go for a drink? I know a safe place close by. You wouldn't be compromised."

A half-smile appeared on Maria's face, and she tilted her head to the side. She put on her best, slightly pleading pose while her heart hammered.

Simone looked at her and sighed.

Phew. Maria's smile was faint. Simone looked weary. There was only one place to go this time of night.

"A drink would be nice." Simone smiled faintly.

Maria indicated to the door. "Shall we?" She reached out a hand and led Simone to the Romeo parked outside.

Simone frowned as Maria opened the door for her. "This is your car?"

"Err...yes."

"You knew where I lived."

"Of course." Maria shrugged. "It's my job to keep you safe." She grinned.

Simone rolled her eyes. "Of course."

Maria noted Simone admiring the white leather seats with her fingertips and smiled. She pulled out from the curb and headed north west, as far from the port as possible. She glanced at Simone, reclining against the headrest. She seemed a little more relaxed. "How was work today?"

"It was fine."

"I need to talk to you about the explosion at the port."

Simone sighed, but Maria continued. "Alessandro is going to be angry that his vans have been decommissioned. He won't be able to transport merchandise for a long while."

Simone looked across at Maria. "Did anyone get killed?"

Maria shook her head. "No, Simone. That is not the Lombardo..." She stopped, the lie scolding her with the orders she had given that would change all that in the near future. What was the Lombardo way?

"But two women nearly died earlier today."

Maria swallowed hard. Simone had heard. Undoubtedly, Alessandro would have been bragging. "Yes, that is the Amato way."

Simone lowered her eyes to her hands. "Yes. My family were killed by them."

Maria reached across and took Simone's hand. "Yes, I know."

Simone lifted her head up and looked at Maria. "Of course. Is there anything you don't know?"

Yes. I don't know you, and I want to. Maria swallowed the mild accusation and smiled. "I'm sure there's lots I don't know."

Simone lowered her head. Maria turned the car down a dirt track, and the softly lit single storey building became brighter. The small lake over which the rear of the restaurant looked came into view as they parked. It had been a long time since she had visited her uncle and aunt's restaurant. The lighting that had been set out around the bank reflected in ripples across the surface, and running water indicated a small fall that fed into the body of water and competed with the incessant chattering of the insects whose day had not long begun. "I had forgotten how beautiful this place is. I think you'll like it." Maria smiled. "I didn't know your family very well, but I recall the incident. Your parents and brother were victims caught in the crossfire. Stefano is in prison for his part in that crime among other related ones. The Amatos owed a debt to your family."

Simone lowered her head. Her hands were shaking. "It was guilt money. They gave me a job and paid me more than I would be paid in any other restaurant in Sicily so I could look after Roberto."

Maria squeezed Simone's hand. "Yes. It's the way they operate."

"It was fine in the beginning. Patrina was kind, and I worked in the kitchens then. It is only recently that Alessandro...that he is asserting himself. He wanted me to work front-of-house at the café, and Patrina gives him what he wants."

"They don't own you." Maria felt Simone's sadness as if it were her own, and the desire to kiss Simone in the darkness and privacy of the car came to her with such force, it took her breath away.

"Alessandro thinks he does."

The desire to protect became stronger as Alessandro's image flashed in Maria's mind. She turned from Simone. "I promise he won't hurt you ever again." She couldn't tell Simone she would dispose of him altogether if she had to. But she would...and without a second thought.

Simone reached up and stroked Maria's cheek. "Thank you."

Maria felt fire in the touch zip through her. *You are so beautiful.* Gently, she ran a fingertip along Simone's hairline and lifted her chin. "Let's get that drink."

17.

"Maria, what a delightful surprise. It has been too long."

The slender, silver haired man held out his arms and smiled broadly as he stepped up to Maria. He tugged her to his chest and held her in a greeting that demonstrated heartfelt affection.

"Uncle, how good to see you. How is Paola?" Maria patted him on the back as she squeezed him. She held his shoulders as she eased out of the embrace and looked into his wise eyes.

He threw his hands in the air with dramatic effect and rolled his eyes. "That woman is getting older and grumpier every year. I will get her from the kitchen."

Maria stopped him. "Later. Uncle Lorenzo, this is a friend of mine; Simone Di Salvo." Maria looked at Simone, and her heart skipped a beat. "Simone, this is Lorenzo Lombardo." She smiled then whispered, "His wife is Paola. She's the chef and the reason people come here." She looked at her uncle and laughed, patting Lorenzo firmly on the shoulder as he rolled his eyes again.

"She is the best chef that no one has heard of," Lorenzo said.

The fondness he held for his wife appeared in the glow in his cheeks and the softness of his gaze. Simone held out her hand and he shook it, bowing his head slightly then kissing both her cheeks.

"Very pleased to meet you, Simone. We rarely see Maria. It is good to know she has friends."

He chuckled and ushered them through the restaurant to a quiet corner with a window overlooking the lake. The night sky looked darker from inside the building and but for the crescent moon and a sprinkling of stars, it would be impossible to see anything at all through the window. Barely perceptibly, trees bounded the small lake in haunting silhouette set against the darkness. Inside, candles remoulded from use flickered on the centre of the tables that diners had recently vacated. The two remaining guests were quietly drinking coffee.

Maria smiled at Lorenzo and waited until Simone sat before taking her seat. "Would you like something to eat?"

Simone hesitated, heat rising swiftly through her and burning her cheeks. She hadn't considered food. It was just short of midnight, and she hadn't eaten before leaving work. She felt awkward that they were inconveniencing these poor people this late at night, but Maria smiled at her as if they had all the time in the world. "A little, maybe."

Maria shifted her attention from Simone to Lorenzo. "Would Auntie rustle up a few nibbles for us? Nothing special, Uncle. Thank you."

He raised his hand and shook his head. His shallow frown didn't last for long, and he broke into a beaming smile. "You cannot spoil my evening. I get one chance in many months to spoil my niece. I will spoil her and her beautiful friend. We are in no rush to close."

Simone blushed. Maria smiled at Lorenzo and Simone felt the tenderness with which she looked at her uncle. Lifted by the unreserved welcome, she relaxed in the seat. Maria smiled at her, and her heart raced.

"Would you like wine?"

Simone's mouth was dry, and the mild discomfort that came with a sense of wanting Maria stirred in her core. "Sure."

Maria indicated to the menu. "You can choose."

Simone picked up the card and studied the short list of options. She looked up and felt the heat of Maria's gaze piercing through her. She swallowed, and Maria smiled with such tenderness she felt moved by her and confused at her inability to process the simplest information. Maria held her under a spell.

"All the wines here are good."

Simone's mouth felt dry. "The house red then." Frankly, she didn't care.

Lorenzo dipped his head, firstly to Simone and then to Maria. "An excellent choice."

He went to the bar and returned immediately with the carafe of wine and two glasses then excused himself to attend to the two customers who were making their way to the door. He bid them a good evening and locked the door behind them. He closed the blinds over the door and the windows that exposed the inside of the restaurant to the car park.

Maria poured them each a glass of wine and leaned back in the seat. She released a long breath and sipped her wine.

Simone watched Maria processing her thoughts in the way the fine lines around her eyes came and went, and the slight movement at the corner of her mouth, and the faintest tremble in her lips before she wetted them. And then Maria bit down as if to control some emotion. Maria's breathing seemed affected, and it was clear that there was a lot running through Maria's mind. "Is everything okay?"

"Sorry."

Maria smiled, and Simone felt the warmth of it move through her. The softness appeared in Maria's eyes again.

"Sorry, I was just thinking. I promise to stop doing that."

Maria's tone was gentle and witty. Simone laughed. "You can stop thinking?"

Maria raised her eyebrows. "Under certain circumstances."

Maria looked at Simone's chest, albeit fleetingly, and Simone felt engulfed by flames. She looked away and sipped her wine. She couldn't even think now, let alone if they had sex. God, she hoped they would. She gulped. And when she looked back at Maria, Maria's smile reached inside her, and her stomach flipped. *Please don't look at me like that.* She cleared her throat and changed the subject. "Were you thinking about the port?"

Maria's expression shifted, and Simone wished she hadn't asked.

Maria nodded. "And other things?"

Simone looked at Maria and felt exposed by the connection they shared. She hadn't experienced this depth and quality of feeling with any of her exes. Not that there had been many, and none of them serious. Maria exuded a quiet, elegant charm. The giddy, light-headedness that came over Simone when alone with Maria left her susceptible and wanting in an intoxicating blend of desire and fear. Maria looked pensive, and the feeling tilted in the direction of fear. "Would you like to talk?"

Maria cleared her throat. "No, thank you."

Suddenly deflated, Simone lowered her eyes. Of course, Maria couldn't talk to her about her work. Maria probably couldn't talk to her about anything. They barely knew each other after all. She picked up her wine and took a sip.

"Hey," Maria said softly.

Simone looked up, and Maria's smile caressed her. The light reflecting from Maria's eyes coaxed her gently back to desire.

"I don't want work to spoil the evening."

Maria leaned forwards and for a fleeting moment, Simone imagined Maria was going to kiss her. But Maria adjusted her position in the seat and sat back. Simone's stomach lurched and disappointment descended like a fine layer of snow.

"Tell me something about yourself. What did you study at university?"

Simone stared over Maria's shoulder, her thoughts heavy with the weight of the time she had tried to forget, and the point at which she had parked her life, her lover, and her studies. Everything she had hoped for her future had disappeared in a flash. The moment she buried her family, she buried her life in a sealed box in the back of her mind. And she had found no good reason to open it since. She looked into Maria's eyes and felt compelled by the inexplicable connection. She took a deep breath and smiled. "I studied Business and Economics at La Sapienza in Rome."

"Pretty and smart." Maria raised her eyebrows.

She hadn't expected that and blushed.

"Did you enjoy it?"

"Yes." She cleared her throat. "My parents had to work hard to afford for me to go."

Maria lowered her gaze and nodded. Simone continued. "I was in my final year when they were killed. I was toying with going on to do an applied Masters in Catering or Tourism." She looked away from Maria and out of the window. "Events took over, and I haven't given it a second thought since."

That wasn't entirely true. She had missed uni...a lot. She had pined for the future she had planned more than she dared admit. And she had missed Alicia during those first months of separation. They had been together since the beginning of their second year. Simone had felt comfortable expressing her newfound sexual freedom with her. Alicia had been frivolous, liberated, and fun to be around, and characteristically nothing like Maria. But Alicia had had no desire to move to Palermo, and Simone hadn't blamed her for that. They had wished each other well, and then, insidiously, Simone's ambition had slipped away. Her role had become focused on looking after Roberto and keeping a roof over both their heads.

She wondered, not for the first time, whether she had sold her soul to the devil. She looked at Maria, and the depth of emptiness in Maria's dark eyes echoed her own unfulfilled dreams. She watched a frown slowly form and narrow Maria's eyes.

"I never wanted to be in this business."

Maria's tone was quiet and reflective, and then her eyes glassed over.

Simone reached across the table and took Maria's hand.

Maria looked at Simone and shrugged. "Life deals us cards, eh."

"Life is shit." Simone shrugged, and they laughed together. The lightness of the moment suspended her contemplative thoughts and warmth flowed into her stomach.

Maria smiled. "What would you like to do with yours?"

Simone sat back in the seat and stared into space. "I would like to own my own café-bar. A small place in a city, close to a theatre for people to come and dine at before they go to the opera or the ballet. With the finest wines, though not overpriced, and traditional dishes from around the world. A place free from the threat of danger. I would pay rent to the landlord and not have to pay for protection." She smiled as she raised her eyebrows at Maria.

Maria winced.

"I'm teasing you."

"It's true though. People pay us rent for protection."

Simone sighed. She didn't want to think of Maria as one of *those* people.

"I prefer to think we're helping them. If we didn't look after our tenants, then the Amatos or others would. And most don't take care of people very well."

Simone's skin prickled. She knew, she worked for them.

"I would like that place too."

Both women turned and looked out the window. Simone sensed the rawness of the sorrow and remorse for the world they had been born into. She hadn't considered that someone in Maria's position would feel as Maria did.

Lorenzo approached the table with a tray of food. A woman equally as skinny as him carried another tray behind him. Maria turned to face Simone and smiled. She felt strange, as if something tangible had shifted between them, and yet she didn't know what. She wanted Maria more. She took a deep breath and turned to face Lorenzo.

"Here she is," Lorenzo said.

For a moment it was unclear to which woman he referred, but Simone felt warmed by his cheery nature.

Maria took the tray from her aunt and placed it on the table, then greeted her with a robust hug. "Auntie. You look beautiful."

Paola brushed Maria away with a disapproving huff. "I am old and have too many wrinkles, Maria. I am lucky to still be here." Paola formed a cross at her chest, then stroked Maria's cheek with tenderness as she looked her up and down, mumbling in Sicilian. "I'm glad you are here. You look very well."

Maria kissed her aunt on the cheek. "You will always be the best chef in Palermo."

She inhaled the complex aromas that filled the room. "It smells wonderful," Simone said. Passion radiated from the old woman's twinkling eyes, and Simone felt embraced by it.

"Don't go telling anyone. We are busy enough, and with nice people who visit." Paola said.

Maria laughed.

Lorenzo put his tray on a stand at the side of the table and nudged his wife away from the table. "Come, come, Paola. Let the ladies eat."

Paola walked towards the kitchen mumbling under her breath, and then stopped and looked over her shoulder. "You come and say goodbye before you go."

"Of course, Auntie. I will wake you." Maria laughed as the two older folks disappeared into the kitchen.

Simone looked at the dishes on the trays. "Wow! This is a snack?"

Smiling, Maria tilted her head and shrugged. "The food here is excellent."

Simone picked up a slice of pizza secca and crunched into the thin crisp base. Fresh oregano danced on her tongue followed by a hint of sweet from the thinly sliced onions and salt from the salami. She watched as Maria took the involtini di pesce spada onto her plate, cut a small slice of the rolled swordfish, and brought it delicately to her mouth. She continued to stare at Maria's tempting lips, yielding with the gentle movement of her jaw. The pizza became dryer in her mouth and hard to swallow.

Maria moaned as she chewed. "This is delicious."

Simone picked up her wine and took a long sip. She looked from one dish to another and plucked a small handful of baked broad beans into her palm. She slipped one into her mouth and crunched. The sweet, nutty taste made her mouth water. "These are amazing. Here, try one." She held the vegetable between her fingers and raised it to Maria's lips.

Maria leaned forwards and opened her mouth, her lips touched Simone's fingertips, and she froze with the electric shock that fizzed down her spine. She could barely breathe, and then she became aware that Maria was still waiting open mouthed. She released the morsel like hot coal onto Maria's tongue and backed away.

Maria flushed.

There was salt and then sweet as Simone crunched. And the taste of lemon that had come from Maria's lips now lingered on her own and infused the nutty taste in her mouth. Her insides flipped, and the moan that escaped her had a deep guttural resonance to it that even she didn't recognize. Maria flashed her an intense look. Heat burned Simone's cheeks. She picked up her glass and sipped.

"I'm glad you like it."

Simone cleared her throat and focused on the meal. "This is exactly the sort of food I would serve at my café." She picked up the bite-size chickpea fritter and dipped it into the ricotta dip.

The warm fritter melted the cool cream cheese, and the flavours burst to life as she ate.

Simone's attention shifted from the sensation in her mouth to Maria watching her. "What would you like to do?"

"Now?"

Simone smiled at the fine lines that appeared and shaped Maria's dark eyes. Had Maria made a subtle pass? The tingling down her spine said yes. "If you weren't in this business? What would you like to do?"

"Ah...I would run an orchid farm."

Simone stared, mesmerised by Maria. She didn't know the first thing about her, but it seemed that everything she discovered was leading her deeper and deeper...towards that broken heart. She would never recover from Maria Lombardo. "You would?"

Maria smiled softly. "Yes. I love anything to do with the preservation of plants or animals. I have a particular affinity with the sea life. I have a pet octopus."

"Really?" Simone whispered. It was the best she could muster. Maria's eyes seemed to darken as she moved towards Simone and then they closed. Warmth lingered at Simone's lips for what felt like an eternity, and her heart seemed as though it would burst if she didn't feel Maria's mouth. *Kiss me.* Maria's eyes opened, and the desire Simone saw in a moment of daring became hesitation. And then Simone closed her eyes and the softness, the tenderest touch to her lips confused her senses into submission. Fragile and fragrant, tender and certain, she caressed Maria's lips savouring every millimetre of her softness, willing Maria to lead her where she desperately wanted them to go. Her lips parted, and she tasted the sweetness again. The firmness of Maria's hand at her neck coaxed her deeper into the kiss. Her breathing came in short bursts, and her pulse throbbed its desires clearly to the rest of her body. Cool air startled her, and she opened her eyes and stared silently into Maria's.

Maria's gaze on her overwhelmed her senses, and Simone's heart missed a beat as she gasped. Instantly, she craved the sense of Maria's lips pressed to hers again and Maria's strength holding her firmly and leading her. She wanted to feel Maria inside her and delight at Maria's naked body touching hers. Her imagination set off sizzling electric energy, and she trembled inside. Could Maria read her thoughts? She closed her eyes as Maria kissed her.

Take me to bed.

18.

Somersaults turned in Simone's stomach as she stepped out of the car and headed into the villa. The thundering in her chest made her breaths short and shallow. She was an emotional wreck in the most exhilarating way possible, both weak and strong in equal measure. Her longing for Maria had increased in the silence in which they had driven home. It had become excruciatingly painful. Maria had only to glance at her, and the throbbing in her core pulsed harder. Maria had driven unbearably slowly for Simone. *Was she always so disciplined?*

Maria closed the door behind them.

Simone moved swiftly and crashed her mouth onto Maria's. Maria's fingers slid through her hair and pulled Simone's head closer. Their teeth clashed and moans of pleasure vibrated through Simone as she tasted Maria's unique sweetness and explored the softness of her lips with her tongue. She could barely breathe, and she couldn't work her hands fast enough. She reached inside Maria's jacket and ran her fingers over Maria's breast. Simone gasped as Maria's nipple responded sharply to her touch. The firmness of Maria's strong feminine form tingled in her fingers and chased fire to her core, and the rapid rise and fall of Maria's chest impelled her to explore every goose bump that blazed across Maria's skin. She eased out of the kiss and pulled the jacket from Maria's shoulders.

She froze. Her automatic response to seeing the weapon holstered at Maria's side jabbed in her gut. She blinked and stepped back still trembling with desire and saw apology in Maria's dark eyes.

Maria removed the holstered gun and placed it over the back of a chair. She lifted Simone's chin and stared into her eyes. "Do you see *me*?"

Simone's sex pulsed at the want emanating from Maria's eyes. If Maria didn't touch her soon, she would explode.

"Do you want *me*?" Maria whispered.

Simone's voice broke. "Yes. Yes, I want you." She stepped into Maria's arms and held her face. She silenced the tremor in Maria's lips with a tender, lingering kiss. Delicately, she nipped at Maria's soft yielding flesh, though she wanted to devour her. The act of restraint increased her desire and with the heat of Maria's breasts pressed to hers, restraint yielded to a deep guttural groan, and she cried out.

Simone moaned again as Maria's hand explored the curve of her waist and slid her hand slowly up her back. Maria eased back and looked into Simone's eyes as she undid the buttons of Simone's blouse. The trembling waved from Simone's stomach to her hands and built as Maria freed the material and admired her breasts and stomach. Maria touched the top of her breast with a light brush of her fingertips, and Simone flinched.

Maria was staring intently at her breasts as she touched her. The tiny hairs on her skin tingled in response, and Simone saw the intensity in Maria's eyes deepen.

"I've wanted you since I saw you at the opera," Maria whispered.

Maria looked up from Simone's breasts, and Simone gasped as heat erupted inside her. She bit down on her lip as she admired Maria's body, the narrow shape of her eyes, the line of her jaw. "You are so..."

Maria silenced her with her mouth and urgently removed her own shirt and bra.

Simone thrust her body forwards and moaned at Maria's warmth. She held Maria's head in her hands, kissed her cheeks and her neck, and ran her fingers through her short hair. As she met Maria's lips again, she lost the power of thought and became lost in her sensual pleasure.

Maria's arms felt strong around her and her kisses fierce as she carried Simone swiftly through to the bedroom. Maria lowered her slowly to the bed, and her kisses became tender as she undressed her and threw off her own remaining clothes.

The scent of Maria flooded Simone in warmth, and she moaned. Maria lifted her high, and she wrapped her legs around Maria's waist. The firmness of Maria's abs massaged Simone's sex and sent a ripple of fire shooting back up her body. Then, Maria flicked her tongue across Simone's nipple, and placed kisses to the soft flesh of her breast, and the shockwaves jolted through Simone and she closed her eyes and gasped. "Please. Oh, yes." She clasped Maria's head firmly to her chest, flung her head back, and rocked her hips against Maria. "Please, fuck me."

Maria slowly eased her body between Simone's soft thighs. The sensation that gripped her halted her breath and for a brief moment, looking at Simone in rapture, time stood still. The profundity of Simone's gratification flowed through Maria's heart. *I am in love with you.* Pleasure, sadness and…deep love inflamed the burning in her core and then an urge to hold Simone and never let her go came. She inched slowly up Simone's body bringing the slightest pressure to Simone's sex. *I am so in love with you.* Maria closed her stinging eyes and kissed Simone's neck.

Simone jolted and released a soft gasping moan.

The scent of Simone lingered deliciously on Maria's skin. The openness that connected them exposed her. But this love could not be denied. Maria tensed her abs and moved gently against Simone, eliciting another gasp from her. She came to Simone slowly and unhurriedly kissed her on the lips, her eyes, and her cheeks. Simone shuddered at Maria's fingertips as she gently clawed the sensitive skin at her hips and inner thighs. She placed tender kisses down Simone's body, enjoying the transformation in Simone's skin as it flared in response to her touch.

Maria inhaled deeply and closed her mouth gently over Simone's swollen clit. Savouring the silky sweetness, she licked and teased, and Simone bucked against her. She nipped and kissed, and Simone cried out. She trailed her fingertips slowly across the soft flesh of Simone's thigh and upwards as she circled Simone's hot wet entrance with her fingers and tongue. Simone pressed hard against Maria and moaned, and Maria eased her fingers into the warmth of Simone's centre and found the silky softness inside her.

Simone threw her head back and gasped. Maria penetrated Simone in a slow rhythm. Simone's hips rocked with her. She moved deeper and explored her softness, and then Simone opened to her and she thrust harder and faster. Simone's breaths came in a sequence of fast and shallow groans, and her movements became erratic. Maria held her tightly and stilled her fingers inside Simone.

Simone cried out. Her body tensed, and she shook violently.

Maria moved up and kissed the tears from Simone's face. Her heart raced, and she felt the lightness and ease of a silk blanket cover her. She cradled Simone in her arms.

"You are delicious," Maria whispered.

Simone's breathing slowed, and the spasms subsided. She moved from Maria's shoulder, lifted her head, and looked into Maria's eyes. She ran her fingers through Maria's hair, eased it back from her face, and looked at her intently. "You are so beautiful."

Maria pressed her finger to Simone's lips, and Simone threw her head back to brush them off. "You are." She took Maria's hand and kissed the fingers that had tried to stop her talking then held Maria's palm against her chest and closed her eyes. "So beautiful."

Maria moved astride Simone.

Simone blinked and opened her eyes as Maria's lips met hers. She slid her fingers between Maria's legs and moaned at the feel of her. "So wet."

Maria rocked with Simone's fingers deep inside her. "You feel so good. Please don't stop."

Simone quickly shifted to her knees. Facing Maria, she wrapped her arm around Maria's waist and slowly entered her. Maria's lips quivered, and her eyes closed.

Simone moaned in pleasure at the warmth of Maria at her fingertips. Soft, and supple, and so delicious, her appetite was insatiable. She applied a gentle pressure that became stronger as Maria bucked against her, and she felt their intimacy in the delicate shudder that floated through her on a delightful, enticing wave. And then Maria entered her and paralysing flashes of bliss spread from Simone's core, and the rush that came with falling over the edge took her by surprise, and the spasms that followed made her legs suddenly weak. She tumbled the short distance from her knees onto the bed, and Maria fell on top of her. Maria shook in her arms, smiled, and kissed her tenderly.

Maria lay on her side watching Simone's eyelashes fluttering with the random movements that came when dreaming. Her skin looked slightly paler in complexion than when in the throes of making love. She smiled with the temptation to reach out and touch Simone's lips, her breasts, and her sex. She would have to contend with the persistent throbbing between her legs. Of greater concern was the disconcerting ache in her heart that seemed somehow deeper and more present than it had been the previous evening.

She slipped out of the bed, put on her robe, and tiptoed into the lounge. Darkness revealed a hint of light on the horizon, tempting the world into morning. Opening the door to the beach, with the warmth of the incoming day on her face, she inhaled deeply. Pesto ran onto the sand, and Maria smiled. The beauty of the cove and her home. Pesto. The love she had for her mother and sister, and her unborn niece or nephew. All of it paled by comparison with the depth of her feelings for the woman lying in her bed. *Simone.* She looked over her shoulder towards the bedroom and the ache in her heart increased tenfold. She would miss her family and her home, but she couldn't live without Simone. The difference was as vast as all the oceans of the world joined together. Perhaps this feeling was incomprehensible to anyone who hadn't known profound love. Yet she was sat on a precipice. Once things had settled down with the Amatos, what then? There was a reason her sex life had been expressed behind closed doors in a secret, silent, and sometimes sordid world, a faceless place in which she could remain anonymous. That wasn't love. She would give up everything for Simone. "I would die for you," she whispered. Simone's hands reached around Maria's waist, startling her.

Maria turned and looked into Simone's eyes, and half smiled.

Simone frowned. "You're worried, aren't you?"

Maria sighed. She couldn't look at Simone as she answered, "A little, yes."

There was no doubting the escalation that the decommissioning of the Amato fleet would trigger. Lives would be lost in the process of trying to achieve harmony with a man who didn't know the meaning of the word and had even less inclination to achieve a positive working relationship with anyone.

Maria's desire to leave Sicily had grown with every action she was forced to take. But she was now torn with not wanting to leave Simone. That loss, her heart would never recover from.

Simone stepped closer and released the cloth belt from Maria's waist. She grazed her skin with her fingertips and watched the goose bumps form. "I don't want to think about that right now." She ran her thumb over Maria's nipple and back again.

A flood of energy zipped down Maria's spine, and then Simone's lips met hers. Maria tugged Simone to her and kissed her lips hard. And then Simone's hand was between her legs and the softness of her touch, and the pressure coming and going, and the sense of Simone's fingers teasing at her entrance brought her to the floor. The tiles were cool against her back, and the warmth of Simone's bare skin moved slowly down her body. She closed her eyes and as Simone's mouth enveloped her sex and her tongue moved inside her, she became consumed by the fire that coursed through her.

19.

Reluctantly, Maria eased out of Simone's arms and wrapped herself in her robe. The sensitive parts of her body hummed and looking at Simone just made the humming stronger, and the tingling turned to throbbing heat. She took a deep breath and smiled. Simone looked irresistible lazing sleepily on the couch. The lightness she felt was tempered too quickly by the impending reality she needed to address. The meeting with Don Chico was in two days. What would be Alessandro's response to the decimation of his fleet? Patrina's revenge. And…the not so small issue of creating a future free from it all. Pesto barked and scratched at the other side of the door. "I need to feed him." She ran her fingers through Simone's hair and pressed a tender kiss to her lips then went and opened the door. Pesto ran in, tail wagging, and bounded towards Simone.

Maria laughed as Pesto licked and nuzzled Simone's neck, eventually driving Simone to her feet. Simone's laughter carried through from the bedroom as she escaped Pesto's attentions and Maria's laugh quieted as she poured two glasses of orange juice and set them on the breakfast bar. She watched Pesto munch his biscuits then turned to Simone as she walked towards her. She looked stunning.

The jogging bottoms sat low on her hips and hung loosely to her bare feet with painted toenails, and the T-shirt stretched across her breasts and revealed the smooth skin that Maria had kissed every millimetre of in the past eight hours. Simone's hair had a slightly wild appearance, and Maria read pure lust in her eyes. Simone looked sexy, and she moved with tantalizing grace. Maria swallowed hard. Her mouth was dry, and desire drove her into a frenzy. "Hey sexy, come here." She held out her arms.

Simone tugged open Maria's robe, stepped up to her, and pulled her close.

Maria's naked skin flamed against the thin material that failed to obscure Simone's erect nipples. The hardness fired electric impulses through Maria and ignited her sex. She groaned at the throbbing. *I have work to do.* She closed her eyes, felt the heat of Simone's warm breath on her cheek, and kissed her tenderly. And when she looked into Simone's eyes, the ache in her chest grew.

Simone smiled. "Good morning, lover."

Her groggy voice resonated through Maria and her skin tingled. *Oh my God!* She smiled at her body's reaction. "Yes. It is a very good morning."

Maria ran her fingers through Simone's hair, tilted her head towards her, and looked into her eyes. She brought to mind the job she needed to do, and the inferno subsided. When she smiled, she sensed the emotional distance she had created between them in her withdrawal. A shield had closed across her heart. It was safer that way. Simone released her and went to the breakfast bar. Maria sensed the hurt in Simone by the jabbing pain in her chest. *I don't want to hurt you.* Tension rose up her spine and strengthened the fortress around her.

She had spent the hours since waking thinking about how to keep Simone safe. She was certain Capitano Rocca had seen them together on the street when heading to the explosions at the port. Rocca would spot Maria at a fucking masked ball. She knew the meaning behind the look Rocca gave her and the tenderness of the touch when Rocca had consoled her after her father's death. But Maria would never seek comfort from that source. It was Rocca's job to know what was going on in Palermo, and for the most part she had proved to be effective at it. And whilst Maria would have trusted Rocca before the recent escalation of events, the fact that her father's death had been designated an accident when the car had clearly been doctored meant Rocca was potentially involved in the cover up. Until she knew the truth, Maria didn't trust anyone except Giovanni and Angelo. And, if Rocca was involved in a cover up and she *had* seen Simone in Maria's arms on the street after the blast, then Simone could be in more danger than she might realise.

Simone sipped the orange juice. "What is it?"

Maria stared over Simone's shoulder to the cove beyond the window. "You can't go back to work at the café."

Simone's eyes rose sharply, and she straightened her back.

Maria looked at her. "It's too dangerous."

Simone sighed. Shaking her head, Maria leaned towards Simone. She put her hands on Simone's shoulders as she appealed to her. "You are in danger at the café, Simone. I need you where I can protect you. Here." She stopped and took a deep breath, her frown deepening as she spoke. "Alessandro is going to be angry after the explosion and..." She turned away from Simone.

Simone turned Maria around. "And what?"

"I think Capitano Massina saw us together last night on the street near your house."

Simone shook her head. "So?"

Maria pursed her lips. "It's complicated. If she suspects you're associated with me, she might not like it." She couldn't tell Simone that Rocca might be involved in the cover up of her father's murder until she knew it for a fact. She still had to tell Simone about the meeting in Italy and the business she needed to attend to in Spain. She didn't want Simone to worry unnecessarily. She would be safe staying at the villa while Maria was on business, and then maybe they could both go to Spain and take a holiday.

Simone nodded, fighting tears, and looking around the room. "Okay," she whispered.

Maria took Simone's hand and interlocked their fingers. She pulled her close and kissed her, then stroked the hair from her face and brushed an errant tear from her face. "You can never go back to the café, Simone."

Simone slipped from Maria's arms and paced around the room with her head in her hands. "What do I tell Roberto? He will ask questions. And what will happen when Patrina finds out?"

Maria intercepted her and tugged her into her arms. "Hey, look at me. It will be okay. I can talk to Roberto. I'll make sure he's safe, Simone."

Simone eased back, shaking her head, and looked into Maria's eyes. "You have no idea the lengths I have gone to, to protect him from Patrina's influence."

Simone stared at Maria, as if it were all her fault and then her eyes softened, and she looked at Maria with wide pleading eyes.

Maria squirmed internally. Prickly heat became intense within her and then punched her hard in the gut. She tugged Simone to her chest to avoid looking at her and closed her eyes. *Fucking hell.* She couldn't conceal her relationship with Roberto for much longer. Simone could read her far too well. And if Simone challenged her and discovered she had been keeping the truth from her, she would never trust her again. Simone would probably want to kill her for involving Roberto in mafia business. Their relationship would be over before it got off the ground. She kissed the top of Simone's head, inhaled the sweet apple scent of her hair, and whispered, "I will make sure Patrina doesn't hurt him." She bit her lip and silenced her concerns.

Pesto bounded through the door and jumped up at Maria's legs.

Simone eased out of Maria's arms, her eyes damp, glanced at the wet dog and started to laugh. She wiped her face and sat at the breakfast bar. Maria felt the distance between them. She passed Simone a cup of coffee. "Do you like eggs?"

Simone nodded and sipped her drink. Maria smiled. "I make mean eggs."

Simone didn't react to the light-hearted comment. Maria moved around the kitchen sourcing ingredients and implements. She cracked eggs and cut up Parma ham, parmesan cheese, and spring onions. A few minutes later, she placed a plate in front of Simone.

Simone looked down at the omelette then smiled briefly. "Thank you."

Maria started to eat. "Would you like to go diving with me sometime? I will introduce you to Octavia." Maria raised her eyes and smiled.

Simone toyed with the eggs with her fork. "Sure."

Maria took in a deep breath and placed her fork on the plate. She couldn't dance around the facts any longer. They would dive, and she would show Simone the reef at some point but polite conversation wasn't going to make the imminent reality more palatable. "Simone, I need to go to Italy on Tuesday for a meeting."

Simone stared at her with a worried expression.

Maria smiled. "I'll be fine." She felt the lie sting her chest. "You can stay here. Would you like to come to Spain with me later in the week?"

Simone stared at her blankly.

"I have to visit our construction business there. It will be a short meeting. I was thinking…maybe we could take a break afterwards. The Pyrenees is beautiful this time of year." She smiled again, but Simone continued to stare at her with a vacant expression. She needed to take the bull by the horns if she was going to distract Simone from her thoughts. "There's somewhere I would like to show you. A surprise."

Simone half-smiled.

"You'll love Spain and the mountain air. It's stunning." Maria's heart raced. "You're beautiful," she whispered.

Simone's eyes flashed with the hint of a sparkle, and her smile slowly widened.

"Will you stay here while I'm in Italy? It will just be one day."

Simone nodded and Maria released a deep sigh. "Good." Maria stood, collected a piece of paper and a pen, and started writing. She handed the note to Simone. "Tomorrow, go and see Doctor Bruno. That's his address and number. Angelo will take you. He will sign you off work. I will speak to Roberto and make sure he is safe. Then go and collect some clothes and your passport from home. We will have a couple of weeks to sort something more permanent out." Her thoughts rambling, she smiled at Simone. "Maybe you can work at the Riverside when all this is over." What she really meant was, it would give her time to sort out how to handle the inevitable fall out with Alessandro and Patrina following the explosions and ensure Simone's safety in the short term. After that, she would rather they escape Sicily together and never come back. But the thought of Simone rejecting that particular offer sealed her lips. The time to ask would need to be right, and this wasn't that time.

Simone tilted her head, a slight frown crossed her brow, and then a smile slowly formed, and her eyes became bright and sparkly once more. She took Maria's hand and brushed her thumb across Maria's knuckles.

"I do trust you."

Maria swallowed hard, trying to ignore the sharp jabbing in her chest. She would deal with the backlash from her lies later. She blinked and redirected her thoughts. "Have you ever been to Valencia?"

Simone shook her head.

"You will love it. Do you know there are seventy-seven varieties of orchid in the region? We could take a tour before going to see the wild orchids in the Pyrenees."

20.

The burning sensation in Patrina's chest flared. She breathed deeply as she watched Alessandro acting out his latest tantrum. He reminded her of everything she detested in her husband. He was vulgar, with gross physical movements and a single point of focus that failed to appreciate anyone or anything in the world that didn't revolve around his precious ego. *Fucking pig.* She bit the inside of her lip to the point of sharp pain then smiled as she reached across the table and placed her hand over his clenched fist. She still needed him and whilst she did, she would do what she did well: play the game and get what she wanted...and that was full control of the Amato business. "Alessandro, darling."

He snatched his hand from hers and stood. She watched him trudge heavy-footed back and forth in the small space between the table and the bar, his eyes making jittery movements. He looked like a man driven to insanity by paranoia. She smiled inwardly at his self-initiated demise. If she had time, she would wait for the drugs to take him to an early grave. But time was something she didn't have. And with the Italians on their backs, time was in short supply for Alessandro too. As long as Chico didn't take her down with him. She clenched her fists beneath the table and took a deep breath, aware that Beto was watching her watching Alessandro.

Alessandro jerked his head towards the new face behind the bar, and the waitress smiled at him.

He looked at Patrina. "And where the fuck is that other woman?"

Patrina picked up her drink and sipped. "She's been signed off with stress."

Alessandro looked around the room. "Fucking bitch. I never liked her anyway. We need to get rid of her, Auntie."

Patrina shook her head. "We have bigger problems to deal with, Alessandro." She didn't much like Simone being around either. And it was Alessandro who had insisted Simone be employed to tend the bar at the café. She was eye candy and would attract the punters. He wasn't wrong. Simone was pretty, too pretty. But Patrina wasn't in a position to challenge him and justified her passivity on the basis of Alessandro's dominance and her need to keep him onside. Self-preservation was the first rule of her law.

Simone didn't really belong in this environment. She never had, and Patrina had done her best to keep her out of the way. Patrina could sleep at night, knowing she had done all that she could for Di Salvo's daughter. But no matter what Alessandro thought about getting rid of Simone, that wasn't an option. Don Stefano had created an obligation to the Di Salvo family, and even Patrina wouldn't renege on the promise her husband had made. Some innocent lives lost in the war were just collateral damage but not that of Adrianu Di Salvo. The man who had served them and been their silent eyes on the street for many years had saved Don Stefano's life. Back then, she had been eternally grateful to the quiet, unassuming man for his loyalty. Now, she would defy anyone who protected her husband from the fate he deserved.

Alessandro sniffed, paced to the seat, and sat down, then his bullish bravado shifted to a confused expression, and the young boy inside him looked at Patrina with wide imploring eyes. He cowered in the seat and as Patrina reached across the table to him, he stiffened his back, and his eyes flashed with something akin to hate.

He leaned on the table and spoke slowly through gritted teeth. "We need to take out the Riverside, once and for all."

Beto looked silently from his boss to Patrina, then lowered his eyes to his drink. He picked up the glass and sipped. Patrina stood, and Alessandro mirrored her movement. She stroked his cheek, drew his eyes to hers, and smiled at him. "Alessandro, we need to keep focused. Getting caught up in a war of this kind will shift our attention from growing the business. To where will we supply the wine if we don't have the Riverside?"

Alessandro reverted to his five-year-old cowering self and nodded.

He fell into Patrina's arms and hugged her tightly. "You are right, Auntie."

She breathed a deep sigh, kissed his head as he comforted himself against her chest, then whispered, "We need to keep Don Chico happy, Alessandro."

He pulled away from her aggressively and threw his hands in the air. "Our goods got blown to fucking pieces last night, Auntie. Chico will be up my backside for payment for merchandise we haven't been able to sell."

Patrina concealed the smile that warmed her chest and frowned. She had a plan. "I know. We need to stall Chico and find a new route into Sicily." She looked into Alessandro's eyes with conviction. "We need to call our cousins in Spain, Alessandro. The Lombardo cement comes in directly from Valencia. If we can infiltrate their supplies, we can keep the casino project alive and transport our other merchandise at the same time." She was thinking aloud and shaking her head as she spoke. *Brilliant.* "Lombardo won't hold up their own goods through the port."

Alessandro revealed his cosmetic smile, and his eyes widened. He turned to Beto. "You need to go to Chico and explain the situation."

Beto stared at Alessandro, and his skin paled. "Going to Chico with this news is suicide, Alessandro."

Alessandro went to Beto, put his hands firmly on his shoulders, and stared deeply into his eyes. It wasn't clear whether he was threatening him or putting on a display of comradery to convey his trust in him.

"If anyone can persuade Don Chico, you can, Beto. You'll make a compelling case, my friend," he said softly.

Beto winced as Alessandro squeezed his shoulder tightly, and his head tilted towards the white-knuckled grip.

Beto lifted his chin. "I'll arrange to meet with Chico."

Alessandro sniffed and wiped his cuff across his nose. His eyes made jittery movements and then settled on Patrina. He relaxed his hand on Beto's shoulder.

"Soon, Beto. Soon."

Beto nodded. Alessandro turned to Beto and patted his left cheek hard, three times. Beto took the blows with gritted teeth, and his eyes watered.

Alessandro turned back to Patrina. "You will speak to our cousins in Spain, Auntie?"

Patrina smiled. *Good. He feels as though he is in control.* "I will talk with Miguel." Miguel Gama wouldn't be her first choice boss to align forces with, but he was the most powerful leader of organised crime in Spain. If they needed to ensure the transit of cocaine to Sicily through Lombardo's cement supplies, then he would be the man who could arrange it. She had another plan though. The price would be high but leveraging Gama's support would benefit them in containing the 'Ndrangheta. She needed this partnership to work to their advantage, for the future…her future. She looked to Beto. "Tell Chico we just need more time. A couple of weeks, if you can get it. Explain that the unions are causing trouble at the port. He needs to know we have that situation under our control."

Beto looked from Patrina to Alessandro then walked from the café like a man heading to the gallows. Alessandro clicked his fingers at the woman behind the bar. She brought over a carafe of wine and set it down on the table. He pawed under her skirt, and she smiled seductively, lowered herself to his lap, and put an arm around his neck. She kissed his cheek. He smiled at her then pushed her away. He poured a glass of wine and slugged it back in one hit, then fire flashed through his eyes.

"That fucking pussy whore needs a lesson, once and for all."

Patrina stared at him, her insides flaming. She would always defend Maria, no matter what had passed between them. She loved Maria. She always had and always would. She smiled through the burning sensation and breathed deeply. The tension subsided a fraction. She saw Alessandro's death in the vision in her mind, and the tension softened. She reached out and stroked the dead man, though his cheeks flushed, and she blinked away her desire. "We need to stay focused, Alessandro."

21.

Maria stepped out of the hire car and walked slowly across the damp car park, taking care to avoid the freestanding water that stunk of urine and glistened with engine oil. Giovanni remained in the car, as instructed, watching her back. She became aware of the rifle pointing at Giovanni from the open window of the adjoining derelict building as she approached the parked car.

The hairs standing to attention on her bare arms and the chill that crawled beneath her short-sleeved cotton shirt had little to do with the slightly cooler weather in Florence and everything to do with the heightened state that came with taking this meeting. The 'Ndrangheta's reputation as the fastest growing organised crime group on mainland Italy had been well earned. She respected that. Everyone knew who Don Chico Calabrian was. He and his crew were feared across the country. But the Lombardos were respected too, and she was banking on that being enough for the Italian gang leader to consider her offer.

She had seen her own death a thousand times over, rehearsed this walk, the foul stench that filled her nostrils, and the cool air brushing her skin. The faces were different each time, but the feeling growing within her was the same. Intense, pervasive, and it wasn't going away any time soon. She forced her ribs to concede to her breath as she approached the parked saloon car.

Three men sat inside the 'Ndrangheta's car and a fourth man stood outside the vehicle. There was little reassurance having Giovanni close by. He would be taken out before her if Don Chico didn't like what she had to offer. Her too. She was relying on tradition. Respect between Dons.

She held out her arms, palms up, and stood a few paces from the vehicle. The young man was fresh-faced, clean shaven, and shorter in stature than her, and no more than twenty, she guessed. As he approached, he looked more terrified than she felt. He stared at her as if assessing how she might respond to his instructions and then tentatively, he patted her down. Gender was meaningless, and she wasn't about to make a point as she would be inclined to do in Patrina's presence. He reeked of fresh sweat and stale cigarettes.

She didn't flinch. He looked to the silhouette in the back of the car, the man's features obscured by the thick tinted glass, and nodded. The man in the back of the vehicle opened the car door and stepped onto the concrete. He straightened his jacket then slicked back his grey hair as he walked towards her. The young henchman stepped back, pulled a gun from his waist, and directed it at her. She gave him a steady look, took a slow deep breath, and turned her attention to the older man in his mid-fifties. His eyes said he had seen life, and his smile said he was in control of his destiny. "Don Calabrian."

His teeth were bright white and his eyes dark as he looked her up and down. "You are every bit as beautiful as I was informed."

Her racing heart stilled with her distaste of him. She moved her tongue around her mouth and parted her lips, then smiled warmly. "You are well respected, Don Calabrian." She held out her hand and tilted her head to him.

He looked at her hand briefly before he shook it, then looked back up into her eyes. "You have an offer?"

"Yes, Don Calabrian."

He shrugged. "Well?"

"We can generate greater returns for your business."

He frowned. "Why should I work with you when I already have an open door to Sicily?"

She looked into his eyes. "I understand. Our family knows the Amatos well." She took a deep breath and rested her hands on her hips.

The man with the gun clicked the trigger back. She looked at him without smiling then turned to Don Chico. "Your recent consignment did not reach its destination."

Chico made a huffing noise and flicked his hand as if dismissing Maria's comment. "That is not my problem."

"Don Calabrian, I know your business partner well. I wish to offer you a better deal and a personal guarantee." Maria waited. The silence was thick and heavy. She already regretted trying to make this deal, and it wasn't even done yet.

"Seventy-thirty."

Her expression remained passive to the demands she could not accept. "Don Calabrian, that is not possible."

"That's my price."

Maria noted the roof of the car park and the hire car in the corner of her eye. She looked to her feet where the steel girders from above her dripped water that splashed on the concrete and tainted the shine on her shoes. She took a pace back to avoid the grime, and the gunman took a step closer. She raised her hand slowly, gesturing him to stop, then looked at Don Chico. Even if she wanted to accept a lesser deal and run, she couldn't. If she conceded too easily, he would lose respect for her. "You have fifty-fifty with our friends. We can honour the same, and we can look at increasing the shipments through the port. We have strong relationships with our cousins in Spain that might be of use to you." She cursed herself, but she had no choice. She had to offer something significant to attract the Don's attention, and she would deal with the consequences later.

She stood still, while the dripping water sounded like thunder in the quiet of the warehouse. She tensed against the pounding against her ribs and inched taller.

Don Chico continued to stare at her. She remained steadfast and resolute in her offer. His eyes narrowed, and she saw a spark of amusement.

His lips curled upward a fraction. "Sixty-forty."

He was toying with her to see how far she would push. She wouldn't be bated. She frowned. "I can't accept that. You understand how it is, Don Calabrian. My men would lose respect for me if I made promises that we cannot deliver."

Don Chico's laugh reverberated around the cavernous space. "You have balls."

Maria half-smiled. "Fifty-fifty."

"Ha. My men would lose respect if I did not improve our situation." He shook his head.

"And you will improve it with access to the Spanish." She shrugged.

He thinned his lips and inhaled deeply. For a fleeting moment, his focus shifted. Maria could see him wavering but waited patiently for his response.

"Fifty-five, forty-five."

"Fifty-fifty and the Spanish connection." Her response was swift and decisive, her gaze unrelenting and showing no weakness. She felt his glare soften.

He lifted his chin and turned away from her. "I will be in touch."

She waited until he was settled in his car with the henchman at his side. The car wheels squealed, and the vehicle sped from the car park, and she breathed in the dank, vile stench that surrounded her. A chill washed over her, bile rose from her stomach, and she swallowed it down. Her hands trembled and her heart thundered as she walked towards Giovanni who stood next to the hire car. She wiped away the sweat that trickled down her temples and nodded to him. Her phone vibrated in her pocket, and she retrieved it.

Giovanni released a long breath and then frowned. "What is it?"

"Beto is on his way to meet Don Calabrian."

Giovanni rolled his eyes.

"I have to get back to Sicily. I have a meeting in Spain, Giovanni. I need you to stay here and watch."

"Okay."

Maria glanced around the car park. "At a distance, Giovanni. Don't compromise yourself." She closed her eyes briefly, not wanting to entertain the possibility of someone taking him out. She wasn't certain she could bear it so soon after losing her father.

22.

The drive from Valencia airport to the Lombardo Cement Works on the outskirts of the city brought a smile to Maria's face despite the large volume of traffic slowing her journey. Tapping her fingers to the music from the radio, she revisited the memory of Simone as she had just left her in the hotel.

Simone's warm, damp skin had shimmered and sweat had pooled in the pit of her soft stomach. Through gritted teeth, Simone had tensed at her touch, and screamed out, and fallen into a quivering heap. They had laughed uncontrollably and kissed until Maria had needed to shower and leave.

Maria's smile softened her vision, and the resonance of Simone in rapture fluttered in her chest. *God, I love her.* She sighed and took a left off the highway.

Beto's image came to her, and the lightness in her chest became suddenly dense. She had noted the way Beto looked at Alessandro. It was clear he had no respect for his boss. Beto wasn't like Alessandro, and he didn't deserve to die for the fat man.

Don Chico hadn't taken too kindly to Alessandro sending his lacky to the meeting. It was a mark of disrespect, and he had put two bullets into Beto as a reminder to the Amatos that they had a debt that needed paying. One week for each bullet, and two weeks to pay what they owed. Luckily for Beto, Giovanni saw the incident and had Beto's wounds tended to before he bled to his death. The fat pig's image lodged in her awareness and a shiver passed down her spine. She hadn't thought herself capable of hating someone as much as she detested Alessandro. Perhaps Vittorio wasn't such a bad judge in this case after all.

She turned her attention to the scenery, the road ahead, and enjoyed the wind on her face. Open fields spanned both sides of the road, and the concrete towers at the plant grew in stature as she got closer. Her thoughts drifted. The air was fresh and clean by comparison with the stench of the car park in Florence. She inhaled deeply. *I have to leave Sicily.* Don Chico type meetings would always be needed in this job and someone would always end up hurt or dead.

She turned into the site, flashed her passport ID to the security guard, and smiled. He opened the gates to the compound, and she drove to the site offices.

Preferring to stand while she waited in the reception, her heart raced with anticipation and hope. She had longed for this moment for as long as she could remember, and now it had arrived. She looked through the large glass panels at the tall concrete towers with large sprawling arms and gurgling chutes feeding greedy trucks that moved slowly across the site. The site was even more impressive close up. The uniformity and precision of the operation brought a smile and warmth settled her.

"Donna Maria."

The deep soft voice came from behind her. She turned and smiled at Rafael's bright eyes. She approached him with open arms. "Rafael. How are you? The family?"

His cheeks flushed as he grinned. "We are all well, thank you, Maria." He pulled her into his arms then held her away from him and studied her. "You look well."

"Thank you." She looked over his shoulder towards the door that led into the hub of the building. "Is he here?"

Rafael nodded. "He has the paperwork ready for you."

She followed him to the director's boardroom.

A short, suited man stood as she entered the room. He smiled at her and held out his hand. She glanced briefly at the paperwork neatly laid out on the table in front of him as she shook his hand.

"Buenos días, señorita Sanchez? It is a pleasure to meet you," the man said.

"Buenos días, señor." Her hands trembled though she didn't let it show. She removed the passport from her jacket pocket and handed it over to him.

He studied the photograph and then Maria's face. He maintained an official, stern look as he opened the documents and transferred the information needed from the identification she had provided to his forms. Then he passed the completed documents across the table and smiled faintly.

"Could you please sign at the crosses as indicated on the forms, Ms Sanchez?"

Maria sat and duly signed each of the forms, and one by one slid them back to him. He took a set of the documents and handed a second set to Maria.

"These are for your safekeeping." He delved into his bag, pulled out two bunches of keys, and handed them to her. "Felicidades, señorita." He packed the paperwork into his briefcase and looked at Maria as he stood. "Everything is in order."

"The transit will progress?" she asked.

"Sì, señorita. We have those details as Palermo with a delivery in two weeks' time. We do not foresee a problem but if one arises, we will contact the offices here as per your request."

"Muchas gracias." She held out her hand. Again, the Spanish language rolled off her tongue as if she were native to the country, and the man acknowledged her as such.

He shook her hand and smiled. "Buenos días, Señorita Sanchez."

Her spirit lifted as the deal was concluded. "Buenos días."

Rafael escorted the man from the boardroom and gave Maria a quick, congratulatory smile over his shoulder as he shut the door behind them.

Maria glanced at the paperwork, and the quivering in her stomach spread to her hands. *Yes, yes, yes.* She looked around the room and through the glass panel that spanned the length of the corridor on the other side, hoping she wasn't being watched. She released a deep breath and clasped her hand to her chest. *It's happening.* She paced the boardroom to stop herself from bursting or voicing her delight with screams that would have made her look a little crazy. She congratulated herself then admonished her overzealousness. She had to maintain her composure. *Discipline. Control.* It might be one small step closer to realising her dream, but the situation was still shrouded in uncertainty. It was too early to celebrate.

Her parents had always known how she craved to leave Sicily. Her father had supported her as best he could along the way, but even he probably never thought she would actually leave. Her mother had made it clear she would rather Maria stayed in Sicily, but that could never happen if Maria wanted to be happy. Had it not been for her father's death she might well have left already. But then she would never have met Simone.

She had spilled her wishes for a different future to Simone without thinking, like picking up on a call with a soul mate she'd known for a million years. *The code of silence was there to protect those you love.* Had she broken the code? Bringing Simone to Valencia and the Pyrenees was a risk. She wasn't thinking clearly. Her actions around Simone defied logic. *This was what love did to you.* It was dangerous to lose her capacity to think and to be controlled by strong emotions. She closed her eyes and prayed she wouldn't live to regret the weakness that afflicted her. The image of the cruiser she had just purchased came to her, and she opened her eyes and smiled.

The Octavia was a key part of the plan. She had done everything possible to ensure the cruiser couldn't be linked back to her. The owner, Mariella Sanchez, was a woman of Spanish origin who would be untraceable should anyone come looking.

She took a deep breath and closed her eyes again. Her heart slowed with her thoughts. She couldn't tell Simone about the boat or her identity. Not yet. It was too risky. She turned as the door to the boardroom opened and smiled at Rafael.

"Congratulations, Maria."

"Thank you, Rafael."

"Please, take a seat. Would you like a drink?"

Maria nodded and a woman came into the room with two cups of freshly brewed coffee. Rafael smiled at her as she set them on the table, remaining silent until the woman had left the room.

"We are increasing cement production as you requested. Shipments will leave twice a week until further notice."

"Excellent. We'll be able to increase the scope of our construction projects." She smiled. "Amato will be unable to build the casino as planned because their supplier in the mainland is unhappy, and our cement will be too expensive for them. They'll go bust, and the project will be abandoned. We will get the tech park reinstated as my father had intended." She sipped at the drink, her thoughts drifting to her execution of the plans.

Rafael took a sip of his drink. "Business is good."

She looked at him with a faint frown. "Everything is secure at this end?"

"Of course, Maria."

"Good." She smiled and sipped her coffee. "Please give my regards to Isla and give Jose and Diego a big hug for me. I'm sorry not to take a longer trip. Maybe next time I can visit them."

Grinning, he reached into his breast pocket, opened his wallet, and pulled out a picture of twin boys sporting broad grins and identical gaps where their baby teeth had not long fallen out. "They are growing so fast."

His cheeks shone as he regarded the picture nostalgically, as if imprinting the memory firmly in his mind. Maria smiled and patted him on the arm. "They will soon be as good looking as their father."

He cleared his throat, replaced the picture safely in his wallet, and stood as she did. "I will escort you down," he said.

She followed him out of the building with the paperwork for the cruiser folded neatly into her inside jacket pocket and pressing stiffly against her chest.

23.

Simone had decided on the drive from the airport that the Pyrenees was, without doubt, the most beautiful place she had ever seen. They had passed beneath the high, snowy peaks of the vast mountain range that touched clear blue skies and driven cautiously down the narrow winding roads that carved their way through forested mountainsides. Kayakers paddled top grade trout streams and rivers which split the slopes and created ravines. Everywhere around them had been wild countryside with numerous species of wild orchid, butterflies, and raptors, though they hadn't stopped to discover the many walking trails.

She had delighted in Maria's animation as she talked about one of the most unspoiled regions of France, the prehistoric caves, chateaus, and the escape routes through the mountains that had served the resistance during the Second World War. Warmth had filled her with the admiration Maria had for the place, and she had wanted the journey to never end.

Now, she sat in the passenger seat of their hire car in the town of St-Lizier, her eyes fixed on the blue door of the estate agent's offices that Maria had just stepped into, and a steady flow of vibration fizzed in her stomach. The mixed feelings had started in Valencia. Excitement in the moments she shared with Maria, and comfort in the privacy of their hotel room, but then a dull feeling had her looking over her shoulder in those moments when she was alone. The hotel had been luxurious, and she had been spoiled with the spa and aromatherapy massage. She had felt safe, and there was no logical reason for the discomfort that came to her. Bizarrely, she didn't even feel anxious in Palermo though she had every reason to. She rubbed her fingers together, interlocked them, and clenched her fists, and the urgency to see Maria intensified. Maria wouldn't be long. She just needed to collect the keys to the property she had planned for them to stay at.

She looked around, and the Roman architecture drew her eye. Looking closely, it reminded her of her visit to the Colosseum while she was at Rome University, though these buildings were nestled within a large national park rather than a bustling and vibrant city. She hadn't considered her personal safety an issue in Rome. In fact, it hadn't become an issue until recently…until Maria. *Maria, Maria.* She was exhilarating to be with, attentive, caring, considerate, respectful, and daring. The idea of losing her clenched her gut until it burned. She closed her eyes. *Enjoy this beautiful place with the woman you love, Simone.* She opened her eyes and inhaled. The air here was clearer, cooler, and a little more humid than Valencia. Tranquillity became tangible in the softening of her eyes as she watched people amble leisurely down the narrow street, chatting and smiling. Reassurance quieted her concerns and breathed deeply to relax her muscles. She sighed.

Maria caught her eye as she exited the building and ran to the driver's door. Simone's heart skipped lightly, and she smiled at the beaming grin that spanned Maria's face as she got into the car and dangled a set of keys in front of her.

"Here, you can be the guardian of these."

Simone grabbed them. Maria held on to the fob, drew Simone towards her, and kissed her. Simone froze.

Maria leaned back, let go, and smiled. "We're okay here. It's safe."

Simone looked around outside the car window, her heart thundering behind her ribs. *Yes, they were.* She shook her head at the realisation of how closeted she had lived. Open displays of affection weren't something she engaged in back home, for her own protection. But she hadn't been openly *out* at uni either. *This is so crazy.* She settled in the seat, closed her fingers around the keys, and released a long slow breath. Maria frowned at her, though she saw passion flash across Maria's eyes as she looked into them. She reached up and traced her face. Maria's cheek was warm, and when Maria took her fingers and tenderly kissed them, Simone stopped breathing and swiftly closed the space between them. Tingling sparked in her lips and swept down her spine and across the surface of her skin as Maria's mouth closed tenderly over hers.

It was a short route to the farmhouse, and yet it was as though the home sat a million miles from everywhere. Set in a meadow of green a couple of kilometres from the main road, surrounded by arable farmland, pine forests, and within the mountain's view, it was idyllic.

Simone stepped out of the car and looked around. She took in a deep breath. Sweet, rich, earthy aromas filled her senses. She ran her hand over the cool stone building. "This place is so exquisitely beautiful."

Maria wrapped an arm around her waist. Smiling, she took in the familiar surroundings and inhaled deeply. "You like it?"

"It's incredible."

Maria took Simone's hand and tugged her towards the door. "Come and see inside."

Simone allowed herself to be dragged, though she still hadn't soaked up enough of the vista to want to move. She handed over the keys, and Maria unlocked the front door.

The single-story building was dark inside. Small windows kept out the sunlight that would too quickly overheat the rooms in the warmer months and stopped the cold penetrating during the harsher winter months. The rustic wood door squeaked as it opened into the main living area where a two-seater, chocolate brown couch and a matching armchair hunkered around a natural fireplace. Dry logs stacked in a neat pile on the hearth waited for their turn to deliver their duty. A beautifully hand-crafted, dark-wood dresser leaned against the main wall, with decorative china artefacts adorning its shelves. A large oil painting that replicated the view across the meadow spanned the chimney breast above the fireplace and could be seen from the adjoining dining room through which Maria was leading her.

Maria placed the keys on the central island and smiled at Simone. The layout bore a striking resemblance to the beach villa, slightly less open plan but remarkably similar. Simone frowned as she compared the two properties in her mind's eye.

Maria's smile broadened and then she went to the fridge. "Would you like a drink?"

She had pulled out a bottle of wine before Simone had the chance to answer and knew exactly where to go for the glasses. Simone's frown deepened as Maria poured their drinks.

Maria's eyes narrowed, and her smile slowly disappeared as she held out a glass to Simone. "What is it?"

Simone stared at Maria, her heart pounding. "You know this place?"

Maria lowered her head momentarily. She took a pace towards Simone, who took a pace away from her.

She looked into Simone's eyes, and released a long breath. "Here, please, take this. Let's talk."

Slowly, Simone took the glass. She put it on the island and crossed her arms. Maria took a sip of the wine, picked up Simone's glass, and headed out the rear door to the patio area that overlooked the meadow. She placed their glasses on the stone topped table and sat, encouraging Simone to join her. Simone sat.

"My father brought me to the Pyrenees when I was four for a holiday," Maria said softly. "I discovered the snow on the mountains and trout fishing in the streams in boots that were bigger than me. I discovered this place about fifteen years ago." Her eyes wandered across the spectacular view. "I fell in love with it."

Simone saw tenderness and longing in Maria's eyes. Maria's lips trembled as they closed and formed a thin line. She looked sad and remorseful, and Simone's heart ached. She wanted to take the pain away.

"The agent looks after it for me. I rarely get an opportunity to visit."

Simone swallowed. She dropped her shoulders, picked up her glass, and sipped her wine. Something was niggling her though she couldn't put her finger on what. Every time she looked at Maria, she melted. Her heart ached in a way she had never experienced, and as soon as Maria was out of sight, she worried for her to the point of a physical pain gripping around her chest. This place was so far removed from Maria's life in Palermo. "Why?"

Maria frowned. "Why what?"

"Why don't you visit?"

Maria looked away. She hesitated to speak, and they sat in silence.

"You can trust me, Maria."

Maria turned her head slowly to face Simone. "You are so innocent."

Simone felt the bolt of rejection locking her out of Maria's world. The tumbling sensation started in her stomach, sparked a fire that flamed inside her, and like the tree struck by lightning, she was beginning to crumble. Tears welled behind angry eyes. "Don't say that to me."

Maria sipped her wine. "My life is always under threat, Simone."

Simone remained silent. Her jaw hurt from her gritted teeth. She'd already worked that out.

Maria flinched. "I'm not who you think I—"

"You think you know who I am?"

Maria hesitated, then started to nod. "You're right." Her lips twitched at the corners, and her eyes narrowed. "We don't know each other at all."

Simone lifted her chin as she glared at Maria, her shoulders rising as if to say, so what? "I know you're a mafia boss, and I also know that you're one of the kindest people I've ever met. You're smart. And you care about people."

Maria looked down at her trembling hands on the table. "I've killed people, Simone." She didn't look up and rubbed at her eyes.

Simone felt the admission like the fracturing of ice when standing in the middle of a frozen lake. Her pulse raced. She should jump back in the car and disappear from Maria's life forever. Instead, her thoughts transformed the feeling into a fierce determination to protect and defend her. "You must have had a good reason, Maria."

Maria slowly lifted her head and looked at Simone. She wasn't smiling. She didn't look relieved at the reprieve Simone had given her.

"Is there ever a good reason to take another person's life?"

Simone nodded with conviction. "Yes, I think there is."

The intensity in Maria's eyes softened and then slowly, a tender smile formed. Simone ignored the quaking in her stomach as she searched for the right words as the disappointment, rejection, and loneliness that she had lived through after returning to take care of her brother flooded her. "We do what we have to do to survive."

Maria sighed and bowed her head. "I can't live in that world anymore, Simone."

Simone reached out and took Maria's hands in hers. These hands had taken life from others, and yet they'd given Simone hope of life, a different life. She couldn't imagine the conflict Maria must have experienced nor the suffering she would endure for the rest of her life. She couldn't take Maria's conscience from her and supposed Maria wouldn't want her to. She could love her though. In spite of everything Maria had done, she would cherish her and be there for her. She would do that.

She cupped Maria's cheek and leaned across the table, and when she met Maria's mouth with tenderness, her heart opened, and she felt Maria curl up inside it. When Simone leaned back, her focus was blurred through the wet sheen covering her eyes. Her voice reflected the painful truth she knew they both shared. "I would rather die than lose you."

Maria looked away. "If anything happens to me, if the situation deteriorates with Amato, you can live here. Roberto too if he wishes."

Simone shook her head, and her eyes widened. "Please, don't talk like that."

Maria looked up and wiped the tears that slipped down Simone's cheeks. "I'm not expecting anything to happen."

You're lying. Maria smiled, and Simone's expression remained etched with concern. Maria cleared her throat and leaned back in the seat and sipped from her drink.

"Hey."

Simone saw a flicker of light in Maria's eyes as she smiled at her. She was trying to shift the subject. The least Simone could do was go with her. "Hey."

Maria pointed. "There's a stream down there. We can fish for trout tomorrow."

Simone glanced in the direction of the forested area.

Maria looked at Simone for a long time and sighed. "You are beautiful," she said.

Heat filled Simone's cheeks and when she smiled, she saw a glint in Maria's eyes.

"Would you like to live here one day?"

"Yes." Her voice sounded as broken as her heart felt. Her eyelashes felt thick with wetness. She wiped her eyes to prevent the burning from becoming another flood of tears. The dark image wouldn't leave her though: Maria lying in a pool of blood, Alessandro standing over her dead body with an insane grin on his face, gloating, and his gun still pointing at her blood-soaked chest. An icy chill shuddered down her spine.

Maria leaned closer, lifted Simone's chin, and looked into her eyes. "I'm sorry."

Simone bit down on her lip as she reached up and stroked Maria's face. "It's not your fault."

Maria squinted. "You could stay here. I will come to you, later, once the business is more stable."

Simone shook her head as her thoughts tumbled into words. "No. I can't do that. I can't leave you. What if you walk away from here and don't come back? I could never live with myself. As beautiful as this place is," she said and gestured to their surroundings, "it's meaningless without you."

Maria took a deep breath. "It could get rough back home. Alessandro is in a lot of trouble with some very dangerous people. I'm trying to settle things, to stop them escalating, but he's crazy and unpredictable, and Patrina..."

Simone watched Maria's expression shift, affection moving swiftly across her eyes to reveal disappointment. She had picked up on Maria's connection with Patrina at the café when Maria had first shown up there. She knew how women looked at each other when there was more to their relationship. Who didn't know what such a look meant? "Patrina...she is in your past?"

Maria bit her lips between her teeth. "Yes."

"Does she still want you?" Simone's tone sounded stilted.

Maria sighed. "Honestly, I don't know. I think she just enjoys having power over me." She shrugged. "Her idea of wanting is controlling someone." She took a deep breath.

"We've known each other for a long time. We were lovers before Don Stefano was sent to prison. Our relationship isn't what it was back then. There is no relationship. She wants more than I'm willing to give her." She looked vacantly at Simone, then her focus returned. "I sold my soul to the Devil, Simone, and now I'm claiming it back."

Who doesn't sell their soul to the Devil? Simone knew that feeling. She rolled her tongue around her lips. Women like Patrina never let go? "She still wants you. I can tell."

Maria shrugged. "She never had me. She can never have me." She took Simone's hand and held it firmly. "I want to be with you."

A sheen appeared over Maria's eyes. Simone closed the space between them and pressed her lips to Maria's, then wiped the tear from her cheek. "I want to be with you, too."

Maria's smile looked weak, and then she stood suddenly and held out her hand.

"Come on, I want to show you something. Do you know there are more than sixty varieties of orchid in the meadows around here?"

Simone stalled. It was hard to adjust to the sudden swings in focus that seemed second nature to Maria. One minute, Maria would be engrossed in mafia business, the next enjoying the delights of a freshly cooked meal, and it was as if the business had never existed. Simone took longer to shift state. But the smile on Maria's face and the way her eyes shone when she was excited felt good. "Uh huh!"

"Come on."

Maria seemed to have gained a second wind in an instant. Simone fought her weariness, stood, and took Maria's hand. If she was honest, she was all orchid-ed out after the tour the previous day. But with Maria's hand in hers, and in this special place, she would go hunting for orchids every hour of every day if that's what it would take to keep Maria at her side. Maria grinned at her, and her hand felt warm and strong. She locked eyes with Maria, and the electrifying effect moved through her like lightning. *Did Maria's breath hitch or was that mine?* Did Maria feel this?

Maria's lips curled upwards, and she looked down the road they had arrived via. "And, more importantly, there is an amazing restaurant just down the road. I booked us a table. Are you hungry?"

Simone shook her head, her core on fire, and whispered, "Not really."

Maria nodded. "Would you like to take a walk first?"

Seriously? How can you not know what I want? Simone tilted Maria's face to look into her eyes and smiled. "Not really." She tugged Maria into her, and when she met Maria's lips in a languid, intimate kiss, she groaned. "This is what I want."

Simone led Maria to a sunspot in the meadow and lowered her to the grass. She lay next to her on her side and ran her fingers through Maria's hair. "You are so very handsome and pretty." She smiled as she lightly traced her fingertips across Maria's eyebrow and down her temple, and then followed the shape of Maria's cheekbones and jaw. Every touch resonated in the electric energy that passed between them. She stroked her thumb across Maria's lips, and she gasped softly. Simone placed soft kisses on Maria's cheeks, her eyes, and then lingered on her mouth and nipped and bit Maria's soft lips. Maria raised her hands to clasp Simone's head, and Simone stopped her. She took Maria's hands and lowered them to the ground and moved on top of her. "No," she whispered. She silenced any potential objection with a deep kiss and when she touched Maria's breast, Maria jerked beneath her and groaned into her mouth.

Whether it was the sound or the sense of Maria's hardened nipples at her fingertips, urgency overtook her and she pulled out of the kiss and stared into Maria's eyes. "I need to feel you."

"I want you inside me."

Maria's voice had a gravelly texture that streamed through Simone in a shower of sparkles. Simone undid Maria's trousers, lowered her clothing, and slipped her hand between Maria's legs. She gasped and groaned as her fingers slid through Maria's silky folds and across her swollen sex. "You are so fucking hot."

Maria groaned and thrust her hips into Simone.

"And so very wet."

Maria jerked her head back and groaned. "Oh, fuck…"

"And so deliciously silky. I'm going to…" Simone entered Maria, and her own guttural groan rendered her speechless.

Maria rocked rhythmically and then lifted her head and cupped Simone's cheek to look at her. "You feel so good."

The intensity in Maria's eyes stole Simone's breath. She silenced her streaming thoughts by kissing Maria firmly on the lips and thrusting her fingers deeper inside her. Maria's eyes closed, and she started to shudder. Simone held her fingers inside Maria, teased her with light touches, and kissed her tenderly, and as Maria reached orgasm, she held her in her arms until the tremors eased.

Simone tenderly stroked Maria's damp cheeks and smiled. "I love you," she whispered. Maria shook her head and tears slipped from her eyes. Simone silenced her objections with a languid kiss, and buried the ache in her heart.

Please, tell me you love me.

24.

Maria stroked the smallest blood-red flower of the orchid and traced the darker red veins shaping its character and differentiating it from its neighbouring flowers. The cultivated orchids were very different to the wild ones in the Pyrenees, no matter how well tended they were. The wild ones seemed to exude energy and freedom. Maybe it was just her imagination, her hopes for her life projected through what she saw in nature.

Heat flooded her as she recalled the precious time she'd shared with Simone in a place free from all this. Her heart weighed heavily. She looked out the window across the city. It really was a stunning place, and yet it had come to represent everything she abhorred. The flicker of hope had become brighter in the past week, just as long as she didn't think about the outcome of the meeting with Don Chico and the incident that had left Beto on crutches. She closed her heart to protect it from the impending sense of doom that was never too far from the front of her mind. She needed to stay sharp.

She wiped the light-green, rubber-like leaf and tenderly removed the finest layer of dust that had accumulated in the short time she had been away. She smiled to herself as she shook her head. Her matri never looked after the plants with the same attention to detail as she did. Pesto gnawed on the stick he'd found on the beach. He had insisted on carrying it with him to the office, refusing to get into the Maserati without his prize. A wave of sadness moved through her, and she pushed it away with her thoughts. *You can't always have it all.* She took a deep breath and rubbed her hand across her brow.

Simone, Simone...why are you so stubborn?

Simone had insisted she had things she needed to do, a house to clean, and Roberto to catch up with. At least Roberto had been briefed by Giovanni. *Damn that lie.* She couldn't hold Simone prisoner at the villa though she seriously wanted to.

An unsettled feeling moved through her. She picked up another cloth and put it down again, then touched the Smith and Wesson at her side. She paced at the rate of her thoughts then picked up another cloth and tended to a leaf. She couldn't sit, couldn't rest. In short, she wished Simone had stayed at the beach where she would be safe.

She turned to the door as it opened, threw the cotton cloth into the bin, and walked to the front of her desk. She smiled at Vittorio and Giovanni as they approached.

Giovanni smiled warmly. "Donna Maria, the break was good?"

His kindness distracted her, and she smiled. "Yes, a very good break and a good meeting with Rafael. But now, we must get back to business." Tension crept up her back, sharpening and directing her attention.

Vittorio bowed his head. "Good to see you back, Donna Maria."

"How's Catena?"

Vittorio smiled. "Good. A little sick, but happy."

"That's good." That *was* good. It was normality of the kind Maria would like to enjoy.

Vittorio hesitated, and his smile disappeared. "Donna Maria."

"Yes, Vittorio."

"Alessandro is not going to pay Don Chico."

Maria expected nothing less.

"Patrina is looking to the Spanish."

Maria rolled her tongue around her mouth as she considered. "That means she will be trying to piggy-back on our supply routes."

Giovanni nodded. "Alessandro is pushing too."

Maria frowned.

"Since we increased security at the Riverside, he sent a small supply of wine and tobacco to Lo Scoglio and Pastasciutta yesterday. The wine is of a much lower quality, and the quantities aren't as high. We refused it, but the managers were forced to pay at gunpoint...I have had the situation taken care of. Security has been increased at all our venues, and the stock has been sent to his customers as a gift. The Romano brothers are behind the deliveries, and Vittorio is going to send them a stronger message. Alessandro is wild. He's crazy, Donna Maria. Something needs to be done before we have the Italians *and* the Spanish on our backs. Chico is not our friend; he just hates Alessandro more than us."

Maria nodded. "I know."

Giovanni held his breath as if he had more to say and didn't know how to say it. "We can't expand the routes for Don Chico's supplies, Donna Maria. It goes against everything we stand for."

Maria took a pace towards Giovanni and placed a hand on his arm. "I have no intention of giving Chico what he wants, Giovanni. We needed to cut that deal to give ourselves time." She lowered her eyes. She wasn't ready to share her thoughts on how they would handle the Chico problem, but it would involve Patrina. Firstly, they needed to silence Alessandro. "Is Beto okay?"

"He will live."

Maria ran her fingers through her hair, pressing tightly to her scalp. "If Chico had wanted Beto dead, you would have brought him back in a body bag. He is toying with Alessandro, but for how long we don't know."

Giovanni looked concerned. "Donna Maria?"

She let go of Giovanni's arm and turned to face Vittorio. "Yes, Vittorio."

"Alessandro is planning to take rent from our tenants. Stracato Street, the bakers, and tailors have been given notice. Next month, they pay him."

Fucking hell. Could this get any worse? Maria stared at Vittorio. "That fucking pig."

Vittorio lowered his head, then looked up. "You know Gavino Romano is as crazy as Alessandro. He is Alessandro's right-hand now."

"What about Beto?"

Vittorio shook his head. "He is recovering. Alessandro has moved on."

Maria worked her tongue slowly around her dry mouth, and her focus remained still and distant. "Vittorio, we need to take down their infrastructure."

"Yes, Donna Maria."

She looked at Giovanni. "Is Roberto doing a good job?"

Giovanni smiled with affection for the boy.

"He is smart. He's collecting rent and has keen eyes on the street. He remembers names and faces well."

"Good. I want every truck in the Amato's supplier's fleet decommissioned. Roberto can help. Vittorio, tell him to be careful. And, speak to the bakers and tailors. Let them know we are looking after them, and that they are not to pay rent to Amato. Any Amato goes near them, or anyone else, we clean up the streets. Understand?"

Vittorio smiled, a glint in his eye. "Of course, Donna Maria. I understand."

"I will speak to Roberto," Giovanni said.

Maria looked from one man to the other. She hesitated, then looked to each of them again. "Simone will be staying at the villa until this mess is cleared up. She can't work at the Riverside, it's too risky. She wants to go into town today. Giovanni, can you get Angelo to take her? Keep eyes on her at all times."

Giovanni nodded.

"I will try and meet with Patrina and see if we can calm this situation before it blows us all out of the water. I want to know the faces of every Calabrian crew we can trace. If they set foot on our shores, we need to know who they are."

Both men answered in unison. "Capisci, Donna Maria."

She turned her back to them and walked to the window, the sound of their metal heels clicking on the wooden floor fading as they went to the door.

"Vittorio."

"Sì, Donna Maria."

She faced the window as she spoke. "Nothing to Catena or Matri. I don't want them worrying."

"Sì, Donna Maria, capisci."

She sighed as the door clicked shut. Staring vacantly, her heart running a heavy beat, her stomach corkscrewed. Slowly she held out her hands and looked at them, surprised to see them remaining still. Her thoughts drifted to Simone, and her heart started to race, though not with joy or the blissful sense of peace and love she'd experienced while they were away together. This was the quality of alertness she had known once before, the time she had referred to when talking openly with Simone at the farmhouse. She had just turned twenty-one, and she had killed a man. That was her first time, and although it hadn't been her last, it was the one memory that lingered. His eyes never closed. They stared at her blankly. There was nothing behind the dark brown irises. His skin paled, and his blood trickled from his nose. Life had drained from him instantly.

She looked at her trembling hands. Simone's face replaced the man's lying motionless on the cold concrete, and Maria's heart thundered, heavy and hard.

25.

Splinters of light lit up the beach and shoreline as Maria drove towards the villa. Simone was home. *Home.* She took a deep breath, and a wave of warmth moved across her shoulders and down her neck. She brought the Maserati to a stop, and the music of Carmen she heard coming from inside the villa made her smile softly. One day she would watch the opera with Simone's hand in hers and savour every second of it. She closed her eyes and enjoyed the delicate fluttering in her chest. The image of Simone in the flowing red dress she wore at the opera came to her. Maria slowly undid the buttons, slipped the dress from her shoulders, and unhurriedly felt the softness of her skin with her fingers and tongue. Maria's pulse raced. She flashed her eyes open, stepped out of the car, and took a deep breath to stem the throbbing between her legs. She entered the villa.

And froze.

Steel tension gripped Maria as she focused on the woman stood staring out of the window towards the beach. Her chest thundered beneath the tightness that clamped her lungs, and she gasped urgently for breath.

Patrina turned slowly. She was smiling softly, disarmingly. Pesto sat in his bed, happily chewing a bone. Maria glared at her. "How the fuck did you get into my home?"

"Someone is getting careless, ma bedda."

Maria's throat constricted as she processed the words. The latch on the door to the beach had been broken. Careless got people killed, and that thought never settled well. Maria cleared her throat, and when she asked again her tone had an edge to it. "How did you get in here, Patrina?"

Patrina glanced out of the window. Lights bobbed on the water, spotting the cruiser that was moored next to the Bedda at the boundary of the cove.

"You think you are invincible and that the cove protects you? I can recommend a good locksmith. You need one."

An icy chill trickled down Maria's spine, then a surge of electric heat shot back up and filled her head with fire. "We had an agreement, Patrina."

Patrina continued to stare out the window. Maria thought she heard her snigger. She clenched her fists to stop herself reaching for the gun at her side. She couldn't kill Patrina though she wished she could. She had drawn a line under that option a long time ago. It was one thing to be intensely irritated by Patrina, but taking her life just wasn't an option Maria could live with.

"I think any agreements we had were annulled when you laid your hands on me...or should I say, your foot?" She turned to face Maria, her eyes darker and colder than a moment ago. "Don't you think?"

Maria refused to acknowledge the comment. She walked to the kitchen to free her muscles from the rigidity that stifled her. She needed to think clearly. Patrina would not have come to the villa without good reason. If Patrina had wanted to kill her, she would have done it already. And Maria didn't believe Patrina wanted to kill her any more than she wanted Patrina dead. Too much had passed between them and despite what had happened, Maria still held a shred of respect for her. "What do you want from me, Patrina?"

Patrina sighed. "I thought you would never ask."

Maria winced. *The fucking game playing.*

Patrina approached the breakfast bar and looked around the room. "This is a nice place. I can't think why you didn't invite me here."

Maria went to the fridge and pulled out a bottle of wine. She grabbed two glasses and placed them on the bar. "We need to talk, Patrina."

"There you go, bedda. We are still like-minds."

Patrina's sarcastic tone was paralleled in the disdainful look she gave Maria as she poured the wine and sipped her drink. Maria glanced at the front door. The last thing she needed was Simone coming home while Patrina was here. She should be back by now. *Where the fuck is she?* She breathed deeply, and her ribs reluctantly expanded.

"Are you expecting someone?" Patrina teased the glass across her lips.

Maria gave her a stern look. She wouldn't be baited. She still held the upper hand, otherwise Patrina would never have come to the villa. She sipped her drink. "You're losing control, Patrina." The smile slid from Patrina's lips, and the lines appeared across her forehead as she narrowed her eyes. Patrina looked older, and Maria noted vulnerability in her unsettled appearance. "Alessandro is bringing your business down, Patrina."

Patrina sipped the drink then rested the glass on the bar. "We need to work together, not against each other, bedda," she said softly.

The tender, almost conciliatory, tone in Patrina's voice turned the chilled wine that had just hit Maria's stomach, even though she knew Patrina was right. She'd had the same thoughts. If they didn't work together, the Italians and or the Spanish would tear them apart. But there were a couple of big issues. Firstly, she didn't trust Patrina, and secondly, she really didn't trust Patrina. She couldn't concede easily, or it would send the wrong message. "Why should I work with you?"

Patrina took in a deep breath and released it slowly, and when she looked at Maria, it was as though she was trying to convey tenderness.

"We had something special, didn't we?"

Maria took a sip of wine. "That was a long time ago, Patrina. A long time ago."

Patrina smiled ruefully. "I know. But something that special leaves an ember that can never be extinguished. It's an eternal flame. I know you feel it too."

Maria shook her head almost imperceptibly. She didn't feel an eternal flame, but it would serve her to have Patrina believe she did. Patrina had comforted Maria after she made her first kill. She had helped her see a different perspective and to recognise that what she had done had served the greater good. Patrina had been the one to clean up the situation and make sure that no route led back to either of them. But Maria had paid a hefty price for Patrina's protection and affection. The pounding in her chest forced her to ask the bitter question that sat at the tip of her tongue. "Did you order the hit on my father?"

Patrina's eyes widened, and she shook her head violently. "What are you saying? No, of course not. The police confirmed it was an accident. The case was closed. No, bedda, I swear I would not do that to your father, you, or your family."

Maria stared into Patrina's eyes. The paling of Patrina's cheeks, the adamant shaking of her head, and the genuine sense of shock she saw in her eyes meant something. She believed her. And not because she wanted to, but because her gut told her. "Don Stefano ordered this?"

Patrina shook her head. She looked dazed. "Um, no. I don't think so. He respected your father."

Maria didn't flinch. "Then Alessandro."

Patrina swallowed hard, and she lowered her head.

"Who is he working with at the DIA?"

Patrina pursed her lips and shook her head as she looked up. "I don't know, but I swear I will find out for you, bedda."

Maria gritted her teeth. "Alessandro."

Patrina nodded.

Maria took a gulp of wine and swallowed. "What did you want from me?"

Patrina hesitated. "If you and I are leading our businesses, peace will be restored, Maria."

Maria's lips curled upwards, and then a frown stopped her from smiling. She shook her head. "You want me to *clean up* for you."

Patrina broke eye contact. She reached for the glass and turned it fitfully. "Some people are just bad for business, Maria. You know this."

"Why don't you feed him to the Italians? Chico will be heading this way if his debts aren't paid, and he doesn't take disrespect too well."

Patrina's skin paled. Maria nodded. "You're worried he'll take you out as well as Alessandro?" Maria raised her eyebrows. "You're probably right."

Patrina's hand was trembling, and she lifted the glass unsteadily to her lips. The look of terror in Patrina's eyes touched Maria. Loyalty? Love? Whatever it was, it was a curse.

"Please, Maria, help me. It serves both our families to restore peace. If Chico infiltrates our ranks, there will be devastation."

Ruining the Amato's business was preferable to taking lives, but Patrina was right about the fact that they were solid when working as a united front in the same way her father and Don Stefano had been. A united front made it more difficult for outsiders to infiltrate.

"Alessandro is refusing to pay the debt, Maria."

"Then his demise will come sooner than he thinks."

Patrina lowered her head.

Maria shook her head. "To think Beto took two bullets for that fat pig. He deserves everything that's coming to him. If the Italian's don't take him out, you should, Patrina."

Patrina's hand trembled around the glass as she whispered, "And I will die, too."

She looked up at Maria, revealing the soul that Maria had once known intimately. Maria fought being drawn into Patrina's world. If Patrina died, that wasn't her problem. Why the fuck did she still care then? She walked to the window, put her hands on her hips, and took a long deep breath. Alessandro was Don Stefano's only nephew and likely to be voted in as the next Don. If the finger for Alessandro's death were pointed in Maria's direction, Stefano would come for her. Maybe Alessandro was working from Stefano's orders to kill her father. Patrina could be way out of the loop. Her father had said that Stefano had lost his way. Maybe he had lost his way enough to order the hit and get Alessandro or one of his men to deliver it. Alessandro picking up the leadership of the Amato clan wasn't an option Maria could live with. If Patrina died, Stefano would find another thug who he could direct from his cell. Having Patrina at the head of the Amato clan was by far the safest solution for them all. Fire burned in her belly. If Patrina didn't take the hit on Alessandro, she would have to. She looked into Patrina's eyes and saw fear. "I hope for your sake that the Italian's get him."

"Will you help me, please, bedda?" Patrina went to Maria and pulled her into an embrace.

Maria stood stiffly as Patrina's hot breath touched her neck. "Now, please leave my house, and never come here again."

Patrina took a step back. The opening of the gates on the CCTV camera drew Maria's attention and as she looked at Patrina, Patrina was looking at the camera. *Fuck.*

"I thought I could smell her perfume," Patrina said.

She looked at Maria with a faint smile. Maria saw the sadness in Patrina's eyes deepen. "You need to leave."

"Please help me?"

Maria looked away. "I will."

Patrina stepped through the door to the beach, and Maria watched her walk across the sand to the motorboat resting on the shoreline.

As the boat sped out to the cruiser, Maria took a deep breath and closed her eyes. Wave after wave of tremors spewed through her gut. Her hands shook, and her legs felt weak. She moved around the room, and the environment felt disconcertingly unfamiliar. Her privacy had been invaded. She felt violated by Patrina and not for the first time.

She went to the bathroom and set a bath to run, then returned to the kitchen and filled a bowl of biscuits for Pesto. He followed her to the balcony. She patted his head as she set down the bowl. The sea danced in quiet nonchalance with the sand, creating faint strips of white at the points where they became one and as she inhaled deeply, the consoling taste of the sea came to her. The familiarity brought a little comfort, and she went to the front door just as it opened.

Simone grinned broadly. "I brought food." She held up the bags in her hands.

Maria smiled and held out a steady hand. "I missed you."

Simone slipped her fingers between Maria's and clasped their hands together. She leaned into Maria, who remained steadfast.

"I missed you too," she whispered, and then her lips met Maria's in a lingering kiss.

Maria slid her fingers tenderly across Simone's cheeks as if exploring her for the first time, eased from the kiss, and moved her thumb across Simone's warm lips. "I ran you a bath."

"I made us food." Simone indicated to the bags, then looked into Maria's eyes. "How was your day?"

Maria smiled and ignored the question. "The food smells good." She peeked into a bag and inhaled, her stomach still turning acid following the earlier disturbance. But she couldn't tell Simone she had no appetite. "Smells really fantastic. What did you make?" She looked at Simone who was looking at her, fully aware that she hadn't answered her question and smiled. "My day was busy. More importantly, how was yours?"

Simone glanced towards Pesto who jumped up as he reached her. She ruffled his neck. "I felt watched all day." She looked at Maria and raised her eyebrows.

You were. "I know. It won't be forever. Come and have a bath with me, and then we can eat."

Simone's eyebrows rose and fell, and a spark flashed through her eyes. She took the bags into the kitchen and then went into the bathroom.

"How was Roberto?" Maria asked as Simone undressed. Simone looked to the ceiling. Maria slipped the dress over Simone's head and trailed a fingertip across her breasts. The texture of Simone's skin transformed, and Maria's breath hitched.

"He seemed a little distant. He's been busy."

Simone's voice was fractured with the distraction. and she groaned as Maria's arm brushed against her. "I have my guys watching him, making sure he's safe. You don't need to worry." She smiled, looked quickly to the rising suds, and stepped into the bath.

Simone climbed in and faced Maria. "He's working very long hours."

Maria reached up and stroked Simone's face, leaned forward, and tugged her closer. The water rose up and broke in a wave. She kissed Simone tenderly, enjoying the warmth of the feeling that floated inside her. When she eased out of the kiss, she looked into Simone's eyes. She needed to address the confinement issue Simone had hinted at.

"You can't wander around town every day, Simone."

Simone lifted her eyebrows and thinned her lips.

Maria ran her thumb over Simone's cheek. "Not at the moment. You need to stay here where you will be safe."

Simone looked down and ran her fingers through the water. "Will it always be like this?"

Maria shook her head. "I know it feels that way. I can keep you safe here." The image of Patrina standing at her window came to her, and an icy chill trickled down her spine.

"I know life is difficult, but I can't hide forever, Maria. I can't live like that."

Maria nodded. "I know. It's just for a little while. Pesto will enjoy the company, and I'll get Giovanni to teach you to fish. I'll spend time here, so we can go diving. We can go tomorrow, see if Octavia is around. Think of it like being on holiday again." She was blabbering. That was new.

Simone tossed soapy bubbles at her and laughed. "You're very convincing, Maria Lombardo." She pressed her soapy fingers to Maria's lips. "I love you."

Maria kept her eyes closed until the intense emotion subsided, and she had sealed Simone's words in a box and placed it in at the back of her mind. *Later.*

26.

A rush of adrenaline jolted Maria awake. She lay still for a few minutes, her eyes wide open, her heart pounding, and her mind adjusting to her surroundings. Hot, soft flurries of air waved up the back of her neck. Pesto's bark resonated a short distance away. Her mouth was dry and swallowing cramped her throat. She blinked, sighed, and then relaxed her weight into the mattress. She closed her eyes and smiled at the heady scent that lingered from their lovemaking. Simone moved, and Maria turned and looked at her. *So angelic.* She slipped her arm under Simone's neck and snuggled her into her shoulder.

Simone moaned into Maria's chest, "Morning," and then hooked a leg over Maria's waist.

Maria teased her fingertips over the line of Simone's hips, though her thoughts still raced from the vivid dream that had propelled her from sleep. She eased Simone's leg from her body, kissed her head softly, and slipped out of bed. Simone groaned and buried her face into Maria's pillow.

Maria put on a robe and ambled to the kitchen. The broken lock caught her eye, and she sighed. She checked her phone. No messages. She took the coffee beans from the shelf, loaded them into the grinder and released the rich chocolate aroma, then set the machine to percolate. Pesto stretched on his front paws and came to greet her with his tail wagging. She opened the beach door to let him run and stepped onto the cool sand.

Giovanni strode up the beach towards the villa. She could tell by the speed and length of his pace that he brought news she didn't want Simone to hear. She jogged to meet him.

"What's up?"

"Vittorio's been shot."

"Shit." She lifted her chin, turned her head to the side, and took a pace back. How the fucking hell had Vittorio got shot? She looked into Giovanni's eyes. "Is he okay?"

Giovanni tilted his head. "He will live, thanks to Roberto."

She frowned. "What the fuck happened?"

"He took Roberto with him to decommission a fleet last night."

Her eyes narrowed further. She glanced towards the closed door of the villa. Pesto was chasing along the beach. "And?" she said, watching the dog paddling.

"Vittorio took out the Romano brothers. They were working out of a garage on the industrial park. Thank fuck he took Roberto with him otherwise he would be the one dead. Gavino sunk a bullet into him before Roberto finished the job. Roberto torched the place and took Vittorio to Doctor Danté. He's in hospital now though. He should pull through, but it's not clear what the impact is. He might have nerve damage."

Maria pressed the tips of her fingers tightly to her scalp, Patrina's plea for them to work together as a team screaming in her head. "It's a fucking mess." The words slipped through her teeth on a sigh.

Giovanni turned and looked out to sea. "*They* needed decommissioning, Donna Maria, not just their fleet."

"I know. It's okay." Maria sighed. The situation was far from okay. The feeling that time was running out had woken her in a near sweat, and it hadn't been from the joy of Simone lying next to her in the bed. Alessandro wasn't going to take this, and the first place he would point the finger was in her direction.

"The police found what was left of the two trucks of wine and tobacco at the workshop. They were in the process of loading a delivery. The 'Ndrangheta will take credit for the hit and burning down the workshop as payback. With Alessandro refusing to pay them what he owes, it's a natural response. They think Gavino was moving up the ranks too quickly. 'Ndrangheta don't like that. They believe in earning the right to lead. Respect is important to them. At least we have that in common, eh?" He laughed lightly.

Maria nodded and gritted her teeth. Pesto ran to her with a stick and dropped it at her feet. She launched it up the beach and watched him run. At least Giovanni had cleared up the mess. The 'Ndrangheta's reputation would only benefit from this scenario. "Good work, Giovanni. Well done."

He looked towards the villa. "Will you both stay here today, Maria?"

She smiled. "We're going to go diving."

His smile slowly disappeared. "We should still expect repercussions."

She nodded. "Alessandro is being elusive. How is Roberto?"

"Roberto is professional. He's fine."

Maria's eyes shifted to the villa. "She's not going to like that he's involved." That was an understatement and another problem that haunted her nights now.

"No."

Maria tilted her chin upwards and closed her eyes. How could she tell Simone her brother had just killed a man? If Simone discovered the extent to which Roberto was now involved, Simone would never speak to her again. The box in the back of her mind was fast overloading.

"Is there anything I can help with?"

She looked to Giovanni then to the villa. "Wait here." She jogged back to the house and returned to him with Simone's passport. "I need alternative documents. Driver's license, everything." She handed him the passport. "Can you get that back to me by the end of the day?"

He nodded.

"Can you get the restaurant to send over something special for dinner? About eight."

"Yes."

Maria looked out to sea, to the edge of the cove. Careless, Patrina had said.

"When are you going to tell Simone about Roberto?"

She breathed into the pressure that compressed her ribs. "Soon."

"I'll sort out the documents." He started to walk away.

"Giovanni."

"Yes, Donna Maria."

"Can you get the locks on the beach door changed, please?"

He frowned.

"Patrina paid me a visit last night." She indicated with her eyes to the right-hand side of the cove where it opened to the sea, where the Bedda was moored.

His posture stiffened. "I'll get the locksmith out here while you are diving. And either me or Angelo will monitor the cove." He looked up to the high cliffs to their right and pointed. "From up there."

She smiled. "Thank you." She could only hope it would be enough.

27.

Yawning, Simone blinked into the early morning sunlight, closed her eyes, and enjoyed the moment of gentle warmth that caressed her face. The sun would burn too fiercely to be savoured later in the day. A rhythmical thud already caught her attention, and she turned to watch Maria sparring. She leaned over the banister on the veranda, and her spine tingled in light waves. She sipped her coffee and found it hard to swallow. Maria danced with the athleticism of a panther and jabbed her gloved hands with the precision of a golden eagle attacking its prey. A light sheen glistened on her toned shoulders and arms, and the beads of sweat on her forehead trickled down her temples. *So sexy.* The thrum between Simone's legs increased, and she cleared her throat and looked out to sea. It did nothing to curb her lust. She sipped her coffee then returned her attention to Maria.

Maria puffed out a short sharp breath with every blow in a rhythmical pattern that she delivered with precision and power. She displayed graceful strength, an unrelenting determination, and ardent self-discipline as she continued to throw punches. Watching Maria, an airy feeling fluttered in Simone's chest, and the pulsing beat lower down her body that Maria had not long satisfied, cried out for release again. She could still taste her, the silky softness that wetted her lips and the precise touch that lit a fire across her skin and shivered its way inside her.

There had been a difference in their love making last night that Simone couldn't explain. A sensual depth and an intensity as if it were the first *and* last time that they would be together. There was an appreciation of every slow moment, every delicate touch, and every lingering look. Maria had been unhurried, tender, and attentive. Slowly, Simone had trailed her fingertips over Maria's firm abs, and Maria's muscles twitched and shaped as they constricted and released. Seeing Maria in bliss, Simone's heart had raced, and then Maria's cries of pleasure had sent electric waves tumbling through her.

Maria landed a final punch on the bag then danced on toes with her arms hanging loosely at her side. Simone smiled. "You look hot."

Maria rubbed her forearm across her brow and puffed deep breaths. "I am."

"I didn't mean that kind of hot." Simone raised her eyebrows and chuckled.

Maria smiled. "Come and have a go."

Simone shook her head. "No thanks."

Maria tucked a glove under her arm and freed her hand, then pulled off the second glove. "Come on, I'll teach you." She ran onto the veranda and swept Simone into her arms, then gave her a sweaty, lingering kiss.

Simone complained as she laughed and batted her away. She looked into Maria's bright eyes, thumbed the crystal beads from her brow and across the top of her lip, then kissed her deeply. Then she pulled out of Maria's hold, and Maria helped her squeeze her hands into the gloves. Simone grimaced. "Yuk, they're disgusting inside. They're wet."

Maria laughed and held out the second glove. "Come on."

She ran back to the bag and stood next to it. Simone ambled towards her. Simone threw a punch that landed like mist on a leaf.

Maria's lips curled softly upwards, and she tilted her head. "Really. You can do better than that. And again."

Simone landed another punch that skirted off the side of the bag.

"Stay focused on where you want to hit it."

Maria looked as though she was taking this seriously and indicated for Simone to try again.

"Keep light on your toes, like you're dancing."

Simone started to bounce on her feet as instructed and focused her attention on a mark on the skin of the bag. She hit the leather softly again, and grinned, then dropped her arms to her side. "The gloves are heavy."

"Gloves up in front of your face, to protect yourself." Maria demonstrated, with her fists adopting a position that blocked her mouth and chin.

Simone groaned and raised the gloves into position.

"Keep your feet moving."

"Oh, my God, there's so much to think about." Simone started jogging from foot to foot.

"Guard up. Now, jab, jab."

Maria demonstrated, and Simone followed the instructions, gritting her teeth as she punched the bag.

"Stay relaxed. You can't box if you're tense, or you'll injure yourself."

Simone relaxed her jaw, and her arms became floppy. Her punch landed softly.

Maria laughed. "You need some tension in your arms, just not too much."

Simone wanted to stop and take Maria back to bed. "This is hard. My arms feel like lead already." She shook her head.

"You want to quit?"

Simone huffed. That was like red rag to a bull. She pulled the gloves up to guard her face, started moving her feet, and landed a sequence of six blows. Then her arms flopped limply at her side and she doubled over, fighting to claim the air her lungs were screaming for. She pulled off the gloves and dropped them. "I'm done."

Smiling, Maria came to Simone and pulled her up into her arms. She held Simone's head in her hands and looked into her eyes as she kissed her cheeks, her eyes, and then kissed her lips again.

Simone gasped and as she looked deeply into Maria's eyes, her heart stopped beating.

Maria smiled as she stroked the hair from Simone's face. "You are so beautiful."

Simone inhaled and licked her lips. They still sizzled from Maria's electric touch and tasted of salt. She cleared her throat and even then, the words croaked out of her. "I need a shower." She moaned at the pressure of Maria's thumb moving across her lips. She saw a sparkle in Maria's eyes that no longer concealed the dark intensity that was always present behind them.

Maria traced Simone's lips with her fingertip. "You have such kissable lips, you know?"

Simone brought her hand to cover Maria's. She kissed Maria's fingers and caressed her palm to her cheek. She closed her eyes and whispered, "Come and shower with me."

28.

The newspaper was proving hard to read and not just because the headlines further reinforced the Amato's impending demise. There was no doubt in Patrina's mind that Alessandro was behind the hit on Don Lombardo. His ambition to build the casino had led him down a greedy path and for that, she could never forgive him. Additionally, no matter which way Patrina tried to juggle the figures, the impact of the explosion, their inability to further the casino project due to a lack of materials, and her need to set aside funds to support her plan to engage the Spanish, had depleted the Amato's liquid assets. *Fucking Alessandro. Fucking numbers.* But the intense feeling of discontent that had disturbed her night was about more than the business. Simone living at Maria's was one thing, but the fact that Maria felt strongly for Simone—she'd seen it in her eyes—had been like a puncture to her lungs. The painful truth had reinforced her sense of vulnerability. She was alone and powerless.

She had spent her life fighting this emptiness, and yet it always returned bigger, and bolder, and more insistent with each reincarnation. It wormed its way into her slowly, burrowed snuggly, and then pervaded every cell of her body. Her sense of inadequacy became stronger with the pressure inside of her head. She had tried to be strong facing Maria. Her heart ached with love looking at her, and then her head flashed with rage. She wanted to scream and lash out at Maria but couldn't. *It's not her fault.* The words were true, but they still warred with the fear that controlled her. She missed Maria more than life itself. Maria had been her rock, her stability, and her strength, though she had never admitted that to her. Now it was too late. The emptiness had become more prevalent since their last engagement, as if the cord from which they had fed each other had been severed. They might as well be complete strangers, except for the other sensation that haunted her nights with a dull, leaden ache that cocooned her heart. She needed Maria more now than she ever had. If they worked together again, they could become close. Age always gave the illusion of time running out, and she certainly felt older, but it was never too late to win back Maria's heart.

Alessandro slammed the door of Café Tassimo and strode towards the table.

Beto jerked to face him as he approached and bowed his head. With his foot in a cast, he shuffled across the bench seat, extended his leg underneath the table, and pulled himself to sit upright.

Patrina glanced up. *At last, he surfaces.* No longer would she hide her contempt for Alessandro to the degree she had. She had tried to keep him sweet, but showing any affection seemed futile in achieving a connection with the man. *He* now needed to toe the line, and *she* would be the one giving the instructions.

Alessandro communicated his demands with a simple flick of his fingers at the barwoman as he ambled past the bar. Patrina stood and greeted him with a kiss on his cheek though it revolted her to be near him, let alone touch him. It always had, though now the feeling was more meaningful and had the attention of her conscience. "I take it you haven't read the news?"

He started to laugh. His pupils were dilated, and the whites of his eyes had streaks of red in them. There was a wild and confused look about him. He had clearly only recently finished partying at the club. He reeked of tobacco and sex. She looked into his eyes, searching for a spark of something resembling comprehension, but there was nothing. She leaned back in the seat and waited until he stopped walking and was just about to sit. "There was an incident at the garage late last night. Gavino and Autustu were shot."

Alessandro stood still, and his features remained unaffected for a time, then he frowned and looked away from Patrina. His eyes darted frantically, and his skin paled. He took a pace towards the door.

"Which hospital?"

He stared at her blankly. She waited until she had his attention, her silence conveying the gravity of situation. "They are dead, Alessandro."

He clicked his neck from side to side and clenched his teeth. "Fucking Lombardo."

Patrina shook her head. "No, Alessandro, this is the work of the 'Ndrangheta. Don Chico is making his promise to you very clear. We need to pay him." Her tone was calm and measured. She knew that Vittorio was being treated in hospital and was under no illusion that he was behind the hit. He had done her a favour. The Romano brothers were unstable, and the last thing she needed on her plate after disposing of her nephew was having to deal with a power struggle with Gavino. She smiled inwardly as she watched Alessandro's appearance shift from rage to fear. He didn't look any more handsome with paler skin and still seemed to lack full comprehension of the dilemma he faced. *Pig.*

Beto looked at Alessandro. "It's true, Alessandro. Chico's men were spotted today at Picasso Plaza. They're staying at the Grand."

Patrina sipped her drink. That knowledge had brought her much pleasure and a little anxiety, which she had reasoned away on the basis that Alessandro was Chico's main prize. The fact that the Italians were in the city served her needs perfectly right now, because aligning themselves with criminal incidents enhanced their reputation, and she would take full advantage of the threat they presented to Alessandro.

Alessandro cocked his head to face Beto, and his lips curled into a vindictive smile. He conveyed distrust in the anger that flared behind his eyes. Beto lowered his head.

"Alessandro."

He snapped his head to Patrina's raised voice.

"We have to pay, or they will escalate." Her tone shifted to concern. She needed him to comply and appealing to his inflated ego usually worked. "I am worried for *you*, Alessandro."

Alessandro swallowed then snapped his head towards the barwoman. "Where's my coffee?"

Beto cleared his throat. "This is bad news, Alessandro."

Alessandro turned to him with dark eyes and placed his hand on Beto's injured thigh. He squeezed hard as he gritted his teeth, revealing the bone structure of his jaw that would otherwise remain buried deeply beneath the flesh that concealed his frame. Beto whimpered as he leaned into the back of the seat and bit down on his lip.

Alessandro glared at him. "When I want your opinion, I will ask for it."

Patrina reached across the table and set a comforting hand on Alessandro's arm, encouraging him to release Beto. She looked at Beto with apology. "I have good news," she said, attracting her nephew's attention.

Beto released a whispered moan when Alessandro let him go and cowered away like a wounded animal. The barwoman approached and set their drinks on the table, looked fleetingly from Patrina to Alessandro, then hurried away.

Alessandro sipped his coffee, dunked a biscuit, and ate it. "Tell me, Auntie, what good news is there?"

"The Spanish." She smiled warmly when he looked up at her, so as not to reveal the lie she was about to tell him. He looked too preoccupied to notice her mild disquiet and too eager to hear good news to ask for any details. She would just give him the numbers.

"And?"

She rubbed her hands together. "We have a deal. The Spanish are confident they can access the Lombardo cargo ships. Twenty-million euros, Alessandro. Fifty-kilos being shipped out tomorrow and arriving in Palermo in ten days. Ten days, Alessandro." She stared into his eyes and caressed his face as she spoke.

Alessandro looked at her, and a spark of light flashed across his eyes as he grinned.

"I just hope you are alive to see it."

His focus became swiftly enveloped by a blank expression, and his eyes widened. Patrina knew fear when she saw it. The lightness she felt in his suffering lifted her, and she concealed her smile. She frowned. "What are you going to do about the Italians, Alessandro?"

Alessandro glanced at Beto. "You deal with them."

Beto pointed to his leg and shook his head slowly back and forth. "I can only watch them."

Patrina shook her head at Alessandro. She wasn't going to let Beto be dragged into a battle that would certainly end in his execution this time around. He, of all the men, respected her and once this problem was sorted, she wanted him at her side. "Our two most talented hitmen have just been murdered, Alessandro, and there is no doubting the lengths Don Chico will go to and the resources he can commission to ensure you pay what you owe. Beto will be executed if he tries to do your job again."

Alessandro slammed his hand down on the table, then tapped his fingers feverishly. He pressed his body back into the seat as if trying to escape his own mind, then his eyes moved skittishly, and he looked around the room.

Patrina softened her tone. "Beto is right, Alessandro. If we retaliate, Chico will annihilate us all."

Alessandro slumped, and his fingers quieted. Beads of sweat covered his face, and a trail of water trickled into the creases in his neck. He released a long breath.

"We don't have the money, Auntie?"

There was uncharacteristic acquiescence in his tone. Patrina stared at him. *Good, he's on the ropes.* "No, we don't. What about your private account?"

Alessandro shook his head as he lowered it.

She straightened her back and took a deep breath. "You will have to go to Chico and ask for more time, Alessandro." A surge of excitement coursed through her.

Alessandro's eyes widened, and the remaining colour slipped from his cocaine-flushed cheeks. He rubbed the back of his hand across his face, glanced at Beto then back to Patrina, and whispered, "He will kill me."

Patrina sighed, and her lips thinning as she frowned. "Well, you had better hope he wants his money more than he wants your scalp." She leaned towards him and patted his arm. She didn't give a shit. Alessandro would get what was coming to him, one way or another. She couldn't wait to see the horrified look on Don Stefano's face as she gave him the news of Alessandro's assassination by the 'Ndrangheta. She felt energised by the thought, and her spirits lifted.

Alessandro looked at her with pleading eyes. "That's too risky, Auntie."

She lifted her chin and stared at him. "I hardly think you are in a position to negotiate, do you?" Her tone was quiet, leaving no room for him to challenge her. She smiled reassuringly. "You have to do this."

Alessandro stood, staggered to his feet, and stormed out of the café without looking back.

Patrina turned to Beto, her chin high. "Keep an eye on him. No deliveries to Lombardo. We stay off their turf, got it?"

Beto's eyes lit up and he bowed his head. "Yes, Lady Patrina."

She smiled and spoke softly. "Thank you, Beto. That will be all."

He edged to his feet, gathered the crutch at his side, and made his way out of the restaurant.

She smiled at the barwoman. "Martina, would you bring me lunch. I'm feeling really rather hungry."

"Yes, of course, Lady Patrina." Martina smiled, and her eyes had the same quality of satisfaction in them that Beto's had had.

She could guarantee Beto's support, even Martina's, though hers was insignificant. She took a deep breath and the feeling of satisfaction relaxed her. With any luck, Don Chico would resolve the Alessandro problem for her and save her the trouble. In any event, she had a plan. *I run the Amatos.*

29.

Maria slipped the oxygen tank onto Simone's back. She tugged the belt to fasten it securely around her waist and then tested air was coming through the mouthpiece. The look in Simone's eyes burned her skin as she worked. "How does that feel?"

Simone was staring at Maria and smiling, and Maria had a very good idea of what had flashed through Simone's mind. With slow deliberate movements, she placed her hand in Simone's and inched closer. She ran her fingertips along Simone's thigh, and as she watched the tiny hairs prickle in response, her own skin tingled with fiery heat. Simone jerked as Maria traced a line across her hip, and her lips quivered and her breath hitched. Simone closed her eyes, and Maria kissed her deeply as she trailed her fingertips back along the edge of Simone's hip. Simone jerked, and groaned, and then jumped out of the kiss and giggled.

"You're a tease."

Maria had never felt more caressed and more loved. "I can't help it. I want you." She grinned like a child who had just discovered a secret and moved her fingers to make Simone writhe again. Simone continued giggling and tried, neither hard nor successfully, to get out of her grip.

The boat rocked under their feet, making it difficult to balance. Maria encouraged the boat to sway harder and continued to tickle Simone until she squealed and made the boat move as if it were on a stormy sea.

"Stop, stop." Simone could barely speak for laughing.

Maria steadied the boat. She reached up and stroked Simone's cheek, and her lips. "You are too tempting."

Simone's eyes darkened.

Maria directed her attention back to preparing for the dive. Simone's sensual gaze persisted, making the task of burying the desire that rendered her senseless and carefree, impossible. She groaned as she lifted the oxygen tank onto her back and secured it into place. She looked into Simone's eyes and swallowed. "Ready then?"

Simone's smile lingered. "Always."

Maria ignored the surge of electric energy that moved through her and instructed Simone to sit on the ledge of the boat. Simone took a deep breath and released it slowly then sat. She wriggled the mask and mouthpiece into place and gave a thumbs up. Maria smiled and nodded. Simone tumbled backwards into the sea.

Maria fitted her mask and tumbled into Simone's stream of bubbles as they rose to reclaim their place in the air that tossed the surface of the water above them. As Maria oriented herself in the water, Simone floated in front of her, moving gracefully, her hair flowing freely, soft and coral-like. She looked to be enveloped in a vacuum, a saintly aura that shielded and protected her. Captivated by the wide, shining eyes behind Simone's mask and the beautiful, loving smile obscured by the breathing apparatus, a jolt in Maria's chest made it hard to breathe. She hoped her eyes conveyed the elation she felt. The look in Simone's eyes softened, and the tingling effect lingered reassuringly inside Maria.

There was something else Maria sensed between them: profoundness, the quality of which could drive her insane. She knew it as the point at which love and loss merged into an absolute realisation that this person in front of her, *she* was the one, the missing piece of the puzzle of her life that would make her world complete. It had been that look in Simone's eyes that had shaken Maria's world and awoken her to the deepest love she had ever known.

Her heart ached as she looked into Simone's eyes with deep affection. Simone reached out, took Maria's hand, and squeezed. Fire rose up inside Maria like a venomous serpent. Overwhelmed by intense heat, she swallowed hard and battled the tears that threatened her vision. She turned her attention to the sea and hoped Simone hadn't noticed her weakness.

Simone stayed close to Maria as they swam in the direction of the reef. Her heart pounded as she focused on the agile movement of Maria's body gliding through the water. The passion she had seen in Maria's eyes had shifted suddenly, and she sensed the feeling of absence she feared could come between them. And then Maria had looked at her with such love and longing, the pain of it ripped through her heart and stole her breath. She would enjoy what she could, for whatever time they shared together, and try not think too much about the future.

Maria looked back at Simone and pointed to their left. Simone's heart fluttered with the sparkle that had returned to Maria's eyes. She stopped and watched the shoal of knife-shaped silver fish as they moved closer and darted around them. She turned to see them go on their way and when she turned back, she locked eyes with Maria, and her stomach swirled and sent a quiver to her racing heart. The excitement and desire felt fragile, and the water in which they swam was an ethereal state of physical suspension. Heaven on earth. She could live here forever with Maria. They could be free and *together*. Safe and *together*.

The look that she had seen in Maria's eyes earlier returned. Worry etched in the darkness behind the flicker of lust. The result was a potent cocktail of disquiet and deep longing. She knew it because she felt it too, and she wanted Maria more than she had ever wanted anyone. Though a most exquisite sensation, it was also painful. She felt the essence of it every time she looked at Maria and every time Maria looked at her.

Maria broke eye contact, and the feeling subsided. Simone could breathe more easily though her heart still raced. She followed Maria, spellbound by the beauty in the underworld that moved around them.

Swimming deeper, the water became darker the closer they got to the black rocks of the volcano. Maria pointed to the white sponges and gorgonian residents of the rocky surface. Orange and purple arms danced with Maria as she weaved among them and waved at Simone as she passed. Maria pointed to their left, to the brown grouper and the damselfish nipping at the coral carpet. Maria indicated to a cave-like structure, and Simone followed her towards it. Maria approached the cave slowly and waved for Simone to come closer and look inside.

Maria turned to reveal the purple-red octopus taking refuge in the darkness of the cave. Simone's eyes grew wider. Simone froze then the ice shattered and formed snowflakes that tingled as they descended through her. *Oh my God.* The small creature's dark eyes seemed to be assessing her keenly as it slunk closer to Maria. All arms, reaching out and testing the boundaries of its environment, it curled a long tentacle around Maria's arm, another searching around her waist and dipping into the pocket of the vest beneath her apparatus. Simone watched Maria being caressed, tugged, and played with, and the air from Maria gushed and bubbled towards the surface. She held back the fizzing laughter that rattled in her chest.

Maria reached into her invaded pocket and pulled out a sealed jar. The octopus claimed it from her with silk-like, pin-point movements. Then it drew the jar closer to it, inspecting the live crabs within. The jar became entwined within its grasp, and its tentacles worked almost as hands and fingers to twist the lid from the jar so the octopus could claim its prize.

Maria held out her hand, and the octopus responded and led Maria into the cave. Watching Maria stroking the creature with tenderness, communicating as close friends would, Simone felt enveloped in tenderness. Her heart expanded and pressed hard against her ribs and sapped her of strength. *I love you.* Maria looked at home in this beguiling place. This was clearly her sanctum of peace, where she was liberated from the darker world she'd unwittingly inherited. In this natural habitat, surrounded by undisturbed beauty, Maria was transformed. She watched, stunned, finding it hard to think, hard to breathe, and impossible to draw her eyes from the woman she would always love.

Maria climbed onto the boat, pulled Simone up, and removed their equipment. Simone stared at her wide eyed and then shook her head gently. Her lips parted as if she were going to speak, but she remained dumbfounded. Maria smiled at her, teased the wet hair to the side of her face, then moved closer and claimed Simone's lips in a tender kiss. Easing away, she looked at Simone with a soft smile.

"You taste of salt."

Simone shook her head. "That was the most awesome experience I..." She stopped speaking, immobilised by the intensity she saw in Maria's eyes. The darkness seemed to have lifted and only lust remained. Simone's breaths came in short shallow gasps, and her chest burned inside. Every sensation she had experienced with Maria as she had watched her beneath the water moved through her in waves of increasing ecstasy. She threw her arms around Maria's neck and kissed her. She buried her fingers into the firm muscle at Maria's shoulder, then moved her hands around to Maria's back and grazed the skin the length of Maria's spine. Maria's moans echoed her want, her need, and she kissed Maria harder. Enjoying the taste of her, the softness of her, Simone's tongue delved and teased, and she slipped her hand beneath Maria's vest and cupped her breast. Maria groaned into her mouth. She ran her thumb across Maria's nipple and moaned as it stiffened against her.

Maria groaned again and eased out of the kiss. She cupped her hand to cover Simone's at her breast and stared into her eyes. Maria's lips were swollen and inviting. There was want in her eyes, and her breathing was rapid. Simone watched Maria smiling at her, and then the intensity slowly drained from her. Maria's eyes closed, and a soft moan sent fire down Simone's spine. Her heart thundered with her confused thoughts. There was no doubt Maria felt as strongly as she did. She had to. But Maria was also concerned about her family and the business. It was her job to take care of them. Loyalty came first. Simone knew and accepted that. Even though Maria had talked of wanting out of the business, they both had to admit deep down, there was no escaping this life. She stroked Maria's face willing her to open her eyes, to share her concerns. "What is it?" she asked.

Maria opened her eyes and sighed. "You."

Her smile was restrained. Simone bit down hard on her lip. She wouldn't accept rejection, not from Maria, not knowing what they shared...and not now. There had to be a reason Maria had lived in relative isolation all these years. She was a gorgeous woman who could have anyone and chose no one. *Why, Maria? Because loss hurts so much? You're not going to do that to me.*

Maria took Simone's hand. She raised it to her lips and kissed the palm. "I want to explore every part of you."

The shudder that vibrated through Simone caught her breath and when she released, heat flooded her. Every cell in her body trembled. *Thank God.* "I want that too," she said quietly, her words barely audible though they resounded loudly in her head as she realised how deeply she'd fallen for Maria.

30.

Simone took a seat at the table at the front of Lo Scoglio café overlooking the square and ordered a freshly squeezed lemonade. Thoughts of Maria made the sun warmer and brought a faint smile that settled inside her. She was in love with Maria, and she felt like a giggly, happy child. But then there was a scary and confusing feeling that disturbed her as it had when they were diving and previously in the car in Spain. She was living a double life with Maria. One part of it she loved and never wanted to end, the other part—the unreachable part that existed in the shadows—she resented.

Diving to the reef had been incredible. Fishing with Giovanni, learning to box, and exploring the cove with Maria had been like living in a fairy tale. Making love with Maria was the most exquisite and insanely delectable experience ever. Maria had exposed her deepest vulnerability in her need for Simone, and it was the most frightening responsibility Simone had ever owned.

And yet there was a quietness about Maria. The code of silence, maybe. Maria never talked about anything to do with her work, except Alessandro, and that was quite normal in this business. But Maria didn't talk about a future either, except the offer she had made for Simone to live in the farmhouse in the Pyrenees...without Maria.

Would life with Maria always be this isolated? She had never lived in seclusion before. Sure, she had never been sociable and had kept herself to herself, but she had always been in control of her choices. She decided what she did and when. Now that option had been removed, the feeling of frustration niggled, and her thoughts raced.

Feeling cocooned, like a baby bouncing around in the womb, was safe and secure. That was a good thing, but it was also suffocating. As beautiful and remarkable as the villa on the beach was, as wonderful as spending time with Maria was, Simone craved to return to her life outside the confines of the cove. The freedom to come and go and move around was living, as she had lived before all this blew up. Perhaps things would still have escalated without Maria's involvement. Alessandro made enemies easier than friends. Maria was a mafia boss, and there were requirements and restrictions that Simone had never been party to before. She didn't relish talking to Maria about her frustrations, but her feelings of incarceration would drive a divisive wedge between them if she didn't address it.

Angelo was the perfect example of that restriction, sitting on the wall that bounded the fountain in the middle of the square, facing the café, and leafing through the broadsheet newspaper though his eyes on her. His constant presence did nothing to alleviate the itch that came with living like a caged animal. She had survived perfectly well in the presence of *these people*, the Amatos, for enough years to know she could fend for herself.

She looked up as the waiter approached and smiled. She studied him as he placed the tall glass on a coaster in front of her. He reminded her of her time at Café Tassimo and the other restaurants she had worked at. He had an easy smile, made whiter by his tanned skin, styled black hair, and eyes as brown as cocoa and as bright as diamonds. In spite of Alessandro's sickening behaviour towards her, she had felt as liberated back then as this waiter looked now. She sighed and smiled at him. "Thank you."

"It's a pleasure." He bowed his head and looked out over the square. "It is a glorious day to enjoy."

She nodded. *Yes, it is.* She leaned back in the seat and lazily scanned the square, focusing on nothing and everything. The whooshing and running water, footsteps on the cobbles; a repugnant smell that made her nose twitch; wafting cigarette smoke hung in the air, swirling, plumes clinging to the person who exhaled it as they walked past the café, then the smell drifted and merged with the fumes of passing cars. The light breeze cleared the air. The aroma of chargrilled meat, fresh herbs, and salad dressing drew her eyes to the plates of food being delivered to the table next to her. This was Palermo, *her city*, and she wouldn't be kept from it.

Her stomach growled, and she picked up the menu and studied the options. At least she could choose what she ate. She lifted her head as the shadow came to rest over her and when she looked up, her breath stalled.

"Hey, sis." Roberto pulled down on the handle of the scooter as he smiled at Simone from the curb.

Simone squinted and grinned at him. The pizza delivery sack hung around his chest. "I didn't expect to see you here."

"I spotted you from over there." Roberto indicated across the square.

Angelo looked up from his paper, and Simone thought she saw him indicate in their direction. Roberto's features became sterner and more focused. Had Roberto acknowledged Angelo? He seemed to be looking to the other side of the square and silently communicating with a group of men Simone didn't recognise. They lifted their chins in response.

She frowned. She could understand he might know of Angelo because Maria was going to keep him safe, and Angelo might have been the one to speak to him. How did he know these other men? Who were they?

He looked up at the café's sign, and his beaming smile returned. "You should stick with our pizza, you know." He winked at her, laughed, and pulled down on the handle again to open the throttle.

Then he glanced out around the square with a seriousness that was out of character for him. Simone dismissed her thoughts. She was becoming paranoid. "Will you be home later?" Why had she asked him that when she wouldn't even be there?

He smiled at her. "Much later. I'll have a lot of deliveries today. Our pizza is the best in town. How is it at Maria's?" His eyes shone as he spoke, and he patted the large bag at his side.

She smiled. "It's good."

His focus became distracted. "Good...right. I have to shoot or this will get cold."

"Sure," Simone said, but he had already swung the scooter into the road. She sipped her lemonade and looked across at the group of men. They didn't look back at her. She sighed, then spotted Maria walking towards her and smiled.

"Hi."

Maria stood with her hands on her hips, and smiled softly then took the seat opposite Simone and glanced around the square. Angelo folded his paper and headed to the group she'd spotted. Simone frowned. Was something going on? And what did her brother have to do with things? She looked at Maria. "You just missed Roberto."

Maria smiled. "How is he?"

"Seems fine. Busy. Interested in what's going on in the square." She watched Maria's facial expression. It remained constant.

"That's good. The pizza business is a good business." Maria leaned closer. Her eyes were shining, and her smile warm. "You look very hot."

The earthy timbre of Maria's voice turned Simone inside out and upside down and swept her deliberations from her mind. The longer she looked into Maria's eyes, the more her skin flared and the more the vibrations fluttered from her core in a constant and increasing flow. A fuse ignited and tingled through to her hands and burned the tips of her ears. She sipped the chilled lemonade. It didn't help.

Maria's smile broadened. She picked up the menu. "Are you hungry?"

Simone clung to the tall glass, determined not to put off what she needed to say. She lowered the glass carefully, turned it on the coaster, and then looked into Maria's eyes. "I need to do some kind of work, Maria."

Maria leaned back and challenged the fire in her belly with a gracious smile. Simone was curious, and that was both a good quality and a dangerous one. Did Simone suspect Roberto's involvement? Maria hadn't expected him to be in the vicinity when she suggested the café for lunch. He was working on Giovanni's instructions, which must mean they had eyes on Alessandro. *Damn it.* At least the men had moved on, so they could enjoy lunch. "I know it's tough, Simone, but things are improving. I have a meeting with Patrina after lunch. I need some reassurances from her, and then maybe you could work at the Riverside. What do you think?" Maria bounced her leg up and down underneath the table. She had sensed Simone's discomfort at being holed up at the villa and that this time would come, and she didn't want Simone to feel trapped. They had at least contained the Amato supply of wine, so there shouldn't be any further activity from Alessandro, especially since his attention was now distracted by the Italian's demands. She nodded with her thoughts. Simone would be safe working at the Riverside.

"Can I?" Simone reached across the table and squeezed Maria's hand, then swiftly returned her hand to her glass.

A deep thud pulsed in Maria's chest. She had seen distress in Simone's expression. *Did you think I would refuse you?* She swallowed before speaking. The truth was, she would refuse if she thought Simone's life depended on it. *This is no way to live, and Simone didn't ask for any of this.* She smiled. "Let me speak to Patrina first, please?"

Simone's eyes sparkled as she grinned.

"I will arrange things with Antonio."

Simone's lips parted and then curled up at the edges, slowly at first. Her eyes flickered, and they looked more alive than Maria had seen before. The bright sunlight revealed rich shades and soft tones. And when a broad grin caused fine wrinkles to dust Simone's cheeks, the tingling started in Maria's neck and swept fiercely down her spine. "Now, shall we eat? I really am starving."

Simone took a deep breath and leaned back in the chair as she exhaled. Maria cleared her throat, picked up the menu, and pretended to look at it, her eyes peeking over the top of it at Simone. "You still look really hot."

The waiter came to the table.

"I think I'll have the skewered lamb." Maria said, looking to Simone as if nothing had passed between them.

Simone looked directly at the waiter. "Me too, rare please."

Maria's cheeks flushed. "And a half-carafe of red wine, please."

The waiter smiled and excused himself, and Maria smiled at Simone. "Why don't you take the Romeo? Then you can come and go as you please." Maria tilted her head from side to side, relieving the tension in her neck.

Simone drew Maria's eyes to look at her. "I promise to be careful. You don't need to babysit me, Maria. I have lived around these people all my life. I can handle myself."

Maria nodded. The smile on her face was slow to form, and she averted Simone's pleading eyes. "I will still need to keep an eye on you though. Just for another couple of weeks until the Italian affair is sorted out."

Simone held her breath and pressed her lips together tightly. "Okay. And when the Italian thing is done, no more baby-sitting. Deal?"

Maria nodded. "Deal." She wasn't convinced. It wasn't that Maria didn't think Simone couldn't look after herself. She probably could under normal circumstances. But the Italians involvement in Sicilian business wasn't normal and if they stayed, it would lead to bigger problems. They were more dangerous than the Amatos, and when the Lombardos failed to deliver their side of the bargain she had agreed with Chico they, *and she*, would be the 'Ndrangheta's next target. *Would the Italian thing ever be done?*

31.

Donna Maria stepped over the threshold into the cathedral and made the customary cross at her chest as she scanned the pews for Patrina. The lamb she'd had for lunch had turned to lead cubes in her stomach. If Simone had noticed she'd only eaten half of her meal, she hadn't commented and for that, Maria had been grateful. The lie she'd told Simone weighed on her mind. She didn't know whether things were improving. Watching Simone drive away from the square in the Romeo had brought a wave of relief though. And then she had received a message from Giovanni to say that Alessandro had just walked away from the Italian's following a meeting on the plaza outside the Grand Hotel. How the man had managed to cut a deal with them she didn't know, but apparently, he had.

She spotted Patrina bowed in prayer and slid into the seat next to her. She knelt, clasped her hands, and rested her elbows on the back of the pew in front of her. She lowered her head to her hands and whispered across the short space that separated them. "Alessandro has more lives than a black cat, Patrina."

Patrina leaned closer and whispered, "I have a plan that will eradicate the problem."

Maria squeezed her hands tightly. She didn't want any involvement with a hit on Alessandro, but in the heat of the moment, and for reasons she couldn't fathom, she had agreed to help Patrina. Acid burned in her throat. "I need to think about…"

"We don't have the luxury of time, Maria."

Maria clenched her teeth. "You're talking about your world, Patrina, not mine. The Italian's are chasing you for money, not me. Remember?" She felt the heat from Patrina's piercing stare and lips that curled into a half-smile. Maria had seen that expression a thousand times. It said, *I know something you don't. I have power over you.* Ice crawled up her spine.

Patrina stared at Maria. "You haven't heard?"

"What?"

"Roberto was just picked up by the DIA."

Maria couldn't decide whether she saw contempt in Patrina's eyes. What did sincerity look like in a woman scorned by life? Had she been stupid to trust Patrina?

"Honestly, I had nothing to do with it." Patrina turned to face the front of the church and returned her tone to a low whisper that could only be heard by Maria. "He was caught carrying a kilo of cocaine."

Maria kept her head down, her eyelids slowly bringing the darkness that would still the fire behind her eyes and quell her distaste for this world.

"Alessandro knows Roberto's running for you."

Maria felt the skewered lamb become a single solid mass in her gut. She opened her eyes and stared at the stone floor and the small firm cushion beneath her knees. What if Simone found out? No, when Simone found out, she would be furious. Beyond furious, she would feel betrayed. *Shit.*

Patrina breathed out a long sigh, mumbled something that ended in amen, and then turned to face Maria. "Simone will find out that you employ her brother. I have no control over that. Lovers always find out the truth, bedda. That's just the way it is." She looked to the front of the church. "You know how hard Simone fought against him working in this business? I considered training him myself in the early days. He was gullible, hungry, and needy. Alessandro didn't think he had it in him, and I felt a sense of duty to Simone after what had happened. You have trained him well, bedda."

Maria blinked then locked her attention onto the priest at the front of the church, feeling small and insignificant. She watched him light a candle and pick up a chalice. Patrina's words echoed in her mind, and Simone's image came to her in the form of her own broken heart, bleeding life from her. She continued to stare, reality entombing her in emptiness.

"You have a shipment arriving in ten days. Alessandro is under the impression that it has our property on it. I have told him we need your assistance for us to reclaim that property before the ship docks at the port."

Maria continued to stare at the priest. "What assistance?"

"I told him we need you with us when we intercept the ship, bedda, in case there are problems with the crew. They will listen to you. Alessandro needs the reassurance of your presence. We will take our boat for the pick-up, of course." She shrugged. "Obviously, if we don't intercept the goods, he thinks they will be discovered when authorities do their rigorous inspection at the port, and you will go to prison. He would rather intercept the drugs than lose them at the port."

Maria cast her eyes down. The gnawing in her gut told her Alessandro wouldn't think twice about wasting her if the opportunity presented itself. "And what will stop Alessandro taking me out?"

"Me, bedda. You can trust *me*. I will take care of him."

There was fondness in the softness in her tone and the slowness in her speech that Maria had known in the tender moments they had shared before. Maria looked at Patrina, pursed her lips.

Patrina stood then stopped and stooped over Maria. "By the way, the pizza boy and the waitress are all yours now."

And there it was...the harsh and vindictive person that Patrina had become was never too far away.

"The Amato's debt to them has been paid in full. I have also seen to it that there will be no more deliveries to your restaurants."

Maria stood. "What did you find out about the car?"

Patrina looked away. "Nothing, yet. Someone covered their tracks well."

"Rocca?"

Patrina shook her head. "I doubt it. She's too loyal to you, bedda. You have that effect on women, didn't you know?"

Maria's focus didn't shift from Patrina. The comment washed over her. She would get to the truth. "There is one more thing."

Patrina slowly turned and looked into Maria's eyes. "What is that?"

"I want you to hand back the casino site."

"So you can build the tech park?"

"You know it makes good business sense for the city, Patrina."

Patrina's lips thinned, and her eyes wandered around the church. "The casino would be better for us."

"For you personally, maybe." Maria's stare hardened. "But I promise you, I'll make sure you are implicated in the death of my father, Patrina, and then your empire will fall. You will spend the rest of your days in a cell."

Patrina's chin rose as she inhaled deeply and her eyelids fluttered. Maria noted weariness in her sigh, and the heaviness in her eyelids as they closed briefly.

Patrina swallowed and inhaled another deep breath through her nose. "I will get the paperwork drawn up."

"It needs to be on my desk before we intercept the shipment."

Patrina nodded. "I will see to it, bedda."

"One last thing."

Patrina waited.

"I need you to deal with Chico. I won't be working with him, so either you pay him and he continues to work with you, or you implicate him and he goes down for the hit. You decide."

Patrina's lips curled upwards and her eyes narrowed. "I need money."

"I'll fund you, but I want him off my back." Maria cursed the need to pay Patrina but with Alessandro out of the equation, she needed Chico distracted one way or another. Patrina nodded. Maria waited until Patrina disappeared from the church. She sat back down. Her head spun at the inevitability of Simone walking away from her. She closed her eyes, and the squeezing sensation in her heart intensified. She clenched her hands firmly into tightly balled fists and cursed under her breath. The feeling became leaden and all-consuming. She bolted from the church and stood on the cobbled plaza and gasped for breath.

Slowly, her focus sharpened and her pulse resumed its normal rhythm, and she noted the Roman architecture, the cobbled stones around the cathedral, people milling around, and cars making their way along the main road. Everything was as it had been when she entered the cathedral. She checked her phone as she headed back to the Maserati. The text she hadn't long received from Giovanni told her what she already knew. She shifted the car into gear and drove to the DIA. Capitano Rocca would be expecting her.

"Donna Maria, I am so sorry."

Maria saw genuine concern in Rocca's dark eyes. "Capitano Massina, I understand there was a situation."

Rocca glanced around the reception room and cleared her throat. "Please, follow me. I have some paperwork I need you to complete."

Maria followed her into a small office and stood next to the table. Rocca reached into a cabinet, placed two sheets of paper on the table, and pushed them towards Maria. She took a pen from her jacket breast pocket and slid it across the table.

"One of my colleagues arrested Roberto Di Salvo this afternoon. He was carrying a kilo of cocaine. This is a very serious offence, Donna Maria. I have taken the case from my colleague, and I will do what I can to help you."

Maria pushed the paperwork away. "I'm not signing anything. Roberto would not have been carrying drugs, I can assure you of that. I want him released and these bogus charges dropped."

Rocca swallowed. "I understand, Donna Maria. But there is also the issue of the substantial sum of money he was carrying, and…"

Maria locked eyes across the table. "I'm sure there was no cash in his possession, Rocca." She smiled. "Who is this colleague?"

Rocca blinked and lowered her head. She moved the paperwork to another spot on the table for no apparent reason.

"Tommaso Vitale. He received a tip off and, in my absence, took the initiative to deal with the situation. I would have stopped this happening had I been aware of it."

Vitale was working for Alessandro. "Rocca, who dealt with the evidence for my father's case?"

Rocca looked up and then looked away. "Umm, I did most of the work, Donna Maria. Why?"

Rocca seemed anxious, but she appeared too sincere to be disbelieved. Still, Maria couldn't dismiss the evidence that said otherwise. "Did Vitale have any contact with the investigation? Any of the paperwork?"

"Yes, Donna Maria. He helped me."

Maria looked for incongruence in Rocca's body language as she asked, "Did you know there was a bullet hole in the front passenger tyre?"

Rocca's head snapped towards Maria, and she stared at her with wide eyes, shaking her head. "No, Donna Maria. Of course, I did not know this. I would have told you if I'd known."

Maria nodded, satisfied she was telling the truth. "Can I take Roberto home now?"

Rocca stood. "I will have him brought to you, right away. I am so sorry, Donna Maria." She stood, pulled her jacket down, and walked out of the room.

Maria waited.

At the click of the handle, Maria stood and when the door opened, she stepped through it and past Roberto before he could enter the room. By the time they exited the building, he trailed a pace behind her. They walked across the car park at the front of the DIA and got into the car. "Are you okay?"

He lowered his head. "I am sorry, Donna Maria… It was a setup, Donna Maria. Alessandro."

She looked into eyes filled with rage, his jaw square and strong. She placed a hand on his sleeve. "I know, Roberto."

His nose flared. He rocked his jaw from side to side and squeezed his words through clenched teeth. "What can I do?"

"You can go home."

He turned his head and looked through the passenger window.

"Your bike has been released from the compound and taken to your house."

He continued to stare.

An image of Vitale, Rocca's partner, came to mind, and she began to formulate a way to deal with him too. "I will have a job for you later, but now you need to rest." She glanced at him and felt the warmth that came with affection. She smiled. "Roberto."

He turned to her.

"You need to be careful."

His troubled expression didn't change. Maria drove in silence. The air was heavy with the unspoken they both knew needed addressing. She needed to be honest with him. "I don't know how to handle this with Simone."

"She's going to be angry with me."

Maria nodded. Simone was going to be furious with her too.

He sighed. "She vowed after our family was killed that I should never be involved in this business. She sacrificed herself to the Amatos, working for them so that I could be protected, you know?"

Maria felt the pain that had crippled her earlier in the church resurrect in her chest.

"She doesn't know I have made my own way. I have worked jobs, independently, but she doesn't know about them at all. I kept it from her, because she worries about me. I have learned skills. I've been fixing cars since I was thirteen, Donna Maria. The pizza delivery is a good cover job, but I'm ambitious. Simone will be angry with me, but I want to work for you. I'm good at what I do, Donna Maria."

"Simone will be angry with us both, Roberto," Maria said softly, barely above a whisper. She hoped that he didn't sense the helplessness she felt. "I have become close to your sister."

He looked down at his hands. "Yes, she has changed too. She is close to you."

Maria didn't hesitate in clarifying the truth. "We are lovers."

He lifted his head slowly and turned to her. "She is happy and safe with you. That's all that matters."

"When she finds out that you're working for me, she'll be angry. She'll walk away."

His eyes widened. "I will talk to her and explain."

Maria shook her head. "Not now. Not yet. We have work to do. Then I will talk to her." She swallowed. "Capisci?"

"Sì, Donna Maria, whatever you think is best."

Maria turned the car into Benitos Street and parked outside Simone's house. It reminded her of the night of the explosions at the port, and the supper they had shared at her uncle's restaurant, and the first night they had made love... She had the sense of falling downwards, and the emptiness inside her became dense and dragged her deeper. She blinked to chase the sensation away and focused on the steady rise and fall of her chest. But the hollowness lodged there and expanded.

She opened her eyes slowly, turned off the engine, and reached up and squeezed Roberto's shoulder. "You are a good man, Roberto. A strong leader. I have plans for you. There are only two people you can trust; Giovanni and Angelo. If you can't speak to me, you speak to one of them. Anything of interest you see, you let them know."

"Capisci. Thank you, Donna Maria."

Roberto entered the house. Maria leaned back in the seat, took a deep breath, and released it slowly. Her eyes stung as she held back the tears, and the tension in her head worked its way from her shoulders to her gut. This was going to bite her on the arse. She buried the scream that had built inside her. She had to be honest with Simone, but how? Simone would feel cheated, violated in the way Patrina had made Maria feel. She slapped the steering wheel hard and pain shot through her arm. *Such a fucking mess.* She closed her eyes and waited for the anger to pass. *I need to explain to Simone before it's too late.*

32.

Maria cruised slowly up the drive and parked the Maserati outside the villa. Noting the Romeo that looked as though it had been abandoned in haste on the driveway, her chest expanded freely, and she smiled at her thoughts. Simone would be cooking or preparing food, her skin darkened from the heat of the day, her eyes bright as they had been when they had parted at the café. Simone would be feeling good after her day of freedom, even though Maria had spent the best part of the afternoon containing her reservations and dealing with Alessandro's crap.

She would make sure Vitale went down for his part in her father's death. She would prefer to see him rot in prison where he would be used to satisfy the men's carnal needs. Death would be too clean and easy for him.

She stepped out of the car and breathed in the salty, warm air. The absence of music stirred her and as she entered the villa, she was met with an eerie silence that made her heart pound. Simone's eyes had a stillness about them, and a chill trickled down Maria's spine. It wasn't the swollen red rings around her eyes or the damp puffy cheeks that stopped Maria in her tracks and had her heart dropping like a stone, it was the packed travel bag at Simone's feet and the keys to the Romeo on top of an envelope on the breakfast bar. Pesto, in the corner of Maria's eye, lifted himself from his bed and stretched. Maria clicked her fingers, and he settled down in his basket.

She took a step towards Simone. "Simone." She held out her hands, palms up, pleading to her as she stepped closer. "What's happened?"

Simone took a pace back and brushed a tear from her cheek. She shook her head and tears streamed onto her cheeks. "How dare you?"

Maria tried to maintain a calm exterior, her stomach spiralling, and her heart thundering. *Simone knew. Fuck.* The constriction in her throat stopped her swallowing, and her lips were dry and unyielding. "What is it?" She saw disgust flash across Simone's eyes. It was everything Maria deserved. But the pain and the betrayal that emanated from Simone, Simone had done nothing to deserve that. Maria had failed her in the worst way possible, a breach of trust. She could never come back from a breach of trust. *This is over.*

"I saw you."

Maria took a deep breath and looked into Simone's eyes as she released it slowly. "Where?"

"Outside the DIA with Roberto. I drove past you, Maria."

Maria heard, "Don't you dare fucking lie to me," in Simone's tone and read the same in her eyes. She bit down on her lip. "I'm sorry. I need to explain."

Simone thrust her hands downwards and grew in stature. "Explain?"

Maria had never heard Simone shout before, and the ferocity in her tone ripped through her heart.

"Explain what? That my brother was talking to the DIA? That you were talking to the DIA with my brother? That my brother had a keen interest in what was going on in the square earlier today. That my brother is fucking working for you. What is there to explain, Maria? Tell me. What is there to explain that the woman I love has been fucking with me all this time? If you really cared about me, you wouldn't have done this. Or is it just Roberto you're interested in to further your business interests?"

Simone threw a double quote gesture, and her eyes looked wild with rage. Maria looked away, every word resonating in the stabbing sensations that penetrated her chest. Hopelessness dragged her down, and the bottom of the pit fast approached. "I should've said something sooner."

"Sooner? You should have left my brother out of your business."

Maria gritted her teeth. *That's the truth.* "I'm sorry, Simone. I was looking after him."

"What, like you're looking after me? If the DIA are talking to my brother, you failed in your duty of care, Maria. Who are you deceiving?" Simone held her head in her hands while she shook. Her skin darkened, her eyes narrowed, and she wiped frantically at the tears as they spilled onto her cheeks. "You're just like Alessandro *and* Patrina."

That stung. Maria jolted backwards, the burning in her chest becoming an inferno and consuming her in swift gulps. Shrinking inside, bracing before the collision, she fought the desire to run, and the desire to escape this world she detested reared up strongly. Right here, right now, she could easily pack her own bag and disappear into oblivion. But she had a duty, a job, and a desire to do right by her family...and by Simone. Running wasn't an option. Her breaths came in short sharp bursts, the assault gutting her with every punch. She had no defence. Simone was right about Roberto, but she was nothing like Alessandro and Patrina. An inner cry moved through her, and it took her all her strength to remain standing and to continue to look at the woman she loved. Simone shook her head at her and looked disappointed.

"If you knew how much I tried to avoid this happening to him."

She knew. She'd really fucked up. She should have said something to Simone sooner. She shouldn't have involved Roberto, but he wanted to work for her, and he was good. She was giving him what he wanted, and who was she to stand in the way of a man wanting to develop a career for himself? She'd done her best to make sure he was ready for the job. She'd made sure he had only taken on jobs that he could deliver safely. Vittorio's little prank hadn't helped matters, of course. But if it hadn't been for Roberto, Vittorio would be lying six-feet underground right now. The boy had skills that could be honed, but Simone didn't want to hear that. Simone didn't want to hear her plan for his future; that he might one day become a Don, a solid second in command at the very least.

Simone picked up the case, and Maria ran to her. "Please don't go, Simone." She placed a hand on Simone's arm, and Simone slowly looked down at it, her eyebrow raised. Maria removed her hand. "Please, Simone." The heat from Maria's chest flared upwards, scorched her throat, and stopped behind her eyes and she closed them for a brief moment.

She felt the rush of warm air move past her, and Simone's perfume faded. Her eyes burned and drove her lids to blink repeatedly. The sea beyond the window seemed blacker and hazier. She turned to the CCTV. Angelo's car pulled up outside the gates, Simone walked through them, and the gates closed behind her. The car disappeared.

Simone had gone.

She stared at the blank screen for an unfathomable length of time and the depth of emptiness she had felt once before, expanded within her. The intensity of it overwhelmed her as it had done back then too. She removed her jacket and threw it to the floor. She walked to the side of the house and, driven by the same fire that she'd felt when Rocca had informed her of her father's death, she punched the boxing bag hard until her knuckles bled. Only then did she drop to her haunches and allow the tears to flow freely. She had found herself a really good girl—the best—and now she'd fucking lost her. Anger aggravated her thoughts, and she screamed. Without Simone's love, life wasn't worth living. *Why does this fucking job, this place, this fucking code, fuck up anything that means something to me? What did I do to deserve this?*

33.

The chill from the space in the bed next to Maria filtered from her fingertips to her stomach as a dull ache of recognition. Every morning was the same routine with the same sense of desolation, and then the tightness and burning accompanied utter self-contempt. She fisted the cool sheet and winced as a sharp pain shot into her wrist. The stiffness in her fingers still refused to cooperate with her mental demands, though there was some small pleasure in feeling the pain she deserved. She had badly strained the ligaments in her hand boxing in anger, but she didn't care about that. Rage flared wildly, confirming that she hated herself, her life, and the torment that ate at her like a cancer in Simone's absence. She launched herself out of the bed, scrambled on her clothes, and went into the kitchen.

Pesto came to greet her with a wagging tail just like every other day. Except it wasn't every other day. It was another day in the absence of Simone, another day where Maria would have to fight her unrelenting inner voice and the incessant erupting negative emotions. *Good girls don't want to be involved with this business.* But she had found that good girl, fallen in love with her, and she had even allowed herself to dream of a future together.

Mechanically, she went through the routine of petting Pesto, filling his bowl with food, grinding the coffee beans, sipping at a bottle of water, and stepping onto the veranda. She glanced around the cove. The sea, as calm as it always was this time of year, lapped reluctantly with tiny waves at the sand. She put on her trainers, a signal for Pesto to join her, and started to jog. Every step was sluggish, her head pounded, and her wrists throbbed. *Discipline is the most important quality, Maria.* Her father's voice reassured her.

She jogged and sprinted to the left side of the cove, took the route inland, up and around the front aspect of the villa, weaving a path to add distance sufficient to exhaust her. Returning to the veranda with a final sprint across the sand, she came to a sudden halt. Her empty stomach didn't stop her body trying to rid her of its liquid contents. Bile rose, caused her to retch, and stung the back of her throat, then stomach cramps brought her to her knees. She buckled over, breathing slowly to stem the shooting pains. Pesto jumped at her, licked her face and hair, and nuzzled beneath her to lift her from the ground, and then yapped into her ear. She lifted her head slowly, held out her hand to him, and stroked him. "It's okay, boy." Easing slowly to her feet, she winced. She made her way to the kitchen and pulled out a bottle of water. She sipped and watched the CCTV. *She's not coming back, Maria.*

She picked up her phone and messaged Giovanni, put the coffee on to brew, showered, and dressed.

The chocolate notes hit her tongue, and the caffeine added an edge to her determination. With the gun resting reassuringly at her side, she pulled a small travel case from the cupboard and moved about the villa.

She slotted the documents Giovanni had arranged for her into the sleeve in the lid of the case. A plain envelope contained a small sum of euros. A laptop held the details of the bank accounts in Switzerland and the legal documents for the property in the Pyrenees and the Octavia. She threw in a set of keys for the boat and left the second set on the bed. She pulled open the drawer to her desk and sighed as she removed the gift. She'd planned to give the surprise to Simone once all the Italian business had been sorted as a celebration for them to enjoy together in the autumn. A sharp stab to the heart reminded her that their past was no longer her future. She hoped Simone would appreciate the gesture, nonetheless. Hovering the present over the case, her hands trembled. She studied the swollen and bruised skin as if it was alien to her and frowned at her fingers gripping tightly and the white knuckles that refused to let go. She turned her head, looked to the ceiling to stem the burning at the back of her eyes, and dropped the package into the case.

She threw in her favourite pair of shorts and T-shirt, the set that Simone had admired the time she had tantalisingly removed each piece of clothing from her body and deliberately tasted every ounce of flesh as she revealed it. A shudder of pleasure came to her with Simone's kisses igniting her skin. She swallowed down the feeling and buried it deep, deep enough so that it might not hurt her. She threw in a new toothbrush, toothpaste, and the bubble bath that Simone had enjoyed and then went back into the kitchen. That was everything that meant anything to her. The sum of the life that mattered sat in a small, innocuous case on the bed.

She located a pen, plucked a sheet of paper from the desk, and set them on the breakfast bar. Slowly she prepared another coffee while glancing between the paper and pen, the walls that had been her home for so long, and the beach and sea. Pesto was oblivious to her fate. She took the cup to the bar and sat staring at the blank white sheet of paper. *How do I write a posthumous declaration of love?* She sipped the coffee, hoping the words would come.

My love, Simone,

Everything I own that cannot be traced is in this case. I give it to you with all my heart. I loved you from the first time I saw you. I'm sorry I failed you, and us. Please, enjoy the gift with an open heart and think of me.

Love always, Maria x

She placed the note into the case, zipped and locked it. With the case in hand and Pesto at her heels, she made her way to the Maserati. Even the hollow emptiness had become a sense of non-existence. She felt nothing. But her focus had never been sharper.

She stood at the window that looked out across the heart of the city, her mobile at her ear. She continued with the call as the office door opened. "Sí, Rafael. Muchas gracias. Sí, Sí. Hasta luego. Caio." Pocketing her phone, she turned and greeted Giovanni with a weary smile. Rafael had at least given his assurance that the shipment from Spain hadn't been tampered with, and she believed him.

He bowed his head as he spoke. "Donna Maria."

"You heard?"

"Yes, Donna Maria. I was very sorry to hear."

She cleared her throat. "We have work to do, Giovanni." Her tone was clipped.

He nodded. She turned away, then turned back and stared at him.

"Angelo has eyes on Simone," he said and smiled softly.

She wetted her lips, glanced at the case at the side of the desk, and took in a deep breath. She picked it up and held it out to him, holding his attention with a determined look. "If anything happens to me, will you give this to her, please?"

She saw his jaw clench as he took the case. She took in a sharp breath that impaled her chest, swallowed down the rising emotion, cleared her throat, and turned back to the safety of the view from the window. "I want you to run the Lombardo business, Giovanni…with Roberto at your side."

The silence drove steel into her back until she couldn't bare it any longer. She turned to face him and stifled a gasp. The rims of his eyes were red, and he immediately averted his eyes.

"Yes, Donna Maria. I understand."

His voice sounded broken with emotion, and she pushed away the desire to console him with a hug. They'd only ever hugged once, and that was at her father's funeral. Perhaps this was another solemn enough occasion, but the moment passed and she simply nodded. "Good, I will let Matri know."

Giovanni cleared his throat. "Roberto?"

"I know Simone is against him working for us, but this is what he wants to do. He is adamant. And he is clever. I'm not going to stop him from living his life."

"He has a good head for business and is personable. A good memory for faces too. And, did you know, he can hit a pigeon between the eyes at fifty metres?"

She couldn't bring herself to smile at his light-heartedness. "I will talk to Matri regarding Vittorio's position with the company, but with his injuries I think he might struggle. He will have a family to look after soon, and I don't want my sister ending up a widow before she's thirty. Maybe we could offer him an office job?"

"I will deal with it, Donna Maria."

His eyes glassed over, and the muscles in his cheeks flickered and tensed. He had lost the battle to conceal his emotions. She smiled through tight lips. "I'm sure everything will be fine, Giovanni. We just need to take proper precautions. It's good business practise." She smiled reassuringly.

A smile appeared faintly at Giovanni's lips and disappeared quickly. "Is there anything else we need to consider?"

She turned to the window. "I have some things stored at the reef," she whispered. Giovanni remained silent. She sighed. "Octavia guards them for me. If..." The words caught in her throat.

"Yes, Donna Maria," he said quietly.

She breathed strength into her tone. "Small things, my will, the legal documents for the villa here, a letter for Matri, some photographs. Retrieve them for me and give them to Matri. She will need them."

"I promise, Donna Maria."

She turned to face him. "Will you look after Pesto for me?"

He nodded.

Remorse coursed through her like heroin through her veins, the damage just as destructive, before she shifted focus. "Keep a watch on the Amatos. I trust Patrina as much as I can, but…"

"Of course."

She smiled and felt a greater sense of purpose.

Giovanni inclined his head. "Simone did not turn up for work today."

She nodded. "I think we can assume she has given her notice. But if she changes her mind, the job at the Riverside is there for her."

"Of course, Donna Maria. Perhaps Roberto can persuade her." He smiled ruefully.

Maria moved back to the window and put her hands in her pockets. "Thank you, Giovanni."

"Bona sira, Donna Maria." He turned and made his way to the door.

Maria stared out of the window. Would this be the last time she looked out across the city from her office window? Had that been her final conversation with the brother she had never had? The leaden feeling in her heart reflected how she felt about the man who had stood beside her all these years. Rooted to the spot with regret, she wiped the tears from her cheeks and told herself there would be other times to come. The heavy feeling became dense with her sorrow as she wished she had hugged Giovanni and told him how much she cared. The tears flowed faster, and she heard herself sobbing.

34.

Roberto paced the small living room at Benitos Street and raked his fingers through his hair. "I told you before, I want to work for Maria." He threw his arms in front of him in a submissive motion, as if pleading for Simone's understanding. "She's been good to me. And I am good at what I do, Simone. This is the perfect business for me. I don't want to be a pizza boy or manage a shop. That isn't progression, that's a life sentence."

Simone's stomach churned. She lowered her hands from her hips and shook her head. No wonder Roberto had become distant. Was this how he'd made the money for her extravagant birthday gift? Bile rose in her, and she clamped her hand to her throat. "Who are you?"

Roberto flicked his hand dismissively at her and hissed through his teeth. She saw darkness behind his eyes and felt the impenetrable distance fortifying between them. In that moment, his demeanour reminded her of Maria's when she was preoccupied with the needs of the business. *Fuck the business that had ruined my life and stole my family.* And now it had ripped her brother from her and driven her from the only woman in the world she had truly loved.

"You want to kill me, Simone? You would have me work in a dead end job for a pitiful wage like our father did? I make more money in a month than I did in a year at the hotel."

Simone's hands returned to her hips as she leaned towards him. "At least our father made an honest living." She tossed her words at him like weapons.

Roberto stood taller and gave her a hard stare. "You know nothing."

Simone turned her back to him. "I'm not playing these games with you."

"Yes, even this house, your waitress job. It was bought with blood money, Simone. We both know that. There's no escaping the fact. *We* were effectively sold to the Amatos. Why?" He started to pace. "You know, it took me a while to work it out. Why didn't Alessandro recruit me into the clan? His men have watched me for years working the streets. You think you had some kind of power over them and could make demands of them? They take what they want, and if they don't take, there's a good reason. Our father passed information to Stefano, quietly and in the background. One time, that information saved Stefano's sorry life. So, out of loyalty to our father, and respecting your wishes not mine, they have stayed away from me."

Simone snapped her head towards him. His words weaved fire through her veins. *No, no, no.* Her father wouldn't have sided with the Amatos. He was a shopkeeper who worked hard to earn a living so she could benefit from a university education. She shook her head, her knees buckled beneath her, and she slumped into the chair. "You liar. You've become just like them." She spilled the words on a wave of fatigue with which came a realisation of the truth.

"Maria is not buying me or you, Simone. And the past is in the past."

Simone didn't look up. She interlocked her hands in her lap.

He sighed and looked away from her. "Maria pays me for a job well done, Simone," he said softly. "I have a career in the business that doesn't involve..."

"Killing people?"

"Vittorio would be dead if it hadn't been for me."

Simone stared at her shaking hands.

"But this isn't really about me, is it? You're not blind. You must see that Maria is in love with you, and it's clear you love her too. I've never seen you so happy. And for what it's worth,

Im glad you're not working for Patrina anymore. Surely love is all that matters. So, why are you here when she is there?" He indicated to the door.

Simone didn't respond. She closed her eyes. She had never thought of Roberto as a romantic, but he was right. In the words that echoed in her heart and released butterflies into her stomach, words that made her head giddy and absent of thought, she knew she was deeply in love.

She itched to go back to the Riverside and back to working under Maria's protection. The surface of her skin prickled at letting Antonio down so soon after starting work there. Then a surge of anger flared within her and fuelled her justifications for deserting Maria. Vindication didn't make her feel any better and dejection resonated through the story she'd fabricated in her mind. "Maria has betrayed me and lied to me. Is that love?"

Roberto shook his head. "She tried to protect you. You know this business well enough. The less you know, the safer you are."

She stood in silence. *He was right.*

"Simone."

She looked at him as every ounce of energy leached from her and lowered her head.

"Maria loves you. She told me herself."

A silent gasp jabbed her. She lifted her head and saw frustration behind Roberto's half-closed eyes, and the walls around her heart crumbled. The exposure left her feeling raw and weak and struggling to process what she had done. Maria hadn't betrayed her. Maria hadn't even come close to being dishonourable. On the contrary, Simone had felt adored and respected by her, coveted in a way that she had never experienced before. She had felt safe in Maria's arms, safe in her presence, and safe just knowing Maria was in her life.

She *had* trusted Maria.

She had no sound reason not to trust Maria.

I'm an idiot.

She saw her own disappointment reflected in Roberto's eyes as he took a pace backwards and shook his head at her. She hesitated to speak, and he turned away and walked to the door. Fire burned with the tension in her throat. She swallowed hard, and it throbbed fiercely.

"Do what you like. But I'm staying in this job, and nothing you say is going to stop me. If you had any sense, you'd go back to Maria now. She made you happy, and she'll keep you safe. That's more than anyone here can promise you." He closed the door quietly behind him.

Simone walked to the window and watched him ride down the street. It wasn't her place to fret about where he might be going or what he might be doing, but that didn't stop her worrying. At nineteen, he was more of a man than many men she knew, and yet he was still a kid to her. She shivered and wrapped her arms around herself.

He had always been street smart. He had an instinct to know which relationships to forge and which to avoid...unlike her. She couldn't deny it; his wit had served him well. It still did. And now, she needed to let him fly. He was right about her taking the offer of support from Patrina, though she hadn't considered that Patrina had bought their silence. But it turned out that was exactly what Patrina had done, and Simone had accepted the deal.

She went to the kitchen and made a coffee. The aroma elicited memories of being at the breakfast bar watching Maria as she prepared food, setting out biscuits for the dog, and tending the orchids on the window ledge.

And then, that dreadful night when she had walked out after seeing Roberto interacting with the men at the square and with Maria outside the DIA. She'd thought about nothing else in the days and nights since. The hours spent moving around the house, fretting, a little too afraid to venture to the plaza now that Angelo wasn't looking out for her, and then tossing and turning her way through the sleepless nights that haunted her.

She rubbed her forehead. Had she known deep down about her father's involvement with Stefano? She had wanted to believe her school fees had been paid with clean money, earned fairly and without detriment to another human being, but Roberto's words tolled bells that she could no longer deny. Maybe the fear that she had carried with her since the death of her family had been too much of a reminder that she too was like the Amatos. She had deceived herself. Their money was tainted with blood, and she had not once declined the inflated salary that Patrina had paid her. She was more like them than she dared imagine and certainly more like them than Maria.

What have I done?

Maria *was* different.

Maria cared.

Maria's protection had given her the space to be herself. She had travelled with Maria and seen the beauty that surrounded her through new eyes and experienced the purest sense of awe and joy. Maria's hand had felt strong and reassuring in hers as they had ventured down the cobbled village streets, and her lips had tasted sweet when they kissed after drinking cocktails and eating tapas. The evening sun had spilled reds and oranges from behind the snow-capped mountains and sparkled in Maria's eyes, and they had danced to music in the street. With Maria, she had lived.

She sipped her drink. Roberto's statement nursed her conscience and eased the pressure in her head. "She loves you and you love her, and that's all that matters."

The sensation of Maria's soft tender mouth exploring her became tangible, and she licked her lips. Her heart raced, and a shudder spiralled swiftly down her spine. She bit her lip as the tingling lifted the small hairs on the surface of her skin.

Love is all that matters.

She lowered her head and closed her eyes. Harsh, prickly heat crawled inside her for the accusations she had levied at Maria in her fit of anger. She'd ignored Maria's tears after attacking her integrity, and she had walked out on Maria without giving her a chance. *She* had failed Maria. *She* had broken Maria's heart. And in doing so, she'd eradicated the only joyful thing from her life.

She shook her head. Just thinking about Maria made her ache with longing. She needed to talk to Maria and make things right between them. She would go back to working at the Riverside, and they would get back to the life they had started to create. The future they might share together was still within reach. Here, the Pyrenees, wherever Maria wanted to go, she would be there at Maria's side.

35.

Simone stepped out of the taxi at the bottom of the road and walked quickly to the gated entrance to the villa. She stood at the security keypad and looked into the camera, fire and ice dancing in her stomach at the thought that Maria might be looking back at her. She wanted to be with Maria so badly...but what if Maria rejected her? Her trembling fingers clumsily pressed the buttons. She squeezed through the smallest gap as the gates started to open and ran up the pathway. She looked at the villa suspended in a soft haze behind which the night sky became intangibly distant and dark. Waves of tingling swept over her. One moment, she was giddy with excitement and in the next, worry took hold. Her head was spinning. Her heart thundered. She was stalling.

She loved the way the bright slithers of light from inside reached out, streaked across the veranda, and spilled into wider path onto the beach. Late, in the blackness of night, the absence of light gave an eerie feel to the cove. She remembered the evenings they shared, strolling along the beach, chasing through the shallow water, and laughing together. She recalled the cool sand on her feet and then her shoulders as they lay together, staring up at thousands of stars. She'd missed Maria's warmth close to her, the softness of her kisses, and the feel of her as she covered her and moved inside her. With a dry mouth, and trembling from her vivid recollections, she approached the front door.

Maria would have already answered the door if she had seen her on the CCTV. She peeked through the window. With no signs of Maria or Pesto, she wandered around to the side of the villa where the boxing bag cast a motionless shadow on the slatted wood. She gazed along the beach, nightfall and the light at her back restricting her visibility, and the emptiness caused her heart to thunder harder.

She stepped onto the veranda and looked through the window into the kitchen and living room. She opened the door and warmth brushed her skin. She closed her eyes and inhaled, comforted instantly by the familiar feeling the villa had imprinted on her. The memory of standing there, with her suitcase at her side, flashed into her awareness and then the scent of Maria came strongly to her. She opened her eyes, looked directly into Maria's, and gasped.

"Simone."

Simone jerked her hand to cover her mouth. "I..." Words wouldn't come.

Pesto's toes clipped the floor as he wandered between them and settled into his bed.

The bathrobe hung freely from Maria's shoulders and revealed her beauty within its opening as she rubbed her hair with a small towel.

Simone tried to avoid staring at her, but her eyes were drawn to the rise and fall of her chest, and the taut muscles across her stomach. Her eyes drifted lower, and she swallowed. She looked into Maria's eyes.

Maria closed the robe around herself and secured the belt around her waist. "What are you doing here?" she asked quietly.

"I'm sorry. I let myself in. I thought. The CCTV." Words tumbled from Simone.

Maria rubbed the back of her neck with the towel. Her dark eyes shone as she smiled. "I was just taking a shower."

"Yes." Simone tried to speak, but her mouth was dry and the words hard to form. "I came to apologise."

Maria's breath seemed to catch, and she looked away before turning and walking into the kitchen. "Can I get you a drink?"

Simone nodded.

"Coffee? Wine?"

Simone cleared her throat. "Wine would be nice."

Maria poured Simone a glass of wine and handed it to her.

Simone frowned. She took Maria's hand and studied the yellow bruising around Maria's knuckles that extended in patches across her hand and up her wrist. She winced, and Simone looked at her with wide eyes. "You're hurt?"

Maria shook her head. "Embarrassed more than hurt. I boxed in anger. One should never box in anger." She squeezed Simone's hand and smiled. "I was angry with myself."

Simone lowered her head. "Me too." She left the warmth of Maria's touch, picked up her glass, and sipped her drink. "I'm so sorry about the things I said."

Maria went to the fridge, pulled out a bottle of water, removed the top, and took a sip. She walked back to Simone and reached up to stroke Simone's face. She brushed a thumb across her lips.

"I'm sorry about the things I didn't say."

Simone shuddered at the tenderness and closed her eyes to the image of Maria's mouth pressed to hers. She moaned as she kissed Maria's thumb and held the palm of Maria's hand to her cheek. The warmth and soapy scent of Maria became potent, and the yielding pressure as Maria closed against her, stole her breath. She opened her eyes as Maria's mouth claimed hers. She fell into the kiss, clashing teeth with Maria then jerked back and giggled with nervous relief.

Maria wrapped an arm around Simone's waist, cradled her head to her chest, and placed soft kisses to the top of Simone's head. She inhaled and moaned at the tingling at her scalp. She slipped her hand beneath Maria's loose robe, and the unique scent of Maria came to her and quickened her pulse. She grazed her fingertips across Maria's back. "I love you," she whispered.

Maria squeezed her tighter. "You can't stay here tonight."

Simone felt the words jar in her chest. She took a deep breath, eased out of Maria's arms, and looked into her eyes. "I understand."

Maria sighed. She brushed her fingertips across Simone's cheek and rested them on Simone's lips. "I have work I need to do tonight."

Simone lowered her head. The heaviness through which her world had just tumbled became dark and impossible to navigate with logical thought. Maria lifted Simone's chin. She stared into her eyes for a long time, breathing slowly and deeply, and then smiled and her eyes turned a shade lighter.

"I love you."

Simone's focus shifted slowly from despair through recognition to hope. A sparkle appeared in Maria's eyes, and her smile radiated love. The pounding in Simone's chest expanded, and the quake that followed trembled through her hands, and her legs felt suddenly fragile beneath her.

Maria's strong arm pulled Simone back into the warmth of her body and then she kissed her on the head.

"I will come and get you in the morning," Maria said firmly. "We can go away and start a new life together. Spain, France, the US, Australia? Wherever you want to go. We can talk about it tomorrow. I have some plans in place already, but we can make our own arrangements. We can do anything you want, Simone. Sicily has no hold over me. Only you do."

Simone lifted her head and locked eyes with Maria.

"Will you come with me, Simone?"

Simone smiled. "Yes."

Maria shifted in focus, and her eyes became more distant. "You need to go home now. I have to work."

Simone shivered with the chill that moved down her spine. "You'll be safe?"

Maria blinked. "Of course."

The trembling imploded within Simone, nausea sat low in her stomach, and dizziness claimed her mind. "I don't want to leave you."

Maria took Simone by the shoulders and forced her to look at her. "Listen. I will be fine. You need to go home. I will come for you tomorrow. Look at me, Simone. I need you to understand. You have to trust me."

Simone looked at Maria, but her eyes wouldn't register beyond the fear that squeezed the life out of her. "I understand," she whispered.

"I'll get Angelo to take you home." She kissed Simone firmly on the lips.

Simone stood dazed as Maria moved around the villa. She turned her head and looked out over the beach and couldn't stop the thought. *What if this is the last time?* When she looked back, Maria was stood in front of her, dressed in jeans, a light blue shirt, and a dark blue jacket that she knew concealed the butt-nosed Smith and Wesson 637. The thought that Maria might be intending to use the gun was fleeting, but the dark knowledge that Maria might murder someone tonight turned her stomach.

36.

The deck of the Bedda rocked gently, moored to the outer edge of the cove where the sea currents were more active. Maria could see to the horizon in all directions, though that distance was limited by the dark sky crowded with stars that crowned her and sprinkled shimmers of light onto the gentle waves below the boat. The crescent moon reflected the black depths of the sea where cargo ships edged along the horizon, a long way off in the distance. The sereneness wasn't lost on her. It was settling. She turned to face the villa. Light beams danced on the water between the cruiser and the shore, and the small motorboat that had been pulled from the water reclined on the beach. On the cliff top adjacent to the shore, Giovanni watched her.

With the Smith and Wesson tucked at her side, the metal warm from the heat of her skin, she closed her jacket and placed her hands in her pockets. Eyes closed, she breathed deeply, slowed her heart, and focused her mind to prepare for what was to come. She had to trust Patrina, but she would do so with one eye on her movements. The small vessel appeared in her peripheral vision long before she opened her eyes fully and turned her head to watch the craft bounce across the water. Her heart thumped out a steady beat, and she took another deep breath, hoping to the fates that it wouldn't be one of her last.

She walked to the edge of the Bedda as the speedboat moved alongside then jumped down and caught her balance before Patrina reached out.

Alessandro's bulk dominated the cabin raised above the bow of the vessel. Behind the cabin were steps to the lower deck on which Maria stood. Breathing apparatus hung, clipped to the outer wall of the cabin, and a narrow ledge bounded the boat's perimeter. More traditionally, the craft would be used for diving and fishing expeditions. It looked the part, should they be stopped by the authorities for any reason. Maria sat on the ledge at the rear of the boat where she could keep her eyes on her two hosts.

Patrina looked at Maria and smiled. The darkness cloaked a steel focus Maria knew sat behind the shine in her eyes.

"All set?"

Maria nodded her head. Her eyes drifted to the water as it sprayed up behind the low freeboard. The temptation to reach down and tickle the surface passed quickly, though the fleeting distraction helped. Patrina walked the short distance across the deck and climbed up the steps to the cabin to talk to Alessandro.

Alessandro eased the craft slowly forwards and guided the boat out to sea. Patrina walked back up the boat and stood next to Maria. She gazed into the sky as if they were about to embark on a luxury night cruise with wine and canapes.

"Beautiful evening, bedda."

Maria's stomach twisted. She remained silent.

"Are you ready for this? I don't want to get too far out to sea. Once this goes up," she indicated to the craft, "the authorities will arrive quickly." She smiled. "He insists on keeping an eye on you, so I need to go and take the wheel."

"Okay." It wasn't that she didn't trust Patrina's word, but she had to trust her gut and that was telling her not to trust Alessandro to play ball fairly.

Patrina went back to the cabin, and Alessandro slowed the boat for her to take the helm. Maria stiffened her back as Alessandro walked towards her. The craft swayed under his bulk. Her skin crawled and something sharp stuck in her throat. She lifted her head and smiled then stood and looked down at him. "Good evening, Alessandro."

He laughed, and ice trailed down her spine. His movements were uncoordinated, and he wouldn't look her in the eye. He was high...and drunk no doubt. He reached out, and she swatted his arm away. The Smith and Wesson jabbed at her side with the sharp movement.

He stumbled, pulled a gun from inside his belt, and shoved it in her face. "I need to fucking check you're not carrying, bitch."

Maria held up her hands and glanced towards Patrina.

Patrina stepped from the cabin. "Of course she's carrying, Alessandro. We will need her help. Put the gun away."

Alessandro glared at Maria and took a step back. "I don't trust the bitch."

His spit struck Maria in the face, and the stench of his breath curdled her stomach. She remained steadfast, watching him closely.

"It will be fine, Alessandro. Please," Patrina said.

Alessandro glared in Patrina's direction. "And I don't fucking trust you, either." He swung the weapon towards Patrina and then swiftly back to Maria. "You think I don't know there's no shipment?" His laugh had an acerbic quality that matched the wild look in his eyes. "You brought me here to kill me. Ha. You think I'm fucking stupid?" He pointed at his head as he spoke and swung the weapon like a pendulum between the two women.

Maria looked into Alessandro's eyes with a hard stare, and as he went to grab her again she moved away. "Of course there is a shipment, Alessandro. I wouldn't be here if there wasn't."

The boat rocked, and he stumbled. He looked for a brief moment as if he was considering Maria's statement, then he narrowed his gaze.

"Fucking bitch."

He staggered again on the moving deck and squatted to prevent himself falling. As the boat stilled, he rose slowly, and focused again on Maria. His eyes looked darker than death itself and he pointed his gun at Maria's chest.

"That was fucking stupid."

Maria stood still with her hands raised. "I didn't..."

"Alessandro, no!" Patrina screamed.

He glanced towards Patrina, and his eyes widened slowly as he registered that she was pointing her Colt .45 directly at him. She started slowly down the steps. He growled and swung his weapon towards her.

Patrina stopped walking. "Put the gun down, Alessandro. We don't need this."

Maria looked for a brief opening of uncertainty in a shift in his demeanour. It didn't come. She appealed to him as she would a genuine friend, though she felt nothing of the sort. "Alessandro, it's okay. We can do this together."

He kept the barrel of the gun pointed at Patrina as he seemed to ponder the proposition. Then his smile revealed the same quality of lunacy that Maria had seen in a man's eyes once before, and he turned the weapon towards her.

"Alessandro, no," Patrina shouted.

A crack as sharp as thunder split the night's silence.

Alessandro moaned out, and then another crack echoed out.

Maria clasped her hand to the fierce burning sensation in her chest, then raw pain ripped a tornado through her, and her legs collapsed beneath her. The hard wood of the deck brought a shock of fire that kindled something inside her, and the gurgling in her throat made it harder to breathe.

A third crack boomed out, and then a fourth, and a fifth.

Patrina's screams resounded in the darkness behind Maria's eyes and then silence took the pain away.

Patrina wailed like a wounded animal fighting for its life as rage coursed through her. She ran to the cabin and stopped the craft, then ran to Maria lying on her side on the deck. Maria's eyes were closed, and blood trickled from her mouth. "Fuck, bedda. This wasn't meant to happen. Stay with me, bedda. Stay with me." She pressed her fingers to Maria's neck and closed her eyes at the slow, light pulse. "Thank God."

She stood and took a pace towards the large lump of flesh sprawled on the deck. His eyes were wide open, and blood seeped from his chest and mouth. "Fuck you, Alessandro. Fucking, fuck you." She raised the gun and with gritted teeth fired another two shots into his body and face. His corpse jumped at the impact. Patrina's mouth closed to the nausea that stung the back of her throat. *You fucking bastard!* She plucked her mobile from her pocket, pressed a button, and held the phone to her ear. "Beto, get out here. Now." She moved around the boat, dousing it with petrol, and scanned the cove for foreign vessels. The bobbing light from the speedboat grew brighter as it drew closer.

The smaller craft rocked the deck as it pulled up alongside them.

Beto made a sweeping glance over the scene and smiled at the sight of Alessandro. "Good."

"We need to get Maria to the beach. She needs help quickly."

"Of course."

Together they eased Maria's deadweight onto the deck of the speedboat.

"One second." Patrina removed a lighter from her pocket, flipped the lid to ignite a flame, and threw the lighter into the film of petrol. A wave of flames chased rapidly across the wooden deck. Beto opened the throttle and steered the boat in the direction of the beach.

Three hundred metres from the burning boat, beyond the Bedda, and inside the safety of the cove, the first explosion came and then a second, bigger and bolder that lit up the sky with a firework display that would be visible to the residents of Palermo. She looked at the wreckage that had become her nephew's final resting place and felt pure pleasure for his deserved fate. The Bedda was also engulfed in flames. That had been a necessary part of the plan to create a diversion and suspicion. A moment of wistful reflection passed quickly and as she glanced at Maria's blood-soaked jacket, tears wetted her face. *Please don't die, bedda.* She scanned the beach and noted the familiar form running towards them. *Giovanni, thank God.*

Giovanni held his gun raised in the direction of the two shadows until they transformed as the light revealed them. He returned his weapon to the holster at his chest and ran to the boat.

Beto landed the craft on the beach. "Giovanni, come quickly."

Patrina saw contempt as Giovanni stared at her. It was justified. This should never have happened. Alessandro must have only gone along with her plan because he saw it as a way to get rid of her and Maria. He would have disposed of their bodies to the sharks if she hadn't fired the first shot.

"What the fuck happened?" Giovanni asked.

Patrina wiped away her tears and her lips quivered as she spoke. "Alessandro shot her. I tried to stop him, but the bastard…"

"Shit." Giovanni reached into the boat and lifted Maria out.

Maria slumped in his arms, and he carried her to the dry sand. Patrina followed him. She put a hand on his arm and looked into his eyes. "She's lost a lot of blood." Patrina blinked and brushed the back of her hand across her cheeks. *Please live, bedda.* Her hands trembled as she sensed Maria's skin was colder to the touch. "Please, make sure she lives, Giovanni." Her voice broke as she spoke, and a wave of uncertainty snaked an icy trail down her spine.

"And Alessandro?" Giovanni asked.

Her discomfort intensified at Giovanni's accusatory tone. She was as furious as he sounded. She shook her head, and her tone held remorse. "There is no problem between us now, Giovanni." She looked into his eyes. "Please, tell her that I'm sorry."

Beto waved towards them. "Patrina, we need to go."

She nodded to Beto, then looked intently into Giovanni's eyes. "Please." She turned away and ran to the boat, tears spilling onto her cheeks. She watched as Giovanni cradled Maria in his arms and walked quickly towards the villa. For the first time in as long as she could remember, she closed her eyes and prayed.

Maria started to tremble with the chill that consumed her from the inside out. The arms around her body were tight, and the pain in her chest increased under the pressure.

"Maria, Maria."

The voice had a familiar tone, although it was faint and hard to determine through the ringing in her ears. She groaned as the fire inside her taunted her with its rhythmical jabbing pattern.

"Maria, Maria."

Giovanni was calling to her. She wanted to speak, but the air wouldn't fill her lungs, and all she could do was gasp repeatedly and hope. The blaze in her chest rumbled and crackled, close to the searing pain. *Open your eyes, Maria. Open them.* She flickered her eyelids, and her father's voice became insistent. *Come on, Maria.* Another stab of pain, and the air stopped coming.

Blood stained Giovanni's hands. He leaned closer. "Maria, what is it?"

Now, now, fight, Maria. Fight. "Octavia," she whispered.

*

Simone jolted at the crashing and banging as Roberto burst through the front door and slammed it behind him. Did he have no consideration for the fact that it was long past midnight? She turned to face him, and the smile slid from her lips as the blood drained from her. He stood in front of her, paralysed, his skin pale and his eyes damp. He gesticulated frantically and looked desperate. *Something dreadful...Maria? No, no.* Simone froze. She stared at him, her eyes wide, and her heart pounding. "What's happened?" The words came slowly, almost inaudibly.

He looked away from her and tears fell onto his cheeks. "The Amato's boat."

Simone's head remained still, and her insides quaked. She knew the darkness that had just descended on her world. It was the same feeling that she'd had at the news of her family's death. Nothing could change it. Nothing would lift it. She could think the words, Maria is dead, but she wouldn't be the one to say them. She couldn't, not out loud. That would be too much of an admission of her worst nightmare coming true. "What about it?"

"It just blew up, Simone. They were all on it; Maria, Patrina, Alessandro."

Simone remained still and quiet. *No.*

Roberto looked at her and closed the space between them with his arms open.

She stepped away from him and raised her hand to stop him from speaking and moving.

"I was working at the port. I saw the explosions. Maria's place is swarming with police. The boat was just off the cove. The Bedda went up too. They're looking for bodies."

Simone walked silently past him in a vacuum. She refused to believe Roberto's lies. Why would he do that to her? No, no. Maria wouldn't have allowed this to happen. Not now. Not ever. She stared out the window, gripped by blindness. Sounds became incoherent, and her inner voice muted. Then the firestorm swirled in her head, and she collapsed into a heap and sobbed.

37.

The carrycase sat open on Simone's bed. Every item had been removed from it and placed carefully on the mattress, each lying next to the other in a uniform pattern that Simone tried to give meaning. But where was the justification, the logic, of a life lost for nothing?

Patrina had approached her at Maria's funeral, but the words of condolence that she had offered had simply fuelled Simone's rage. *How is it the evil people in the world survive and the good die young?* Patrina had just blinked and nodded at her as she had levied her verbal assault. If Simone had had the energy and a weapon in her hand, she would have finished the woman there and then.

Time heals. She shook her head and wiped her eyes as she scanned the items for the hundredth time. No length of time could take away the pain of losing the most precious person in her life.

There was no joy in the routine of studying the contents of the case, but the ritual had become a part of her life. It brought her closer to Maria and for a short moment, her heart felt light and warmth comforted her. She picked up the envelope with the letter inside it and re-read it. Three months, and still the paper fluttered in her trembling hand and shook her core, as it had done the first time that she had read the note. She caressed the words with her fingertips, reminded of Roberto's comment.

"You should go. She wanted you to have all of this. That's why she gave it to you."

She put down the letter and picked up Maria's clothing. The softness tingled her fingertips, and she pressed it to her lips and inhaled the scent of it. Tears spilled onto her cheeks and soaked the material. She closed her eyes until the feeling passed then folded the items and set them back on the bed. Her eyes stung, and she swallowed back the lump that had become a permanent feature in her throat. She tried to smile at the black and white photograph of Maria, but her heart hurt too much. It was an image intended for a passport. Maria looked so serious, so dark and moody. What Simone wouldn't give to see that look now. She stroked the stern features and placed the small image carefully back into the case. The absence of Maria came to her in a shock wave as she covered the image to protect it. Trembling, she picked up the small package and emptied its contents on the bed. The flight tickets would take her directly to Paris, where she would check in at the Ritz. From there, she would walk a mere five-hundred metres to the Palais Garnier. She would go to the box at the southern entrance. The performance, Swan Lake.

The rawness felt like an open wound being prodded with every memory, every thought, every glorious feeling shattered by reality was a pain Simone would take to her grave. She couldn't imagine a time when she wouldn't feel tortured by loss. Their relationship was cut short before it had time to grow. If Maria had gone with her that night, if they had run away together there and then, they would be together now. Maria would be alive. Sobs rocked her body, and tears flooded her cheeks. She let them flow. She drew in a long deep breath and released it slowly. At least Maria had escaped the mafia, although she had paid the ultimate price.

She studied the legal documents for the farmhouse. She smiled to herself. Maria was Mariella Sanchez. The property, the boat that Maria had commissioned that Simone would find moored in the port of Valencia, and the Swiss bank accounts. All of it untraceable. Maria, Mariella. She liked the way the name rolled off her tongue. She smiled at the passport with her own image in it and the unfamiliar name, Simonet Begnoit, issued in

France. Maria had taken care of a new identity for her too. Maria had planned for them both to leave Sicily without being traced.

She looked up. Roberto was watching her, his smile looked wistful, and his eyes weary with sadness.

"You have to go, you know? You can start a new life where you will be able to live openly and freely. You can be yourself."

She lowered her head. She only wanted to be herself with Maria. The idea of any other lover wasn't an option.

He went to her and lifted her to her feet. "Hey, what is there to lose? Worse case, you take a holiday and you come home again. You've always wanted to see the ballet. Maria wanted that for you too. Why don't you do it for her?" He shrugged.

He was trying to smile, trying to be upbeat, she could see that. His eyes conveyed quietness and the steadiness that came with the responsibility he held. She had noticed that quality developing over the past months, and especially since he had taken the position as Giovanni's right-hand man and started working on the construction of the tech park. He had grown up to the point of being unrecognisable to her. She stroked his clean-shaven cheek and smiled with a heavy heart. He was still her baby brother, and she would always love him for that. "It won't be the same without her."

"I know." He pulled her into his chest, held her tightly and pressed his lips to her forehead. "I love you, sis. I'm so sorry. I really liked her a lot," he whispered in a broken voice.

Simone closed her eyes. *I loved her more than life.* She pulled away, took a deep breath, and stared into his eyes. "I love you too."

He brushed a tear from her cheek. "She wanted you to have a new life, a good life."

She sighed. "I know."

He stroked the hair from her face.

She sighed. "I will go to the ballet."
He let her go and smiled. "It will be good for you."

38.

Simone ambled slowly up to the doors of the Palais Garnier, becoming more breathless as she adjusted to each aspect of the stunning Napoleon III style architecture. Statuesque, symmetrical columns formed the front façade, gilded figural groups crowned the apexes of the principle façades on the right and left side, and sculptured bronze busts of many of the great composers were located between the columns. It was striking as a building and inspirational as a representation of history.

She stood and stared upwards, inhaling the warm, slightly humid Parisian air. The low, evening sun tingled her back and shoulders, and a light breeze refreshed her skin. A dark-haired woman wearing a suit caught her eye as she walked past in the direction of the theatre's doors. She sighed and closed her eyes. The woman didn't look anything like Maria.

She took a deep breath, climbed the steps, and entered the opera house. Vast columns of gold towered above her, painted ceilings looked down on her, and bright light poured through her, illuminating the substantial central staircase that peeled off in two directions forming a bridge to the various theatre entrances. The back of her eyes burned, and her throat constricted. The awesomeness of the building's magnificence was lessened considerably by the absence of Maria. Pleasure and sadness vied within her. *Maria would want me to enjoy this.*

Simone shielded her heart with her hand and stood, transfixed by the intensity of the lively ambience in the foyer. She gazed around. A myriad of voices came and went. People moved around her casually, studying the ticket in their hands and pointing to the appropriate entrance for their seat location. Reminded of her need to find the box, she gathered herself and walked over to a woman dressed in an usher's uniform. She held out her ticket.

The woman's uniform was smartly pressed, and she offered a warm smile. "Please, follow me."

Simone followed her up the stairs and then peeled off to the right. The woman opened the door and entered the box. Simone hesitantly stepped inside.

The scene of her wishes struck her, Maria's perfume came to her, and her eyes darted hopefully around the small space, hoping for the illusion to be true.

A bottle of champagne rested on ice in a silver bucket to the side of a table. Two crystal glasses shimmered in the subdued lighting. Two high-back chairs decorated in ornate gold leaf trim and deep red suede leather were placed next to each other, the arms touching, orientated on a slight angle so that they were both directed towards the stage.

She swallowed back the wave of sadness, turned swiftly to face the usher, and forced a smiled at the usher. The woman smiled back at her. It was probably the same smile she gave any guest. Polite but lacking.

"Are you expecting a guest this evening, madame?"

The question was perfectly normal, but it cut Simone in two, and she could barely breath to answer. "Um, no."

"Very well, madame. Is there anything else I can get for you?"

Weakness moved through Simone, and she felt her knees giving way. She grabbed the back of the seat and took a slow breath. "Could I have a glass of water please?"

The usher frowned. "Is everything—"

"Yes, I'm fine, thank you." Simone smiled and stood taller. She let go of the seat. The usher smiled and closed the door behind her. Simone turned back to the auditorium and stepped closer to the edge of the box. She scanned the bustling movement around her as guests took their seats in the circle and stalls below her. The warm air was constant, and perfumed, and heady. She closed her eyes and brushed her fingers across the gold trim. The sensual feel of the suede against her sensitive fingers caught her breath. She stiffened her back and her eyes opened. The image of Maria came to her in a flash of desperation, then it disappeared. She searched the auditorium and became quickly overcome by a dense feeling of exhaustion. Anger boiled below the surface of her unfulfilled wishes. She sat, closed her eyes, and inhaled deep slow breaths. *Why did I come here?*

Musical notes started up in harmony from the pit at the front of the stage; violins, joined by wind instruments, and then percussion, and Simone's heart eased into a soft, gentle rhythm. She opened her eyes and stared at the stage. The increasing complexity of the sounds, the musky scent that was the building's unique signature, and the subdued lighting that seemed to compliment the orchestra's resonance as they prepared for the first act, swept her away.

Then the music shifted in tone, sending a message to those who lingered to take their seats, and she smiled. Mumbling voices became quieter, deeper in tone, and the lights dimmed lower. A hum of anticipation arose from below her, lifting the air to dance around the room.

Simone didn't respond to the soft click of the door.

The glass of water appeared in her peripheral vision and was placed on the table. The fingers clasped around the glass registered as vaguely familiar, and then there was the unexpected pressure on her shoulder that jolted her to look up. She blinked repeatedly, then the force of her head spinning fully around in recognition threw her to her feet. Her hand smothered her gasp. The thundering behind her ribs pounded erratically. No words came to her. She became rigid, and no breath moved within her. She stared wide eyed and trembling.

No, no. it can't be you.

The thought had become concrete in her mind, but she couldn't trust her vision. This was a mirage. A dream she so passionately desired to be tangible. She shook her head and stared intently.

Maria smiled at Simone and looked into her eyes.

The black tuxedo with a crisp white shirt and a bright red bowtie, just as Maria had worn the first time that she set eyes on her looked very real. Simone reached out and tentatively made contact with the fine material. She swept her hands slowly over Maria's body, warm to the touch. She inhaled sharply as if she were taking her final breath. She shook her head and took a step back. She leaned forwards and blinked. Then a flash of fire rose up, and she slapped Maria around the face.

The sting burned and watered Maria's eyes, and she cupped her cheek. "I'm sure I deserved that." She smiled as Simone gasped and then tumbled into her arms. Simone caressed her cheek frantically, earnestly, and then tenderly, and it felt so good to be touched.

"Oh my God, I'm so sorry. I didn't mean to... What? How?" Simone stuttered.

She shook her head, and her fingers trembled as she touched Maria's face, her head, her shoulders, and her neck. Maria took Simone's hand and placed it against her thundering chest. "You feel it beating?" Simone was looking her up and down, shaking her head, and frowning.

"You're alive?"

The confusion Maria saw in Simone's eyes seared through her chest and clamped her heart. "Just about." Her dry mouth and tight throat and the fragility in her own voice, reflected the uncertainty she had lived through in the past months.

Simone's hand tensed, and her eyes narrowed, and then her teeth clenched. Maria feared another slap was coming and braced herself. And then Simone pulled back.

"Why didn't you contact me?"

Simone's tone held frustration and concern in equal measure. Maria's lungs deflated from the punch, and she hoped Simone could see the ache in her heart that she would have to live with for the rest of her life. Profound sadness radiated from Simone's eyes and ripped through Maria like locusts stripping a field of corn. She turned away and swallowed hard. "I must have no contact with Sicily, Simone. None."

Simone's stare deepened the wound in Maria that would never heal.

"What about your family?"

Maria bowed her head and inhaled deeply. "It was the only way, Simone. My mother always expected this time would come." *She will grieve.* "I took an opportunity that arose to create a future." Maria felt the pressure tighten against her hand, and her heartbeat thumped harder against her ribs. Pain and joy burned behind her eyes. She tugged Simone to her chest and blinked as a tear slid down her cheek. Simone's hair felt soft and silky at her fingertips. She kissed the top of her head.

She hadn't forgotten how incredibly beautiful Simone was, but the intensity of the feelings she had for Simone had transformed during her time convalescing. Simone had given Maria the will to live despite all the odds against her. She had taken a huge risk, against medical advice, to be treated on the Octavia as she and the doctor travelled to Spain. If she had gone to hospital in Palermo, she would never have been allowed to die. Being here, now, was nothing short of a miracle, and the money that had changed hands had been worth every euro.

She closed her eyes and breathed in the scent of apple blossom. *So delicate, so sweet.* Slowly she opened her eyes and held Simone closer. "I nearly didn't survive. If I'd tried to contact you, you would have been in danger. The only people in Sicily who know I am alive are Giovanni and the doctor who treated me. Both I trusted with my life." She lifted Simone's chin and kissed her. "I am Mariella Sanchez now."

Tears trickled onto Simone's cheeks. "In my world you died and left me."

"In my world I died and became reborn." Maria thumbed the wetness from Simone's cheeks and smiled. "We can have a life together, Simone."

Simone sniffled and her eyes reflected the soft, ambient light as she cast them over Maria's face. Maria kissed Simone's fingers and held them to her lips. "You wore the red dress." She admired the soft curve of Simone's breast and the prickling of Simone's skin under her fingertips. As the shade of Simone's soft flesh darkened, Maria felt a rush of heat cover her. Simone gasped. Maria tugged her closer. She reached her hand around Simone's head and ran her fingers through her hair, and when she brought Simone's lips to hers, it felt as though they tingled. *So soft. So tender.* She groaned and bit Simone's lip. *So real.* The musical notes echoed distractingly around the auditorium. She released Simone and looked into her dark eyes. Her lips trembled and the urge to kiss Simone was strong.

Simone appealed to Maria through a frown as she shook her head. "Don't you dare do that to me again."

Warmth settled like a blanket around Maria's heart. She kissed Simone to quiet her and smiled. "I promise."

Simone leaned her cheek against Maria's chest. "I want to hear your heart beating again," she whispered, "just to check I'm not dreaming."

Maria's spine tickled, and then softness enveloped her as her thoughts drifted to the night to come. Simone would explore the sensitive scars on Maria's chest, and she would tell Simone everything she could remember about the incident on the boat.

Rafael had kept Maria informed. Vitale had been arrested for his involvement in covering up her father's death, and although Alessandro wouldn't ever be charged with Don Calvino's assassination, he had paid the price and justice had been served. Two of Don Chico's henchmen had taken the fall for the hit on Alessandro and Maria on the basis that Chico stayed out of Sicily. Who knew how long Chico would comply? But Patrina had taken control of the Amatos business, and she would incriminate Chico if he broke their agreed truce.

Tonight, she didn't want to talk. Maria wanted to hold Simone if she wanted to be held. She had nothing to hide from Simone. And while it might take Maria time to adjust to her newly found freedom of expression, she would talk openly with Simone about anything and everything. *No more secrets. No more lies.* No decision would be taken without Simone being a party to it.

The future she had fashioned while in the hospital bed filled her with vibrant energy and something too profound to be labelled. *I love you.* She squeezed Simone tightly, hoping she felt it too.

The ballet drew Maria's attention. White swans glided and twirled gracefully around the stage. She had seen this moment from as far back as she could remember, long before meeting Simone. Her dream had come true. Her heart sang in harmony with the musical notes reverberating around the auditorium, and she smiled at Simone. "Will you enjoy the ballet with me?"

Simone nodded. Maria saw the answer to the other question she intended to ask flash through Simone's eyes. "Will you spend a lifetime with me?"

Simone bit her lip harder. The fizzing inside Maria intensified. She stared at Simone. *Amazing.*

Simone turned from the stage and looked at Maria. "What?"

Maria's smile broadened. "Nothing." She continued to stare at Simone. *Stunning.*

Simone kept her eyes on the stage. "Watch the ballet."

Maria continued to stare at Simone. She couldn't take her eyes from her. She wanted to hold her and never let her go. *Later.*

Simone turned to look at Maria and gasped softly. Maria smiled at the longing she saw in Simone's eyes. She took Simone's hand in hers and intertwined their fingers and met Simone's quivering lips with her own in a delicate kiss. The intensity of the vibration that moved through Maria watered her eyes, and her voice broke.

"I am so in love with you," Simone said though her words were muted by the booming orchestra.

Maria smiled and turned her attention to the ballet, enjoying the sensation of Simone's hand in hers, Simone's love caressing her heart. *I know.*

About Emma Nichols

Emma Nichols lives in Buckinghamshire with her partner and two children. She served for 12 years in the British Army, studied Psychology, and published several non-fiction books under another name, before dipping her toes into the world of lesbian fiction.

You can contact Emma through her website and social media:

www.emmanicholsauthor.com
www.facebook.com/EmmaNicholsAuthor
www.twitter.com/ENichols_Author

And do please leave a review if you enjoyed this book.
Reviews really help independent authors to
promote their work.
Thank you.

Other Books by Emma Nichols

Visit **getbook.at/TheVincentiSeries** to discover The Vincenti Series: Finding You, Remember Us and The Hangover.

Visit **getbook.at/ForbiddenBook** to start reading **Forbidden**

Visit **getbook.at/Ariana** to delve into the bestselling summer lesbian romance Ariana.

Visit **viewbook.at/Madeleine** to be transported to post-WW2 France and a timeless lesbian romance.

Visit **getbook.at/thisisme** to check out my lesbian literary love story novella.

Visit **getbook.at/SummerFate, viewbook.at/BlindFaith** and **getbook.at/christmasbizarre** to enjoy the Duckton-by-Dale lesbian romcom novels.

Thanks for reading and supporting my work!

What's Your Story?

Global Wordsmiths, CIC, provides an all-encompassing service for all writers, ranging from basic proofreading and cover design to development editing, typesetting, and eBook services. A major part of our work is charity and community focused, delivering writing projects to under-served and under-represented groups across Nottinghamshire, giving voice to the voiceless and visibility to the unseen.

To learn more about what we offer, visit: www.globalwords.co.uk

A selection of books by Global Words Press:
Aventuras en México: Farmilo Primary School
Life's Whispers: Journeys to the Hospice
Defining Moments: Stories from a Place of Recovery
World At War: Farmilo Primary School
Times Past: Young at Heart with AGE UK
In Different Shoes: Stories of Trans Lives
Patriotic Voices: Stories of Service
From Surviving to Thriving: Reclaiming Our Voices
Don't Look Back, You're Not Going That Way

Self-published authors working with Global Wordsmiths:
John Parsons
Dee Griffiths and Ali Holah
Karen Klyne
Ray Martin
Emma Nichols
Valden Bush
Simon Smalley

Printed in Great Britain
by Amazon